Beyond Blood

Sharon A. Crawford

blue denim press

Beyond Blood

Published by Blue Denim Press Inc.
First Edition
ISBN 978-1-927882-01-6

Cover Design—Joanna Joseph/Typeset in Cambria and Garamond

Library and Archives Canada Cataloguing in Publication
Crawford, Sharon A., 1948-, author
Beyond blood / Sharon A. Crawford. -- First edition.

Issued in print and electronic formats.
ISBN 978-1-927882-01-6 (pbk.).--ISBN 978-1-927882-02-3 (kindle).--
ISBN 978-1-927882-03-0 (epub)

I. Title.

PS8605.R44B48 2014 C813'.6 C2014-905005-4
C2014-905006-2

Dedication

To my son, Martin Crawford, for his support of my writing, and particularly with the computer-related paraphernalia, when I go into a Luddite panic. Without his help and understanding, I couldn't use my laptop, and my blogs would be non-existent. Also a special thanks for booking my boarder, her cat and me into a hotel during Toronto's ice storm, December 2013.

And to all my cousins in Ontario and Michigan who supported my writing, especially my debut short story collection. Special thanks to Gene in Michigan who made it his business to let all his friends know about *Beyond the Tripping Point.*

Other Works by Sharon A Crawford

Fire Underneath the Ice, a novella co-authored with Rene Natan under the pseudonym R.S. Natanevin, Rogue Phoenix Press, 2010

Beyond the Tripping Point, a collection of crime short stories, Blue Denim Press, 2012

Prologue

Him:

He had a big pimple. That would never do. All the makeup in the world wouldn't hide it. And hide it he must. He needed to blend in with everyone else ... a nondescript guy going about his business ... until it happened and afterwards. Especially afterwards.

He scratched the offending bump on his cheek, but that only drew blood. His blood. He grabbed a tissue and started dabbing, but the blood soaked into it. The more he dabbed, the more the blood poured out from the pimple. Crap.

Somewhere he had read that cold water stopped bleeding. He grabbed a couple more tissues, soaked them under cold running water, squeezed out the excess, and applied them to his cheek.

Half an hour later, he was ready—plain white T-shirt, denim cut-offs, short hair combed back, and old sandals. He pushed a plain black cap onto his head and took a last look in the mirror. The pimple now resembled a colourless bump thanks to the concealing cream he had stolen from Jessie's dresser.

He forced a smile, slung the backpack over his shoulders, careful that the knife inside didn't brush his back. He had better uses for it. As he thought about all these uses, his smile widened.

He strode through the doorway humming Bobby Darin's ***Mack the Knife****.*

***Dana*:**

I pushed the door open, staggered onto the balcony and shoved the door shut behind me.

Clutching my arms together and leaning against the wall, I took several deep breaths, but still had the shakes. I willed myself to calm down as my eyes scrutinized the balcony table.

Her body sat hunched over the table. From the door she appeared asleep. The dim light from the overhead lantern cast sufficient shadows to hide the knife. I tiptoed towards the table, telling my heart to put on its brakes, but it remained in the Indy 500. I touched her wrist. No pulse. Dead. What was the matter? Hadn't I believed my own brother? Sweat started forming at my hairline. Pushing back my short bangs, I stepped behind her. The knife was wedged in her middle back with only the handle protruding. I leaned against the wall and tried taking deliberate breaths, but my heart still raced, and the sweat underneath the roots of my hair threatened to erupt into a waterfall. Just the hot, humid night, of course. But I switched my eyes to the peripherals.

The cement floor with its all-weather green rug. The solid oak door. The iron balcony railing and above. But the eyes could play tricks on you, especially when partnered with the mind. Despite the stars, everything seemed darker than the night. The closest stars seemed to take on shapes. Faces. Faces of little boys. I couldn't seem to get past those little boys—Aaron, Jimmie, and David, their features swirling around in my head, David's looming larger and closer. Reminding me of what had happened.

The boys were all gone away now. Would they come back? Alive?

Especially David.

My son.

Chapter One

Mid-afternoon, Wednesday, August 12, 1998

Dana:

I still wasn't sure we were making the right decision. Especially with a six-year-old boy in the picture. And we would be dealing with criminals.

I took the last sip from my second coffee and tossed it in the nearby garbage bin. Today was my day off. From force of habit I sat in the Thurston Mini-Mall on a bench facing Chalmers Shoe Store. I nodded at Ray Chalmers as he adjusted a pair of runners in the window. He gave me his usual scowl in return. On my lap lay a sketch pad and on the bench, a piece of charcoal, my regular tools for recording sights and sound. I had started drawing the shoes in the window but my mind kept straying to Friday evening when Bast and I would be launching our business: The Attic Investigative Agency. Yesterday morning, we had taped a live interview with Christine Bellows, the Thurston Morning Show host on CKNT. Again I wondered if we were doing the right thing, considering our circumstances—Bast, a former crime reporter and me, a part-time mall security guard in plainclothes who occasionally freelanced for Lawrence and Orley. I also had a six-year-old son.

"Mommy, Mommy. Look what Uncle Bast bought me."

I put down the sketch pad as he charged over and shook the contents of a plastic bag onto the bench. A stuffed beaver, complete with teeth, tumbled out. At least it wasn't a racoon. They were all on our roof. Bast was continually chasing them away.

"Oh my, David," I said.

"His name is Beechnut." David grinned.

"How many do you have now?"

"Ten. And I'm not stopping until I get a hundred. Debbie says that's a good number."

"Oh she does, does she?" asked my fraternal twin, appearing with a bag of hamburgers from the A & W. "Where does she think we'll put them?" He smiled. "She'll have to take a few home with her each time she finishes looking after you." Bast sat down beside me. He glanced at my sketch pad. "I see you have a thing about shoes."

Little did he know. Once I could figure out why that particular red and white sneaker Ray had been fiddling with looked out of place in the store display, I would tell him. It wasn't just its colour as it sat among pink, white and blue sneakers. Something else was off.

Or maybe it was me, getting antsy about Friday.

"No, Bast, just doing my job."

"Which one?" My brother's lip curled up. "Artist or snoop?"

"Bast!" I shook the sketch at him. Then dropped it as I heard the caterwauling coming down the corridor from my left.

"Help. He's gone. Jimmie's gone. Somebody call the police." The woman's voice was high and shaking.

I swung around.

It was Debbie, thrashing her arms around and running like somebody lit by a firecracker, sending mall shoppers scurrying away in all directions. Ray jumped back from the store's window display, but seemed to get a grip on himself when Bast reached Debbie and grabbed her arms. Bast tried to lead her over to the bench. They careened into a fellow in a white T-shirt and black cap who was strolling by. His backpack whacked Debbie's left arm. Bast glowered at him, but Debbie didn't seem to notice as the fellow kept walking. Bast led her to the bench. She didn't sit, just glared at me as if I wasn't there and continued screaming and dragging Bast into her jumping-jack motions. I could feel the collective breath of the other shoppers. A quick glance showed them standing still as if stopped by a force field.

"Jimmie's gone," Debbie said, and I turned my head back towards her. "And it's my fault. I was babysitting him and I left him. It's my fault."

"Take it easy, Debbie. Look at me; it's Dana." I stood up and put my hand on her other arm. She lowered her voice to a murmur but continued squirming. I felt a tug from behind and turned around.

"Mommy, what's wrong with Debbie?" David's face was paler than chalk.

Debbie looked down and seemed to see us for the first time. She and David locked eyes. Debbie's mouth formed an "oh" as she lowered herself to her knees and covered her face with her hands.

"I'm sorry, David. I didn't mean to frighten you. I didn't mean to let it happen to Jimmie. I didn't mean ..."

"It's okay," I said, looking first at Debbie and then at David. I hugged him. "David, Debbie has had a bad experience, but she's going to be okay. Uncle Bast and I will get to the bottom of this. Can you sit quietly with your new beaver while we do this?"

"Okay, Mommy."

Getting to the bottom of this wasn't a one-step process. Debbie's story came out in gasps and pauses.

"I was babysitting Jimmie ... as a favour to Mom ... One of her friends was stuck ... her oldest child was rushed to the hospital with appendicitis and her husband's away on business ... and Jimmie ... well, he's hyper and he kept running around their house yelling and screaming, so I took him here." Debbie tore at her hair.

"I had to go to the bathroom so took him in the Ladies. I left him playing with the soap container while I went inside the stall ... I heard the washroom door open—it squeaks ... and footsteps. Jimmie yelled 'let go of me' and there were scuffling sounds. By the time I'd pulled up my jeans and ran out of the stall it had gone quiet and *Jimmie was gone ...*"

Bast patted her shoulder. "Take it easy. Now, was anyone else in the washroom when you came out of the stall?"

"No, and no one when I went into the stall either. Oh my God." She continued yanking her hair and started rocking on her knees. "I should have kept him home."

"Yes, you should have if you're looking after a child," a stern female voice said from behind me. "I wouldn't want you babysitting my grandkids."

I swung around to face a skinny grey-haired woman who towered over me. Her thin lips were clamped together as she marched closer and wagged her finger at Debbie.

"Ma'am, calm down." I said. "I'm from s ..."

"Good God." Another woman gasped. "There's been a kidnapping."

A baby began crying.

"Call the cops," a shaky voice said.

Call the cops; call the cops. It rose like a call to arms, drowning out the squawking baby.

"Quiet!" I yelled.

The disjointed roar stopped abruptly. I took a deep breath.

"My name is Dana Bowman and I'm with security at the mall. I will report this. The police will be here soon. Meantime, please stay put and stay calm."

The crowd began shuffling and murmuring, but soon settled down, except for the grey-haired lady. Her face boiled up into an angry scowl as if someone had stolen her thunder, her authority.

"Ma'am." I faked a smile. "Why don't you help keep an eye on everybody else to make sure they don't leave?"

She glowered at me, nodded and positioned herself on the far side of Debbie and Bast as if to include them in her watch.

I turned to Bast and whispered, "I'm also checking the Ladies. I'll call you on your cell."

"Mommy, can I come with you?" David asked.

Shit. I didn't want a repeat of Debbie and Jimmie.

"David, why don't you stay with Uncle Bast and help cheer up Debbie."

"Okay, Mom. She can play with Beechnut."

I left him, dangling the new stuffed animal in front of Debbie's face.

Upon reaching the side corridor I called Barney Bevens, head of mall security, and my boss. He said he would call 911 and report it as a probable kidnapping. I turned into the side corridor—empty. For a place where someone came screaming out of a doorway, you'd think there would be people nosing around. Or at least the security guard currently on duty. Hopefully security caught something, but it looked dark. Shit. I made a mental note to tell Barney that yet another camera was on the fritz. A twinge of guilt hit me, as this was my security turf. But it *was* my day off. I pushed open the door to the Ladies.

Two women stood in front of the sinks, one washing her hands, the other combing her short blond hair. The stalls were empty.

"Hi. I'm looking for a friend. Did either of you see a young woman, late teens, long black hair? She would have been with a little boy about six or seven?"

"Nope," they both said.

"Did you hear or see anything unusual around here in the last few minutes?"

"Nope," the hair comber said.

"Why are you asking all these questions?" The other lady moved to the right and pulled a paper towel from the dispenser and started wiping her hands as if she was Lady Macbeth. "You a cop or something?"

"Or something, maybe." I noticed the overturned soap dispenser at the sink where she had stood.

"Was that soap dispenser like that when you came in?"

"Yeah, it was. Some stupid kid probably did that." She scowled in disgust. "Some people's kids are no better than their mommies."

"Wait a minute." The other lady stopped mid-comb. "I remember hearing somebody yelling like a banshee just before I came to the washroom. I was back by the Zellers, but it looked like a bunch of people were crowded around the end of the main hall. Then it got silent and the crowd seemed to move on, so I gave it no further thought."

"How long ago was this?" I asked.

"Maybe five to ten minutes." She shrugged. "I wasn't keeping track of time."

"Okay. Please stay put."

"Look, what's going on?" Ms. Handwasher asked. "If you're not a cop, who are you?"

"I'm security, so I'm telling you to stay put."

Ignoring their gasps, I hauled out my cell and called Bast, then Debbie's mother, my friend Madge. My call went into Madge's voice mail.

The police arrived. A constable shepherded us out of the washroom. While giving my statement, I could hear the din coming from the main area. When the constable took us there, it seemed as if the whole Cooks Regional force—uniforms, plainclothes including two from Forensics who headed for the washroom—were present. The mall went into lockdown, and the police told us to stay put and keep quiet until Detective Sergeant Fielding and Detective Harker from Major Crimes arrived. That set some of them off again.

"What?" A woman shrieked from the back of the crowd. "My daughter is in Zellers. Oh God, I don't want her to get snatched."

"How long do we have to wait?" a man asked from behind me. "I have to pick up my son from school and take him to soccer."

"What?"

"How?"

"Please stay calm," said one of the uniforms. "You are in no danger."

"But my daughter is in Zellers," said the woman. Her voice had now hit the shrieking level. "She's not here with us. Someone could be taking her this very minute. Someone do something. Someone ... oh, please ... someone ..."

One of the constables broke through the horde over to her. In the space between the turned heads I could see her, hands over eyes and body rocking sideways. The constable touched her arm gently.

"Ma'am, I need you to calm down. Can you do that for me? I will go to Zellers and bring your daughter to you." He lowered his voice and I didn't hear the rest.

"Dana." It was Barney. "I'll speak to you later." Then he strode towards a man who was obviously a plainclothes walking towards us and began talking to him. I turned towards the shoe store.

A uniform with his back to me was questioning Ray Chalmers. His words weren't audible, but his face appeared drained. I glanced at Bast who had an angry look on his face. David was tossing the beaver around and running after it. Debbie stood with one of the constables, who seemed to be blocking her access to anywhere. I picked up on Bast's anger, or maybe it was my own, and stomped over to Debbie and her guard.

"Constable," I said. "I'm with mall security and I'd like to have a word with Debbie."

"Sorry, you have to stay apart until Fielding gets here."

"Fielding? Who is this Fielding?"

"You don't really want to know that." My brother's voice sounded from behind. I swung around. Bast had his hand on David's shoulder which seemed to have calmed him until he saw me.

"Mommy, I want to go home. Beechnut wants to go home." He started shaking the stuffed animal in my face. "Can we go home now? We're very tired."

"Sorry, you have to stay put."

"Want to go home. Beechnut is tired." David started waving the beaver in the constable's face."

"Shut up kid. We all want to go home." This from Soccer Dad.

"Why don't you shut up, you moron?" a raspy male voice said.

"What did you call me?"

The crowd started to shake and sway. A man with an enormous beer belly thrust his way through and over to Soccer Dad.

"You heard me," he said shoving a fist at Soccer Dad. "A kid has been kidnapped and all you can think of is going home?"

"All right break it up," a constable said as he and another uniform separated the two men, and led them away.

"It's okay, folks," said the plainclothes who had been talking to Barney. "I'm Detective Paul Harker from Major Crimes. Detective Sergeant Donald Fielding has been held up at headquarters so I will be running things here. Now, who first reported the kidnapping to mall security?"

"I did," I said. "Dana Bowman here—from security. I reported it to my boss."

"Ms. Bowman, I'd like a few words with you."

"My son, David ..."

Harker pointed to his left. Barney was leading David towards the end of the mall—probably to his office.

"We can talk to your son later." Harker shrugged, dismissing David as unimportant. "Now Barney tells me you're some kind of undercover security here at the mall. I don't want you meddling in this. Just answer our questions, tell us what you know, and let us do our jobs."

The man would never be handsome even if he deleted the glower. The attitude also needed more than fine tuning. I almost didn't mention the security camera on the fritz by the washrooms, but I got over it fast. A child was missing, probably kidnapped.

"There is one thing," I said.

We could leave, finally, after answering numerous questions and practically signing our lives away. But there was nothing for them to have on us, or was there? I looked over at Debbie, now being interrogated by Detective Harker. I couldn't hear their words, but from Debbie's slow footsteps back each time the detective's mouth moved, it couldn't be good news. Harker wore a perpetual frown which expanded into a grotesque moving mouth when he spoke.

As we exited the mall, I tried Madge again on my cell.

"Madge, where are you?" I said into her voicemail. "Something is happening to Debbie. Call me."

Chapter Two

Evening, Wednesday, August 12, 1998

Bast:

Bast paced around in the attic inside the agency's main office, complete except for a few bookshelves and books, of course. He had debated whether to place his crime writing books and newspaper clippings on the shelves, but what the hell. They were his past and his ticket of experience into the detective business. He couldn't remember writing about child mall kidnappings, though.

His pacing brought him to his desk. He sat down and booted up the desktop PC. He checked the home phone line and it was clear, so he dialled up and opened his Netscape browser. He did a search for "mall children kidnappings." A short list popped up and he began clicking on the links, one after the other.

"Bast, Bast." His sister charged into the room. "Come on downstairs and see the news on TV. They just announced the headlines and will be going into the story in a minute."

"There's something here, too." Bast pointed to the small screen and began reading out loud. "A boy was snatched from the Shawnhessy Centre Mall in northwest Toronto and police ..."

"There's another one?" Dana stared at him as if stymied. "God, that makes three."

"Three?"

"Yes, the newscast downstairs said that the one here in Thurston was similar to one in east end Toronto."

Bast stood up from his chair so fast it fell over. The two charged downstairs to the living room where the newscast about the kidnappings was just getting underway.

Breaking News flashed across the TV screen.

A blond male in his mid-30s began speaking.

I'm standing in front of the Mini-Mall in Thurston, just north of Toronto where a six-year-old boy disappeared this afternoon. (A headshot of a boy with mousey brown hair appeared at the bottom right). *Jimmie Halpern was at the mall with his babysitter, Debbie Sangwell, when he disappeared. The 19-year-old-babysitter had left the boy alone in the main part of the Ladies Washroom while she was in a stall. She heard the washroom door squeak open and then Jimmie screaming "let me go." She rushed out of the stall but found the boy was gone and it was now quiet. There was no one else in the washroom. She started screaming and ran out into the corridor. Police swooped down on the mall but could find no trace of Jimmie.*

This incident is similar to two that occurred recently, one in the East End Toronto Centre on July 22 and one in Shawnhessy Centre Mall, in Toronto's west end, July 29. In all three cases, the child was a boy of six or seven with his mother or in the Thurston case, a babysitter, who had gone into the ladies washroom with the boys. The boys stayed in the main washroom area while the mother or caregiver was in the stall. During that time, the ladies heard the washroom door open and the boys scream "let me go" or "leave me alone." When the ladies rushed out of the stall, they found the boys gone.

The camera cut to Detective Harker.

"Not that jerk," Dana said. She looked over at Bast. "What? You look like a ghost that died."

"Sh."

We are looking at the records of all pedophiles in the area and beyond. We are also checking out mall video tapes. In the meantime we urge parents to keep their children, whether boys or girls, under close supervision and if you have to use a public washroom, make sure you have another adult whom you know with you to watch your child. If anyone has information, please call police at 911.

The camera cut back to the reporter.

We'll keep you up to date when we have more information. This is Charles Haas at CKNT. Back to you Morgan.

Thank you Charles. In other news ...

Bast hit the remote and stood up.

"Hey, I wanted to get more information, Bast."

"They told us all they know. Let's check on the other kidnappings online upstairs."

He took the stairs two at a time. From below he heard Dana call, "We have an elevator installed now if you're in such a hurry."

"I need the exercise," he said over his shoulder. Running up two flights of stairs seemed quicker than standing in an elevator. And he had to get away from that newscast. He felt ashamed that it wasn't just the story that started his insides churning.

He was already scanning the online news list for more stories when his sister stomped into the room.

"I get it now, Bast. You knew that the elevator wasn't working properly. Did it ever occur to you that I might like to know too?"

"Huh?" Bast turned towards her. "The elevator's not working?"

"The door doesn't close on its own, and then the elevator jerks, like it has a bad case of the jitters and lands with almost a thump. I was sure glad to get out of it."

"Okay, I'll call Trillium tomorrow. And no, I didn't know it wasn't working because I haven't used it yet. Now, let's get back to these other mall kidnappings." Bast swung around and began staring at the computer screen.

"Jeez, Bast. Just because you're taller than me doesn't mean you have to get all huffy on me."

"I'm not getting huffy. Right now these kidnappings are more important than a malfunctioning elevator."

"Yeah, well don't forget we have a big opening reception for our agency in two days. We don't want any of our guests getting stuck in the elevator."

Bast jerked up from his chair and glared at Dana. "Okay! I said I'd call the guy tomorrow. Can we leave it alone for now?"

"All right. Keep your voice down. You've probably woken up David. I'm going to check on him."

Bast glared at her as she attempted to stomp out of the room without making any noise. He heard her footsteps head for the stairs and turned back to the computer. Sweat formed at the roots of his hair and beard, and his armpits were damp. He ran fingers through his beard and turned back to the screen.

"David's fast asleep and hugging Beechnut," Dana said from behind. He hadn't heard her come in. "And all nine of the other beavers are lying on both sides of him on his bed."

"We'll just have to get David a larger bed."

Dana laughed and Bast knew the air was cleared ... for now.

Dana pulled up a chair beside her brother. "Okay, Bast, move over." She began clicking on links. Let's check out these news reports."

They read.

On the *Toronto Daily Herald* website archives:

Photo of a boy with black hair and a woman both smiling.

Six-year old boy kidnapped from east end mall washroom July 22, 1998

Jason Shake

Staff Reporter

It was supposed to be a belated birthday treat for seven-year-old Johnny Corvette, who was sick in bed with the flu on his birthday two weeks ago. But a trip with his mother to buy a train set turned into a nightmare.

"We stopped at the Ladies washroom," his mother Alicia Corvette, 28, said. "I left him in the main area with strict orders to stay put while I was in the stall. One of the other ladies washing her hands even said she'd watch him. I heard her heels clacking and the door open. Then it ... the door I mean, opened again and Johnny started screaming, 'Don't hurt me; please don't hurt me. Let go of me.' I charged out as soon as I could and he was gone. No one else was in the washroom. So I ran out and started screaming."

That's when security intervened and called police. Police locked down the mall and interviewed those present. No one saw anything or heard anything beyond Alicia Corvette's screaming.

"I thought she was a madwoman gone berserk," said Gretchen Sinclair, 84, who was shopping for a birthday present for her granddaughter.

"This is a nice mall. We don't get this kind of thing happening here," said mall manager Gordon Falconie.

Asked to describe the woman in the washroom, Corvette said she was about 30, with short blond hair and wearing denim shorts and some sort of tank top or t-shirt and high heels. Corvette couldn't describe her face but thought she might have been wearing sunglasses.

Police are urging parents and caregivers to keep young children in their sight at all times when shopping at malls.

"That's rather short," Dana said.

"Yeah, it doesn't tell us too much." Bast stroked his red beard. "Let's look at the west-end Toronto story."

We did, and it was almost a repeat scenario except the location and date and boy kidnapped—Shawnhessy Centre Mall in northwest Toronto, Wednesday, July 29, 1998. He wondered if there was any significance in the one week gap—and the boy, Aaron King was six. Again, a photo at the top, this time of a boy with red curly hair. Here too, a woman washing her hands in the washroom was supposedly keeping an eye on the boy, but Aaron's mother was so distraught she couldn't remember if the woman was young, old, blond or grey. The Thurston mall story showed up in the *Toronto Daily Herald* home page.

"A week apart for the first two, but two weeks between number two and number three," Dana said. "And it's also just outside of Toronto. I wonder why."

"It could be some sort of a pattern," Bast said, frowning. "Now in this part about today's kidnapping, Debbie comes across as an irresponsible flake." He turned toward Dana. "Are you sure you want her to continue looking after David?"

"Yeah, I suppose so. She's always been good with David. No problems. And Madge is my best friend. She helped me when I was pregnant with David and after."

"Dana, don't take this the wrong way. I respect your loyalty to your friend, but Madge is in her mid-40s and has a hell of a lot more experience with kids than her daughter."

"Are you calling Debbie incompetent?"

"I'm not saying ... I'm only ..."

"Spit it out, Bast. What exactly are you trying to say?"

Her cell rang before he had a chance to answer. Dana opened it.

"Hello," she said. "Yes. Yes. Oh no." She mouthed "Madge."

He turned towards the computer again and started doing more research. But he knew he needed to talk to Debbie again.

"Madge wants us to investigate," Dana said.

Bast swung around and looked at his sister over by the doorway.

"Find Jimmie?" he asked. "He's not her son. What does Jimmie's mother want?"

"Not exactly, although that would be part of it. Madge wants us to exonerate her daughter."

Chapter Three

Just after midnight, Thursday, August 13, 1998

Dana:

Thud.

The latest Peter Robinson crashed to the floor. I jerked awake, bolted up, yawned and turned two sleepy eyes towards my digital. 12:23 a.m. glowed in red.

Thud.

This time the sound reverberated up the heat vent from down below. What was Bast doing in the basement at this hour? Or David? More noises resembling the squish of feet on cardboard and paper, followed by a splash, propelled me out of bed and into the hallway. I peered up the attic stairs. Not Bast. His door remained closed.

My heart hammered into overdrive. I sped barefoot into my son's room. He lay sprawled on top of the covers, Beechnut in hand and the other beavers now on the floor. A light snore emanated from the bed. I grabbed David's water gun and closed his door behind me. More scrapings and thuds from below convinced me no time existed to refill the gun. Hopefully the gun's size would distract the intruder and freeze him into temporary immobility. I shook the gun against my T-shirt, pushed my black bangs off my forehead, took a deep breath and charged down the two flights of stairs.

No one.

The window over the laundry tubs hung open inside the room, its screen shredded. Scratches showed on the frame near the broken lock. To the window's left, bold red letters on whitewashed walls screamed "Detectives get out." Then my nose picked up the sickening smell and I followed its trail to the left laundry tub, peered down and gagged at the stench.

A hunting knife lay on its side. A red mass spilled from the blade and trailed onto torn papers piled at one end of the tub. The end of one paper showed the tip of a running shoe. *My* sketches. Black hairs curled around and out from the blade. An eyeball peeked out from another paper fragment. I sucked in air, jumped backward and charged up three flights of stairs. When I reached the attic floor the alarm system for the business kicked in. Over its sirens I banged on Bast's locked door.

"Bast, wake up!"

After several calls, the door slid open, and my usually calm brother peeked out.

"What the hell, Dana? Get that thing away from me. And keep it down. You'll wake up David." He held his hands over his ears and scowled down at me.

I glared into his puffy eyes and pointed the gun down. A little leftover water trickled onto my bare feet.

"Someone's broken into the house," I whispered.

"What, the offices up here?"

"No, stupid, the basement. Oh, shut that damn thing off."

"Oh." Bast reached inside his room, pulled out the remote and punched in the alarm controls.

"Where?" he asked.

"The basement. He's gone but he left a bloody mess."

"You went down there without calling me? We're supposed to be a team."

"You wouldn't have woken up in time."

"All right. Cool down. Did you see anyone?"

"No."

"What about the elevator?" Bast scratched his right ear and frowned. "Or did you go downstairs in it?"

"No." I shrugged. "Remember. It's not working right. It's ..."

"Mommy, Mommy what's going on?"

"Shit. David's awake." I charged down to the second floor to calm my son.

An hour and a half later I sat on the bottom basement step and huddled in the oversized sweatshirt I'd grabbed just before the uniform cops arrived. My chin rested in my hands and I involuntarily sighed. I averted my eyes from the sign and looked towards the tub. Underneath it, more of my old sketches moved down from the attic lay in a tattered heap.

"Why, Bast?"

Bast stood, stroking his red beard as he eyed the two Forensic detectives—Stewart and Tractor. Tractor dug into his Ident. Kit and when Stewart finished shooting his camera at the tubs and wall, Stewart dusted around the window and tub for fingerprints.

"Why?" I repeated.

"Why what? The break-in, the crap in the tub?"

"Both and messing my sketches up."

"Are you sure you didn't leave your sketches like that when you took them downstairs?"

"No."

"Take it easy, sis." Bast sat down beside me. "Just be thankful it was downstairs, not up in the office or in David's room. At least you got him back to sleep, although telling him his uncle had a nightmare ..." He chuckled.

I glared at him. "Sorry, Bast, This B and E's got me rattled—on top of the mall kidnapping and Debbie. Some detective, huh? And the business isn't officially opened until Friday. Why would anyone break in here before then?"

"Leave it to the cops," he said.

"What? We open an investigation business and before it's official, we're broken into and a sign says to bugger off."

"The offices weren't broken into, Dana. It was our home."

"Yeah, but the warning was for us, the private detectives."

"Well, you know, that might just be a ruse, or pure frustration on their part. You did interrupt them when you stomped down the stairs. And they didn't take it up to the offices."

"Maybe there was some confusion about which floor our business is on. Nothing seems to be missing, but we get a threat and that ... that bloody mess in the tub. Somebody doesn't like us." I shivered.

"Ahem, excuse me, ma'am."

Stewart and Tractor stood before us. Stewart's camera bobbed on his pot belly. Tractor, a pockmarked fellow with a receding hairline, cleared his throat.

"I've dusted for fingerprints and footprints and I'll need to take yours for elimination," he said. "We'll also need to take some of the sketches with us."

"Fine," I said.

As he was finishing, Stewart said, "Ma'am, the window over the laundry tubs is your point of entry. Hey, Marsden." He turned back to the uniform cop, one of the first on the scene. "I'm going to give Fielding a call. He better see this. Make sure ..."

"Fielding?" Bast asked. "He's Major Crimes. What's he got to do with this?"

Stewart's mouth zipped up and his eyes stared right through Bast.

"Oh, the last B and E like this, the homeowner surprised the suspect and got knocked around a bit," Marsden said.

"Cut it, or you'll stay in uniform the rest of your career," Stewart said. He forced a smile as he turned to Bast and me. "Not to worry. No one's been hurt here." Then he turned back to the constable and continued with his orders. "Marsden, make sure everyone stays put until Fielding gets here." He nodded at us. "I'm going to check the elevator."

"I'll check outside," Tractor said. "What's the easiest way to the backyard?"

"Up the stairs, through the kitchen and out the back door," I said.

Stewart smiled as he yanked out a cell phone from his jacket pocket and started punching in numbers. I moved off the stairs to let him and Tractor get by. When they left, I dashed over to the laundry tubs. I wanted to see what "this" meant.

"Ma'am, don't touch anything," Marsden said from behind.

"I just want to look, not touch. I think I got that right."

"Detective Stewart said ..."

"Oh, screw Stewart. Listen, you just keep guard like he said. I'll do my looking, and if you don't tell what I did I won't tell what you didn't do. Deal?" I smiled up at Marsden.

"But ..." Marsden began.

"Look, I can tell him you let me all over the evidence. That should keep you in uniform for many years." I smirked.

He blushed. Bast chuckled. Marsden took six steps backwards, then stood at attention like the raw recruit he probably was.

I sucked in my breath and inspected the left laundry tub. Knife, blood, hair and eyeball, make that two eyeballs, lay as before; so did the sketches. The hairs curled around the knife seemed too thick for human hair. A cheap wig perhaps? But whose eyes? The blood had even splattered into the right laundry tub, colouring the T-shirts and the water they soaked in. To the left of the tub on the floor, a white pile of paper scraps beckoned me. Closer inspection revealed that they were more sketches, torn into jagged pieces and dumped. No blood. I crouched down and began fingering a few scraps.

"Ma'am," Marsden said.

I turned towards him. "Remember our agreement."

"You said look, not touch."

"That was the mess in the tub. This is on the floor. We had no agreement about this."

"Better listen to her," Bast said.

I swung around. He still sat on the bottom step, his arms folded and the corners of his mouth arched in amusement.

"All right," Marsden said. "Five minutes. You have to finish before Fielding gets here."

"Fine." I returned to the floor and tried to piece the sketches together. "Why would someone rip up my sketches of shoes? Chalmers's runners. What the hell does that have to do with the threat and the blood, a knife, eyeballs and a clobbered homeowner? How's he doing anyway?" I turned around to Marsden.

Marsden merely grunted. His face resembled a bonfire.

"Take it easy, Dana," Bast said. "The cops will find them."

I moved towards the sign. From behind, someone cleared his throat followed by Marsden's whispered "drop it." I did and the papers scattered at my feet. As I headed for the stairs, a large black shoe, followed by another, stepped down.

A man in grey pants and navy blazer moved towards Bast. Bast inched away.

"Dana," he said. "Meet Detective Sergeant Donald Fielding of Major Crimes, Cooks Regional Police Force. Fielding, Dana Bowman. When Fielding is in charge he likes to be where the action is, especially if the conditions are offbeat." Bast sneered.

I held out my right hand to Fielding. He ignored it and Bast. I dropped my hand as Fielding nodded. With his barrel-chested frame of about 5'9" Fielding didn't dare do more. He made Bast look like a pogo stick. Fielding opened his mouth.

"D ... D ... Dana Bowman?"

Marsden studied his notepad. I merely smiled, then stared directly into Fielding's eyes. Deep blues—cold eyes—stared back. I glanced over to Bast and back to Fielding. A chill appeared to drift between them. This could get interesting, as we would probably have to deal a lot with this Fielding in our work.

"Ms. Bowman. I understand you and your partner here are opening a private investigation business, Thurston's first." He pointed to the wall message. "Know of anyone who wants to stop you from opening your business?" he said in a clipped English accent.

"No. And we're a branch of Lawrence and Orley, Private Investigators in Toronto, Vancouver and Montreal."

"Ah, yes, Lawrence and Orley, I've heard of them," Fielding said. "Tough, but good reputation, insurance investigations, surveillance, missing persons and the like. Orley's dead now, I believe." Fielding rubbed his square jaw. The man could pass for handsome except for that jaw. It jutted and showed signs of late-day stubble.

"Yes, pardon?" I realized Fielding was asking more questions.

"I said 'What is your end of this investigative business?' I understand Mr. Overture, here, has a shall we say mixed background as an investigative crime reporter. But where do you come in as partner in an investigation business?" Fielding stared down at me and I drew myself up to my full four feet eleven inches.

"Dana is my sister, my fraternal twin," Bast said. His sneer was more pronounced.

"I ... I ... d ... didn't m ... mean it that way," Fielding said. Maybe the man only stuttered when on unsure grounds.

"Hey, my sister has freelanced for Lawrence and Orley. She also caught that kleptomaniac in the Mini-Mall last year. Don't you dare short-change her."

The look Fielding gave Bast almost made the devil appear angelic.

"And where did you say you now live, Mr. Overture?" Fielding asked.

"I didn't, but since you ask, here. My room's on the third floor, the same floor as the agency. The way I see it, this is a house break."

"No, it's the business," I said. "The note in red ..."

Footsteps thumping down the stairs interrupted me.

"Don." Stewart addressed Fielding. "There's a strange old woman with a flowered straw hat at the front door. Says this house has been in her family for years and demands to see Ronald Bowman."

"Good Lord, Great Aunt Doris," I said.

"Dana, is that you down there?" Aunt Doris tended to bellow. "Where's Ronald? Mercy, what is going on here? Police all over the place. In George Howard Bowman's house, God rest his soul. This can't be good for David."

George Howard Bowman was Ron's late father. Aunt Doris had a habit of treating him like dead royalty.

"In the basement, Aunt Doris. The place was broken into."

Aunt Doris perched three steps from the bottom with hands on hips. Her face made a gargoyle look like a runner-up in a beauty contest. As usual, the Great One had piled on the powder over wrinkles and floppy cheeks, and her mouth was redder than a clown's on parade. Tractor stood at the top of the stairs and shrugged his shoulders.

"Gracious, Dana, don't shout," Doris said. "You would think Ronald would have you trained, by now."

"Ron and I are divorced." I glared at her, the family fossil.

"Well, I never. I come for a nice friendly visit and look what I find." She huffed and turned to Bast. "And what are you doing here in Ronald's house, at this hour? Shouldn't you be down in Toronto with all the other queers?"

"Aunt Doris, Bast bought Ron out?"

"You mean he helped you steal the house from Ronald."

"Excuse me, Aunt Doris, but we've had a break-in here and Detective Sergeant Fielding was asking us some questions," Bast said.

"You haven't answered mine. What right do you have here, Sebastian?" She jabbed his chest with her finger.

"He lives here now," I said.

That seemed to set everyone off.

"What? Does Ronald know?" Aunt Doris asked.

"That's right, Dana and I are ..." Bast said.

Fielding raised his hands. "Hold it," he said.

Silence. Fielding took charge.

"Now, Aunt Doris, is it? Officer Marsden here will take you up to wait in the kitchen. Then, after I question this couple, you can sort everything out with them. Marsden?" Fielding nodded to him. "A word with you first."

The "word" seeped out in loud whispers. "Find out what that old biddy really wants here at 3 a.m." Then, a smile, and "that's right, Aunt Doris, you go upstairs with Officer Marsden. Now, Mrs. Bowman, is it? Oh, I'm sorry. You're divorced. Ms. Bowman and Mr. Overture. Perhaps we could clear up this matter of the B and E. You first Ms. Bowman."

I preferred the man when he stuttered. Now he sounded colder than marble. My face flushed but my bones registered below zero. When he switched to questioning Bast, I edged towards the pieces of sketches on the floor.

"What anyone would want with shoe sketches, just some off-the-cuff etchings I did while working at the Mini-Mall," I muttered.

"Excuse me, you can't go there yet." Stewart interrupted my musings. I'd forgotten about him and Tractor.

"You guys finished here?" I asked.

"Not quite."

I stepped back and stared past the laundry tubs up at the window and tried to ignore the stench. "He must have lots of muscle, and not the flabby kind, to jimmy it like that."

Stewart's face registered a smile. I moved over to Bast and Fielding.

"Detective Sergeant Fielding," I said.

"P ... p ... pardon?" Fielding stopped mid-sentence to stare at me.

"Was this window pried open? My ex and I hadn't been able to budge it for years, and Bast and I just use the other window for air."

Fielding put on latex gloves, strode over to the tubs and peered up. He dabbed his right forefinger along the window frame and lock spot, reached under the window and slid his finger along. Then he moved his finger under his nose and sniffed.

"It appears to have been oiled rather recently," he said. "Inside and outside. Did either you or your brother oil that window lately?"

Chapter Four

A few hours after dawn, Thursday, August 13, 1998

Dana:

I awoke to a lumpy beanbag, a large one, jumping on my legs. "We had a buglary," David said.

I did not need that at ... my bedside clock showed 8:30, but it was difficult to see with my left eye still glued shut.

"We had a buglary. Mommy. We had a bug ..."

"Burglary, David. Don't be vulgar."

"What's vuglar, Mommy?"

I rolled my eyes heavenward.

"David, your mother's trying to get some sleep." somebody whispered from the doorway.

I sat up, rubbed my eyes, hugged my son, and looked up. Debbie, stood in the doorway. A little colour appeared on her face, and she smiled. Her long, dark hair sparkled in the morning light. Better than yesterday or even last week when she looked washed out and seemed to have no energy. Her dilated pupils had me thinking "drugs" and Madge ransacking their bathroom cabinet. She had found only a bottle of Tylenol with Codeine. When Madge stormed over here and shook the bottle in Debbie's face, she had merely shrugged her shoulders and mumbled, "I had a headache, Mom."

Now, Debbie bubbled over with good cheer. I wondered if it was forced.

"Morning, Dana. Mom and I came over to catch up." A hint of scared, out-of-control Debbie from yesterday flashed briefly in her eyes, until a smile appeared. "When the dragon lady answered the door I knew something was up. So, I tried to keep David out of your room."

I rubbed my eyes again. God, did I really deserve one of Aunt Doris' long visits?

David was now quiet and sitting on my bed. At the mention of his name, he started fidgeting.

Debbie turned her attention to David. "Hey, young man, why don't you get your water gun and go out in the backyard? I'll join you in a few minutes."

I nodded at David, tousled his hair, and gave him a light tap on the back. "Good idea. I have to shower and dress. But I'll join you two a bit later, okay?"

"Mawm? O—kay." David made a face and lumbered out of the room. I knew he was only faking it. He loved playing with that water gun.

"Bast told me about the burglary," Debbie said. "Mother's downstairs in the kitchen now, with your aunt."

"Oh, God."

"Not to worry. Mother overruled Aunt Doris. She's even got your Great One helping to make sandwiches for tomorrow night, with Bast's homemade bread, no less. He's on his daily run. But he said something about checking with a friend at headquarters about something, then running a few errands including getting a new lock for that basement window and someone from Trillium is supposed to come today to fix the elevator."

"Well that friend won't be Fielding. Debbie, did Bast mention this Detective Sergeant Fielding who's investigating our B and E?"

"Yeah, a little, something about him thinking it was an inside job. Anyway, I better get outside with David. See you in a bit."

Last night—no—earlier this morning, once the police left, I had dragged myself back to bed. Great Aunt Doris and Bast had still been up but probably not for long, given Doris's antagonism towards Bast. Crap. How long was she going to hang around?

After a yawn and a stretch, I stepped out of bed, visited the bathroom, and opened my exercise mat. Kim Robertson's *Tender Shepherd* played on the ghetto blaster. I steepled my hands, and with the *Salutation to the Sun*, began my daily Yoga meditation. When marriage to Ron had descended into nothingness, Yoga classes had been the way to find my centre more than to centre myself. Bast could run marathons, but quiet daily beginnings of deep breathing and slow stretching suited me better.

The Yoga session ended with lying on the mat and tightening, then relaxing each muscle frame. Afterwards, followed by a quick shower and dressed in jeans and a T-shirt, I headed downstairs to the cacophony in the kitchen and nodded towards the two sandwich-makers. Through the window I saw David and Debbie playing catch in the backyard.

Grabbing a coffee, I tiptoed down the basement stairs to the laundry room for a daylight look. The window and window ledge felt greasy and dusty. An inside job, Fielding had insinuated when he'd examined the window ledge. He meant Bast. Although agreeing with Fielding that it probably had something to do with the agency's opening, no way would I believe Bast responsible. Fielding probably didn't like Bast because he was gay. I knew better than anyone, except Bast himself, how much he suffered. Our parents, now both dead, had kicked him out of the house at 16, when they found he preferred teenage boys to teenage girls. "Look on the bright side," I had told them. "You never have to worry about him getting some girl pregnant."

Now to the business at hand. The left tub still showed signs of the night's bloody contents. I breathed heavily while plucking out a minute hair left behind. It felt coarse. Holding it up to the window didn't provide any answers so it went back into the tub. Next focus was the sign. In daylight, the red didn't look like blood. I traced the letters. Spray paint maybe. This guy certainly didn't want us in business. Did he have something to hide? I returned to the window and wondered why the culprit would bother to oil the window from the inside or did that occur earlier in the week?

Who had been in the house lately? Let's see, building inspector, fire department inspector, plus a host of friends and acquaintances—Debbie, Madge, Gerald "Stringbean"

Lawrence, Lois Chalmers aka The Pres. of the Mini-Mall Merchants Association and The Fashion Shoppe owner; oh, and Ray, her husband, trailing behind Lois as he usually did. And Rita Brooks, the old lady next door, to say she and her husband, Randall, couldn't make it for the agency opening. She had stayed for tea, but that was in the kitchen. Bast had been up and down to get tools to fix up the attic. But I would not believe him capable of staging a B and E. And David, trailing after him. A six-year old? For Christ sake, Dana, get a grip.

A scream shot in through the open window. I ran up the stairs and collided with Aunt Doris in the kitchen. A bowl of wrapped candy flew out of her hands and crashed to the floor.

"Mercy," she said. "That bowl was a Bowman antique." She stared at the broken pieces as if she had lost a gift from British royalty.

"Oh, stuff it Aunt Doris." I dashed outside to more important concerns.

Madge and Debbie sat on the back porch steps trying to calm down a howling mass in their midst.

"Uncle Bast killed the racoon with my water gun." David hiccupped. He flailed his arms out and whacked Madge in the right eye. Her head snapped up and her hennaed hair flared out, like a mad scientist's. She grasped David harder causing him to stomp his right foot.

"David," I said.

He looked up. The arms and feet stopped.

"Mommy, Uncle Bast killed the racoon. It's covered in blood. Mommy, why did Uncle Bast kill the racoon with my water gun? He could've just chased him off the roof." David hiccupped again.

"It was awful." Debbie leaned against the railing and squinted at the morning sun.

"When I came out they were just running," Madge said.

"Please." I held up a hand, walked over to my son, motioned for him to sit down on the porch step and pulled him close. "Tell me what happened, David, from the beginning."

"Me and Debbie were playing ball and the ball went under that big tree in the back. I ran to get it and when I crawled under its branches ..."

"Yes." I stroked his blond hair, Ron's blond hair.

"There was this poor little racoon lying there all covered in blood. Mommy, why did Uncle Bast kill the racoon?"

"Show me." Standing up, I extended my hand. David grabbed it and I yanked him up.

"Well, I never," Doris said. She stood in the doorway and pointed her finger. "He's just a child."

"Right, Aunt Doris, my child." I bent down to David. "Are you ready to show me?"

David pulled me towards the back end of the yard. At the snowball tree, he pointed to the ground. I swallowed saliva, got down on my knees, lifted the branches touching the ground, crawled underneath and looked down. Well Fielding and company, guess you missed this. An adult racoon lay splayed on its back, dried blood spread over its stomach. I crawled closer. Bald patches mingled with black fur. The eyes were missing. The laundry tub flashed into my mind and the bile started up my gullet. Even a trouble-making racoon didn't deserve this inhumane treatment. I coughed and backed out to where David stood, a worried look on his face.

"Mommy, why did Uncle Bast kill him?"

"David, your Uncle Bast didn't do this."

"Yes, he did, with my water gun."

"David, come here."

"No."

"I know this is painful, but you've got to get this straight. Let's sit down here for a minute first." I stepped away from the tree and sat down. David followed but he remained standing at a distance.

"Okay," he said. "Show me Uncle Bast didn't do this." He pointed to the tree, shuddered, moved closer and huddled down beside me.

"All right." I put my arm around him. "What do you fill your water gun with?"

"Aw, that's easy, Mommy, water." He squinted up at me.

"Okay, and when you and your friends shoot your water guns at each other what happens?"

"We get all wet."

"And does anyone bleed?"

"No, it's only water. Oh, I see." And his frown turned to a smile.

"You see now that Uncle Bast couldn't have killed the racoon with your water gun."

"Yeah. But who did it?" The frown returned and his shoulders tensed under my arm.

"Someone else, and I don't know who, after your Uncle Bast chased it off the roof with the water gun. We have to call the cops now."

"Why, Mommy?"

"Because someone killed this racoon and that's cruel and against the law."

A mini-repeat of last night followed, except the crime scene had moved outdoors.

No Marsden this time, but an older constable, Nancy Nivens, who gently asked David about his find. Then Stewart and Tractor showed up. Did those two ever sleep? Tractor said "Ma'am" and nodded. Stewart merely smiled. The duo stepped outside. Through the kitchen window, I saw them stride over to the snowball. Tractor pointed, and both stared at the tree. Stewart bent down, crawled underneath, soon coming back up and dragging something with him. He stood up and stared again at the tree and then down. He appeared to measure the distance from the tree's branches to the ground, which seemed silly as it was crawl-space only. He took some photos and my gaze returned to Nivens questioning David. Footsteps clomped up the porch steps; the screen door slammed and Stewart stepped inside the kitchen. He punched numbers on his cell.

"Detective Sergeant Donald Fielding?" he said into the phone.

I had no intention of waiting around. Right now, David needed a diversion, not Fielding.

Chapter Five

Morning, Thursday, August 13, 1998

Bast:

Bast parked his Honda behind Cooks Regional Police Headquarters. He needed some information from PC Joseph Oliver, the Records Bureau supervisor. As he pushed open the main door, it hit a mass.

"Well, well if it isn't Thurston's favourite crime writer."

Bast looked up and could feel his face turn the colour of his hair. All he could say was "Charles."

"Nice running into you, too," Haas said. "Come to visit your good friend Oliver?"

Haas's face wore a smirk, and Bast wanted to shove his fist into it. Now where did that come from? Dana was the one who wore her emotions on her sleeve. He was the twin who held it in.

"Sorry, didn't see you," Bast managed to say. He backed away from the door.

"Next time, look first. You'd think after last year you'd have learned that." Haas finished pushing the door open and strode out.

Bast let out the breath he had still been hanging onto. Now all he needed was to run into Fielding.

Luck seemed to be with him as he found Oliver doing front-desk duty.

"Hey, I hear you and your sister have been in the thick of it—first a kidnapping at the mall and then some vandalism at your place." Oliver smiled and stretched his thin fame. "And your nephew was present for both?"

"Yes, but he slept through the 'buglary' as he called it. But he was right there after the kidnapping when Debbie lost it." He scratched his head. "I have my doubts about her as a good babysitter for David anymore, but then she seemed to be more in her usual spirits when she came by with her mother this morning." He leaned forward onto the front desk and looked around. No one else was in sight. "Oliver, I need a couple of favours: first, I need you to okay me getting in at the hospital to talk to Jimmie Halpern's mother. Sorry I can't say more." He looked at the frown on Oliver's face. "It's client confidentiality."

"And second?" Oliver asked.

"Some more information about a string of B and Es in Thurston over the past few weeks. One of the constables at our place last night let that slip and also that one homeowner had tried to stop the burglar and got bumped on the head."

"Hmm, I think I know which constable that is. Don't say." Oliver waved his hands. "But he's right. There's been only a bit of it appearing in the press. We want people to be aware of what's going on but we don't want to alarm them."

"What aren't you telling me?" Bast whispered.

"The assaulted homeowner isn't the only thing." Oliver leaned forward and placed his hand beside his mouth. "Now, this is confidential, and I'm only telling you this as a friend and because you no longer write crime stories. At some of the places broken into, part or all of a dead racoon was found on the property somewhere. I'll e-mail you the report details."

It was all Bast could do to drive to Thurston General Hospital. He kept thinking of Oliver's information, the eyeballs and animal hair found last night in the laundry tubs, and the much alive racoon he had chased off the roof with David's water gun the other day. He felt sick. But he was here to talk to Jimmie's sister and mother.

He took deep breaths as he headed towards the elevators. This time he saw him first—Fielding was just exiting the elevators. He was talking on his cell, then closed it and hurried towards the front door without looking Bast's way. Something must be up.

But not with Jimmie Halpern's mother or sister Shawna. Twenty minutes later he sat in the car in the hospital parking lot and played back part of the interview tape.

Bast: "Did Jimmie mention anyone strange watching him—at school, maybe, or when playing on the street?"

Mrs. Halpern: "No." Bast could barely hear her voice. She sounded like her whole life had been wrenched from her.

Bast: "What about you, Shawna? See anyone unfamiliar hanging around your house at any time? Or following you or Jimmie home."

Shawna: "Nobody strange. And Jimmie didn't say anything to me about anyone watching him at school."

"Does Jimmie play baseball or is he on any sports team?"

"Soccer," said his mother. "He had ... has a good ... a good kick. I can't do this. I'm sorry." Her voice trailed off and was replaced by sobs.

Shawna: "You better go."

Bast: "Thanks for your help. I hope the police find your son soon."

He had said that not only because he wished it to happen, but he wanted them to gather he wasn't butting in on any police investigation per se.

Too bad he would have to change his mind in the next 36 hours.

Chapter Six

Late Morning to Early Evening, Thursday, August 13, 1998

Dana:

I grabbed our swimsuits and some towels.

"Expect us back at suppertime. And don't forget the guy is supposed to be coming to check out the elevator," I told Aunt Doris, ignoring her open mouth and turning to Nivens. "Fielding can talk to us another time. He'll probably be here for the agency opening tomorrow night. Madge, you and Debbie hanging around for a bit, or what?"

"Only until police are finished with us," Madge said. Then, she lowered her voice. "I have to go over to the hospital around noon."

"Hospital? Oh, yeah, Jimmie's sister and mother."

"Yes, that too." Madge screened her mouth with her right hand. "It's Thursday, one of the two abortion days at Thurston General and my day to picket."

"Oh, yeah, I forgot."

"We right-to-lifers have to save as many as we can from the surgeon's knife."

I heard an intake of breath from behind, so turned around, expecting to see Aunt Doris, but Debbie stood a few feet away.

"You okay?" I asked.

"Yes," she said, attempting a smile. Her face had that chalky look from a few weeks ago and her hands wavered around her stomach. As if aware of their movement, she moved her right hand up to her head and shoved a hair strand behind her ear. "Guess yesterday is still bothering me. Well, I have things to do, so better get going. See you later, Dana. David, I'll be here to look after you tomorrow evening. Mom." She grabbed her purse and hurried out the door.

"Teenagers? Who knows what they're thinking." Madge shrugged.

"Okay, I'll see you later, Madge. Take care this afternoon." I nudged David out the front door.

"Car or bikes?"

"Bikes," David said.

We grabbed our bicycles from the front porch, dumped our swimwear and towels into the baskets and walked the bikes down the steps. We climbed aboard and sped down Maitland St. towards Grainger Park.

Grainger Park swept in a semi-circle around an inlet of Snow Lake on the edge of Thurston. The lake derived its name from its dawn mists, which resembled snowstorms. It wasn't like that now, just peaceful blue, the calm broken only by the occasional quack of a swimming duck and the cries of human swimmers. David peddled determinedly beside me, his eyes straight ahead and teeth clenched. I relished my time with him. Because working full-time was necessary to make ends meet, we had limited moments to spend together.

We peddled past the dock and the idle sailboats and rowboats rocking on either side, proceeding to a building sporting the sign "Refreshments/Change Rooms." We parked our bikes, ducked inside and donned our swimsuits.

You would think with a lake, a pool wasn't necessary. But the pool was reserved for one purpose, to teach people to swim. Since water and I hadn't exactly been friends as a kid, I was learning to swim better now, with David. These days swimming lessons emphasized survival swimming. We had learned the automatic float. Today, we tried the dog paddle. Although David paddled fast and easy, my paddle resembled more of a sad dog's flop. Still, the cool water proved refreshing, even if the lessons weren't.

Afterwards, we stopped at a hot dog stand for lunch and cycled home.

It never occurred to me that today's activities would come back to bite me in the face.

Back home the elevator repair guy hadn't shown up so I left Trillium a voice mail message. Bast had the desktop computer open upstairs to a message in the company e-mail inbox. OliverJ@aol.com had e-mailed that since mid-June there were 13 B and Es, four with mutilated racoons (three left on the back porch; only ours under a tree). The other 12 reported stolen jewellery, loose cash, stereos and camcorders. The only vandalism was broken door locks and glass. Ours was the sole basement entry.

"What about the clobbered homeowner?"

"The last place before this one, the homeowner, a man about 40, surprised the suspect," Bast said from behind. "He heard a noise, went to investigate and got clobbered for his efforts. He's okay, but didn't see the suspect."

"Was that a racoon place?"

"Yes. Oh, I fixed the lock on the basement window." Bast stroked his beard. "Might be a good idea to casually sound out our guests tomorrow evening. Some of them might have seen something but didn't report it."

"Maybe we can drum up a little business, as well."

Too bad I didn't know what type of business, or I might have cancelled the open house.

Chapter Seven

Early Evening, Friday, August 14, 1998

Dana:

We *almost* postponed the open house. The body of a young boy, around six, was found dumped in a shallow creek just north of the Toronto/Cooks Region border. Bast and I had looked at each other as the morning newscast blared from the kitchen radio.

Jimmie Halpern?

Aunt Doris had immediately stood up from the table and led David from the room, muttering, "Not for this little boy."

The 12 noon newscast on CKNT TV contained more information. The body was still unidentified, but it had black hair. Jimmie Halpern's hair was mousey brown. Johnny Corvette had black hair. The murdered boy was probably from Toronto but the dumping point was in Cooks Region.

Bast and I decided to go ahead with the Attic Agency opening in remembrance of that poor boy and a reminder that we needed to help keep Thurston safe.

And find Jimmie Halpern.

And in doing so, get Debbie off the suspicious police hook.

After supper, Bast parked our cars in the Brooks's driveway to give our guests more space, and I turned the air conditioning units on in the attic. Debbie came over to babysit David during the open house. Instead of her usual jeans and T-shirt she wore a long flowered dress.

"Nice dress," I said. "Dressing up for the occasion?"

She looked a little pale again but managed a smile with her nod. She cajoled David upstairs to his room with the promise of an adventure with Beechnut and then a scary story.

Grabbing my cell and heading upstairs to the bedroom, I poked my head inside the closet and pulled out a simple sleeveless turquoise dress. Fielding would be there, no doubt to question us about this morning's discovery. I discarded the turquoise dress in favour of a red V-necked mini-slinker dress, skipped the pantyhose and was about to slide my feet into sling-back pumps when a loud "Dana" roared up from below.

"Damn. What now?" I rushed down the stairs, bare feet making the trip fast and me furious. At the bottom, Aunt Doris grabbed my arm and dragged me to the side entrance.

"The elevator doors don't close," she said.

"Well, press the close button for Christ's sake."

"Dana, your language. I did press. Nothing happened."

After giving the button a few hits and the door didn't obey, I stomped out, muttering, "I'll get Bast to call the elevator company ... again. Bast!"

"Done," he yelled back a few minutes later. "Left a message."

Back in the bathroom, I shook my pumps at my scowl in the mirror, then slid them on.

By 8 p.m. the guests began trickling in. Bast stood outside the gate directing them to the side entrance where I stood, now smiling and repeating, "The elevator is temporarily out of order."

"You and Bast go on upstairs and join your guests. I'll play door person." Madge grinned. "And, this should take care of your elevator problem." She propped up a hand-printed *"Sorry, Elevator Out of Order"* and handed me a duplicate sign. "For beside the elevator."

I smiled back and waved Bast towards me. The cacophony wafted down from above as we climbed up the two levels of self-contained stairs, a remnant of bygone days when the Bowman ancestors had servants with attic quarters. Some of the guests mingled in the hall reception area. Voices drifted out from the office. Bast went in to greet the guests there while I moved around in reception, nodding and shaking hands and keeping ears open for random comments.

"Just what this place needs. You know I don't feel safe walking along Main St. at night anymore. And the police never seem to be there when you need them." Freda Barnes, a retired librarian, shook her walking stick. "My next door neighbour found a dead racoon on her back porch last month. Horribly mutilated it was. And she had her VCR stolen. Then my neighbour across the street also had her house broken into just last week. Took a pearl necklace her late husband gave her. Real pearls." She pounded the stick and scowled into my face. "You should do something about this, Dana. The police can't seem to stop it."

I opened my mouth, but could only emit a "well ..." when Eric Campbell's voice boomed from behind.

"Didn't Dana catch that shoplifter at the Fashion Shoppe?" the Chamber of Commerce president asked. "You know, the one there was all that fuss about; she turned out to be a kleptomaniac or something."

"Oh." Freda scowled at Eric. "If it isn't dim-witted police, then the culprit has some disease. As if being sick is any excuse for breaking the law." She turned away in disgust while I listened for more comments.

"Where do you think they're going to get clients? I mean, we're only 30 miles north of Toronto."

"I wonder why they put the business way up here," squeaked an elderly male voice.

I moved into the office where some of the crowd gathered around the punch bowl and food. A young man wearing a black cap and carrying a black backpack strode past me and up to the food end of the table. He seemed familiar but I couldn't place him.

"The cheese is good—Havarti, Swiss, Gouda, Brie," Lois Chalmers said as her red-gloved hands used Bast's kitchen utility knife to cut small slices. She handed one to the black-capped fellow who took it absently. He seemed pre-occupied with staring at the knife. A shiver slid down my back. I turned my attention back to Lois.

The rest of her garb matched the gloves—a narrow floor-length gown in a black and red abstract design, a jacket hung over a nearby chair, while a small black purse dangled from her left shoulder. She put down the knife and pushed the platter down under the nose of her short thin husband, Ray. Lois had a food fetish and was always trying to fatten up anyone whose major apparel consisted of skin and bones. Once when running into her in The Fashion Shoppe while working undercover in the mall, I had reminded her that slim ruled in fashion. That got her off my case. Along with feeding people, Lois liked nothing better than raking in the profits. We may have had to associate in the mall, but tonight I just couldn't make the effort. Lois, apparently had other ideas, for now she headed my way, but not before setting the cheese platter down on the table.

"Dana, there you are." She wore the fake smile that didn't reach beyond her upper lip.

Oh, oh. This couldn't be good.

"Can we go somewhere more private? We need to talk."

"How about out on the balcony?" Once there, I asked, "What's on your mind?"

"Dana, Mr. Bevens and I had a little chat after the mall kidnapping and we decided that it might be a good idea if you took a leave of absence from your undercover job."

"What?" I stared open-mouthed at her.

"Nothing personal, but Mr. Bevens and I thought there might be a conflict of interest because you know Debbie Sangwell and that makes you close to Jimmie's kidnapping, so-to-speak. Wait a minute, I'm not finished." She waved her hand at my attempt to say something. "This isn't permanent. Mr. Bevens and I would be interested in hiring your Attic Agency on contract in future, but after Jimmie's kidnapping is sorted out. I know you'll understand." This time her smile barely made it to her top lip.

"Fine," I said between clenched teeth and stomped back inside. Lois wasn't giving it to me straight, so a little talk later with Barney Bevens might be in order.

Bast stood over by the punch bowl, ladling a cupful of punch. He wore his usual dress suit of jeans, golf shirt and dusty grey sneakers. His cell phone peeked out from his back pocket.

"Hey teetotaller, it's got vodka in it," I said.

"Oh, no, not your famous vodka, orange, and lemon punch." Bast clutched his stomach.

"Aw, come on. With all these people breathing and the AC, the vodka's probably evaporated. Quit grabbing your stomach and pour me one."

He did. I took a sip and smiled.

"Where's Aunt Doris?"

"Over there on your right."

My next swallow nearly gurgled into a choke. Stringbean Lawrence and Great-Aunt Doris sat closer than my black cropped hair and gave conversation a new meaning. Stringbean had slung his arm loosely on the couch behind Great Aunt Doris. And she lapped it up like an old fool, if that smirk on her face spelled anything. I wondered how many rosaries she would feel necessary for penance when her common sense reappeared.

"Are you responsible for this, Bast?"

"No, I merely introduced them. They appear to be in the same general age bracket. She seems neglected by the opposite sex and Stringbean, well, he does ooze the charm. Unlike ..."

"Unlike who? Detective Sergeant Donald Fielding? Where is the man?"

"Do I detect disappointment in your voice?"

"Of course not. Don't be silly. I just thought ... You said he likes to be in the thick of offbeat crimes." My face felt hot.

"He's probably busy with that little boy's murder."

"Of course." I glanced at my watch. "Perhaps we should do our speeches and get Stringbean to say a few words."

"Good idea. I'll gather the bunch outside."

Bast returned with Madge and the rest of our guests, followed by Charles Haas and a man carrying a video camera with CKNT across the side. I closed the door behind them.

Bast and Haas glared at each other and Bast cleared his throat. After a minute of silence to remember the murdered boy, and a few words from me, Stringbean took over.

"That is one reason we've opened a branch of Orley and Lawrence Investigations—The Attic Investigative Agency here in Cooks Region—to find missing children and prevent what happened today."

"Well you didn't, did you?" Haas asked. "The police found him—dead. What do you have to say about this?" He turned his head. "Bast Overture?" The CKNT camera swung over to my brother.

I slammed my drink down on the desk. The glass toppled, sprawling its orange contents over the plate of nearby sandwiches and sending the utility knife to the floor. The cheese platter remained intact. A horde of eyes turned from Bast to me. I smiled and excused myself with an "I'll get a rag and more sandwiches."

The crowd began talking at once and Stringbean was just calling them back to order as I closed the door.

Halfway down the first stairway a noise came from below, like two people running; next, muffled voices, followed by silence. Then it sounded like a tap dripping in the second floor bathroom. I charged down the rest of the stairs, opened the door to the main part of the house, entered and listened.

Nothing.

The door to the bathroom hung open and the inside stood empty. Same for my bedroom and the guestroom. David's door was closed but I didn't want to disturb him and Debbie. Probably Debbie in the bathroom before. Guess David was asleep by now, and knowing Debbie, she probably sat sprawled in the rocker in his room. Like me, Debbie was a reader, except our tastes differed. Shrugging, I descended the main stairway. Was that the elevator door opening? I flew, two steps at a time, nearly tumbling over the last one, and ran along the hallway, cutting through the kitchen and stopping suddenly inside the agency's side-door entrance.

The elevator doors were open. Madge's "out of order" sign lay in front.

I jumped over the sign into the elevator and pressed "close doors." No action. Scratching my head, I stared at the ceiling as if the answer would flash from above.

The sound of a car backing up came from outside. A look out the front window showed only the parked cars. I picked up a plate of sandwiches from the kitchen table and returned to the attic. Several guests milled in the hall reception area and the agency office door stood open.

Inside, Bast and a tall, thin fellow hovered by the desk. The black-capped fellow was nowhere in sight. I placed the sandwiches on the desk and slid out my right hand towards Mr. Thin.

"Excuse me, I'm Dana Bowman."

"PC Joseph Oliver." He held out his bony right hand and we shook. Up close his face appeared more sunken. Middle age or jaded resignation?

"Oh, then you must work with Fielding?" I smiled at him.

"Not exactly. I'm in charge of the Police Records Bureau."

"Oh, sorry. You know Bast?"

"Yes. We met when he worked as a crime reporter. Nice quiet fellow. Very troubled, though. I didn't mind giving him some information, off the record." He chuckled at his own pun and continued. "Until Fielding came in one day and the atmosphere became charged." He chuckled again. "Fielding can be very big on protocol, and young Bast didn't fit in with what he thought was right. But I suppose I shouldn't be saying such things to his sister."

"That's okay."

More guests drifted out towards reception and the hall. A cell phone rang. Lois opened her purse and put her cell to her ear, turning her back to everyone. She was now gloveless. I munched on a sandwich and followed the others and had just started saying something to Eric Campbell when a whirlwind swooped up the stairs and crashed against me. Eric grabbed an arm and steadied the whirlwind. Debbie. She brushed off Eric's arm, seemed to lose her balance, then staggered towards me. She leaned in, almost falling against me, and dug her long fingernails into my left forearm.

"David's gone," she said and burst into tears.

Chapter Eight

Evening, Friday, August 14, 1998

Dana:

"Gone? What do you mean?"

She released my arm. Behind blinking eyelids, her pupils stared stark, dilated, in a face the colour of whitewash. I grabbed her shoulders and shook her.

"What do you mean 'gone?' " Like Jimmie? *Don't even go there.*

"Let Debbie explain," Bast said from behind, so I dropped my arms.

"David was hungry, and we went down to the kitchen to get something to eat." Debbie jumped around just as she had done after Jimmie was kidnapped. "Then we heard the elevator going down to the basement." She brushed her hand across her nose."Before I could stop David, he ran down the basement stairs. I ran right down after him and the window in the back was broken and David was being dragged out. And I ran through the broken glass in my running shoes and climbed up onto the laundry tubs and looked outside. Someone in sweats and a baseball cap was hauling him away. I must be a curse on little boys." She paused, tried to take a deep breath and burst into full tears. "I'm sorry, Dana. I tried to stop them, but they were already going over the wall, and I tripped on something as I went through the open window." She pressed her hands to her eyes. Her whole body trembled.

Madge rushed to her daughter and put an arm around her.

I couldn't say anything. I couldn't move.

"That's enough for now," Madge said. "Come on Hon, let's go sit out on the balcony and get some fresh air. Could we have a glass of cold water or juice?"

"Good idea," said Lois. She moved over to the other side of Debbie. "There, there, deep breaths." She wore a fake smile as she put a proprietary arm around Debbie.

Bast poured water and handed the glass to Debbie. Her fingers slipped and she almost dropped it. Lois and Madge led Debbie out onto the balcony. Bast pulled his cell from his pocket and hit three numbers.

"I'm reporting another boy kidnapped, my nephew," he said.

That jolted me into action. I tore down the stairs, crashing against the door to the main part of the house, staggered through after opening it, thundered down the main stairs to the front hall and into the kitchen to the basement door. On the way down, my right heel slipped. I missed the last two steps and landed on my ass, so yanked off the offending shoes, flung them away and stood up. My knees shook and I crumpled, but only for a few seconds. David was missing. Grasping the railing, I eased myself up.

The laundry room presented almost a repeat of the previous night except for the window—it had disappeared, as had the screen. So much for Bast fixing the lock. My sketches again were strewn across the floor, this time mingled with glass pieces. Moving forward to get a closer look, I forgot my shoeless condition until my left big toe hit the glass shards. That didn't stop me from climbing up the laundry tub. I leaned over and peered outside to see what Debbie had tripped over.

David's Beechnut lay on the ground atop the window frame.

David couldn't sleep without a stuffed beaver against his face.

If I could only reach the beaver David would be all right. I leaned forward a little more. My right hand slipped. While grabbing the window ledge and manoeuvring backwards, the same foot reconnected with the glass pieces. A noise overhead interrupted my rude reply. Gritting my teeth, I charged upstairs to the kitchen.

"Where are you going, young lady?" Great Aunt Doris asked.

"When did *you* get down here and what are *you* doing here?" I glared into her gargoyle face.

"I couldn't stand the crowd upstairs. So I came downstairs for some air and to make some tea."

"Then you don't know. David's gone. Didn't you see him, then Debbie fly by a few minutes ago?"

"David? Well, I did stop in the powder room, to freshen up."

"So you saw neither David nor Debbie?"

"No. Dana. Just what is going on?"

"I told you, David's gone. He ran downstairs and according to Debbie, someone must've dragged him out the laundry room window. And you saw nothing? And heard nothing? And you are making tea?" I scratched my scalp.

"Tea is much better for you than alcoholic beverage."

I sighed and shook my head. "Where's Bast? Where's Stringbean?"

"Who?"

"Gerald Lawrence. The man you were getting cosy with upstairs."

"Dana, your language. Really. What would Ronald say? And Gerald is a very nice man. Which is more that I can say about your brother, the Bast."

"Aunt Doris, Gerald is technically our boss. Bast and I are a branch of his business in Toronto."

"You mean that nice man, Gerald, is a detective." She spat out the last word like it was a worm.

"Why Aunt Doris. Didn't you hear his speech? Or were you too busy staring at his face to hear the words? Come on. Snap out of this morality bit. David's gone; you saw nothing; you heard nothing, so you might as well continue making tea for everyone. Good idea." I patted her on the shoulder, although I felt more like kicking her in another part of the anatomy.

"Oh, dear. Ronald should know." She wailed like a pig in agony.

"Just hang in there, Aunt Doris."

Then I beat the Olympic record upstairs to David's room. Well, I am a mother and mothers also have hope.

The top of the bed showed empty. Ditto underneath, except dust. The closet yielded only David's clothes, the floor his train set, and nine stuffed beavers. *Alice in Wonderland* lay open-faced on the rocking chair. The closed window shut off any remaining hope. I stumbled out of the room and into the bathroom. Nothing except the mirrored face of a mother sliding into her own quagmire. This time David wasn't playing hide and seek.

The guestroom, Great Aunt Doris's temporary room, showed nothing out of place but a rosary slung over the lampshade. Maybe she was afraid she'd lose it if she couldn't see it. I dashed into my room, giving it the once over, then headed up to the attic offices. Quiet filled the reception area. Voices spewed from the office. Stringbean stood in the doorway and beckoned. I hobbled over and peered in. Oliver appeared to be questioning the guests, but he moved like a slow screen. When I opened my mouth to speak, the only sound was an ocean thrashing inside my head. The guests swayed and I followed suit.

When I opened my eyes, I was sitting in a chair. Somebody was forcing a glass against my lips and urging me to drink. After a few sips, I coughed, shivered, and looked up. Stringbean wrapped his jacket around me.

"You've had a shock, Dana," he said. "Oliver is moving your guests to reception. Bast called it in and the police should be here soon. They'll hunt all over town until they find David." He patted my arm.

"Where's Bast now?" It slid out as a rasp.

"Right here." My brother pushed past our milling and staring guests. In his hand he held a wet cloth. He bent down and wiped my foot. I stared down at the forgotten cut.

"Bast ... David's new beaver ... it's outside the window downstairs."

"Take a deep breath, sis."

I sucked in air and felt a rush to my head. "Beaver," I repeated.

"When?" Bast asked.

"A few minutes ago."

"Hmm." Bast stroked his beard. "Look, I was just outside checking in the driveway and heading for the back when I saw lights shine from the street. When I turned around I saw a small two-door dark—maybe green car, probably a Toyota, pull out from a parking spot across the street and drive off."

"Did you see who was in it?"

"No, it was too dark and I wasn't up close. But when it passed under a streetlamp I saw only one head, the driver's. He appeared to be wearing a baseball cap, and dark glasses. But I did manage to make out its licence plate, LTD 888."

"Could be coincidence," Stringbean said. "A neighbour going out, curious about all the cars and activity here. I'll check Motor Vehicles Registration tomorrow. Of course we have to report this to the police, but it doesn't hurt to get the information ourselves."

"You better stay put, Dana, and relax here until Fielding arrives," Bast said.

"Fielding?" I jerked up in the chair. "He's coming?"

"Yes, I asked for him, although the uniforms should have been here before now."

"Fielding," I repeated.

"I know. Even though I hate his guts, he's a good cop, in his own way. Just likes to run the whole show, and be the main star. He does have a good track record."

"You mean we're just going to let him do all the work. Bast, we can't just sit here."

"I know, Dana. But you're in shock. Let the police do their job tonight, and in the morning we can jump back in again. I can talk to the guests. You can go through the neighbourhood and talk to the neighbours who aren't here tonight. See if they saw anything. They know you and David. Maybe some will tell you more than they would the cops. Come on, Dana. We'll also have that licence plate number. Oliver is no friend of Fielding's. He'll help us where he can."

"I think I'll rest for a few minutes until the cops get here." I attempted a weak smile.

"Good idea," said Bast.

He left me alone in the office but the last hour must have caught up with me, because I missed the next few minutes.

Oliver was telling everybody to stay put. The voices tunnelled into a radio left on low and I drifted off ...

Somebody was shaking me.

"Dana, wake up."

"Huh? Bast? What the ...?"

His face resembled an Albino's in reverse.

"David?" I bolted out of the chair, almost knocking it over.

"No, it's Debbie."

"What? Has she disappeared too?"

"No. She's dead, face down on the table on the balcony with a knife sticking out of her back."

Chapter Nine

Later Friday Evening, August 14, 1998

Dana:

I pushed the door open, staggered onto the balcony and shoved the door shut behind me.

Clutching my arms together and leaning against the wall, I took several deep breaths but still had the shakes. I willed myself to calm down as my eyes scrutinized the balcony table.

In the dim light from the overhead lantern, Debbie seemed hunched over the table in sleep. The light cast sufficient shadows to hide any knife. I tiptoed close and touched her wrist. No pulse.

"*Debbie's dead.*"

Bast's words reverberated inside my head, sending my heart into overdrive. I shuffled behind her, almost jumping at the knife wedged in the middle of her back. Only its handle protruded like an obscene intrusion. I stepped back, again leaning against the wall and tried taking slow, deliberate breaths, but my heart and lungs wouldn't cooperate. Sweat formed underneath the roots of my hair and threatened to spill down my face. The hot, humid night, of course.

I looked at the surroundings.

The balcony walls, brick on three sides with wooden slats in the middle, showed no signs of recent disturbance. Moving closer, I peered over the balcony top, careful not to touch the wall and checked the front lawn below. Nothing. But on the second floor balcony, which jutted out just under a metre kitty-corner from the attic balcony, a small container lay sideways near the front railing. The overhead light wasn't the brightest but the container resembled a prescription bottle.

I couldn't stay here any longer, so I pushed open the door and stumbled into the hallway.

Silence from the few guests still milling around greeted me.

"It's kind of hot out there." I shaped my lips into a weak smile. "Better to stay in here. Think I'll get some tea. Would you like some more tea? I'll be right back."

I hurried towards the stairs and charged down until a sharp pain in my left foot slowed me to a half-run, half-stagger to my room.

Removing a plastic bag from a drawer, I placed a hand inside, and headed into the hallway towards the second floor balcony. Sirens sounded and car doors slammed below. Crouching down, I picked up the empty prescription bottle, reversed the plastic bag over it, and returned to my room. I stared at the bag and bottle combo in my hand. Why were they there? Shrugging, I grabbed my oversized purse and shoved the bagged bottle inside. The cell phone followed. After snatching a sweater, I slipped into a pair of Chalmers's runners and headed for the stairs. Fielding's voice chewing out an underling reverberated up the stairwell.

"You should've been here right after Communications dispatched it."

"But sir, we were stuck at that big traffic accident on 87. And there are a lot of domestics tonight. And ..."

"All right. Get upstairs and get everyone downstairs. I have to seal this place off." Fielding stared up at me. "Ms. Bowman, what are you doing upstairs? I hope you haven't been interfering in police business."

"Of course not." I clutched my bag.

"Purse, sweater. You planning on going somewhere?"

"Well, with my line of work, I know you'll want to get us out of the house, I mean with a murder."

"Murder? I was called on a kidnapping."

"Yes, murder, too. Debbie Sangwell was murdered on the top balcony. We just discovered the body and I was going to call it in when I heard the sirens."

"We? Who's 'we?' "

The clamour from above answered his question.

At the top of the attic stairs, a constable gripped Bast around the shoulder and shouted at several guests milling behind him. Fielding pounced up the stairs, two at a time.

"Clarke," he yelled up the stairs. "Clear all these people out of here. Is anyone on the balcony?"

"No, sir," Clarke replied from above.

"Good. Where are the paramedics?"

"They've been called, sir," Clarke shrugged his shoulders.

"Good," said Fielding. "You." He pointed up to Bast. "Were you out on the balcony?"

"Yes, me too," I said.

"What?" Fielding scratched his left ear. "Clarke, take them all downstairs. You and you," Fielding pointed to Bast and me, "I want to talk to first. Clarke, send a couple more uniforms up here and Detective Stewart when he gets here. You people up here, follow Clarke. And where is Madge Sangwell?"

Fielding questioned me first, then sent me downstairs, but I waited until he finished with Bast. At the kitchen doorway, I whispered to Bast, "Wait; I need to find Madge before that insensitive detective sergeant does."

"Dana, she didn't stay long outside on the balcony after she took Debbie there. She and Lois came in a few minutes later. Lois went into the bathroom on the attic level. Debbie was alive then, because she was standing in the balcony doorway saying something to Madge; I couldn't hear what. Madge replied; then she headed downstairs and Debbie went back out on the balcony. That's the last I saw of Madge, or of Debbie alive."

"Make sure you tell Fielding that."

"I did."

We entered the kitchen. A uniform cop attempted to get Aunt Doris to sit down, but she kept pointing her finger in his face. Another uniform was trying to move my guests out. Lois bent over into the fridge's interior, hauling out extra sandwiches, which she shoved at the cop. Her hands now wore the red gloves and her jacket was draped around her waist. Ray sagged against the wall, his gaze fixed on the ceiling. Aunt Doris poured a cup of tea and tried to force it into his hand. She looked up and saw me.

"Dana, is something else wrong?" Doris asked. "You look a little peaked."

"Oh, no, quite all right. Just police business."

"Well, I never, in all my years, and in George Bowman's house. If only Ronald were here. That poor sweet child. And his mother with a scarlet dress up to there."

Oliver and another uniform entered the kitchen from the hallway. There was no sign of Stringbean and Madge. I made shushing motions to Aunt Doris and tried to get Oliver's attention.

"Where's Madge? Stringbean?" I mouthed the question.

Oliver shrugged. His colleague placed an arm on his shoulder and motioned him to the hallway. I followed them and almost collided with Clarke, Stewart and Tractor as they charged up the stairs. I mingled with the rest of my guests as we were ushered outside. Aunt Doris still hung onto the cup and appeared to be trying to pour its contents onto one of the uniform cops. Trying not to think of David, I glanced around for Madge, but couldn't see her. Fielding came out and motioned from the top of the veranda steps.

"Ms. Bowman, do you have a recent photo of David?"

I removed a couple of photos from my wallet and looked at them. Was this all that remained of my son?

"Ms. Bowman."

"Right." I handed him the headshot.

"Thanks. Now, Ms. Bowman, I need a place to operate from for now until our mobile crime unit is free. One of your neighbours?" He glanced at 8 Maitland St. "Who lives there?"

"The Brooks, but they're an elderly couple, probably gone to bed."

"Ms. Bowman, with your background, you should know I have to seal off the crime scene and that's this house. I will establish a command post next door at number 8 Maitland. We'll be getting a court order to wiretap your business line for the kidnapper's call as that's the number on the agency sign out front. You have your cell for call forwarding?"

I patted my purse, nodded and gave him the number, moved backwards and leaned against the veranda railing.

"With kids, it's hard," Fielding said.

"What would you know?"

"I have a daughter. She's grown up now, but ... keep your cell phone close."

The guests milled about outside with a few uniforms trying to keep them in order. Already the yellow crime scene tape was up around the house. Fielding barked orders at a couple of the uniforms to do a door-to-door and steered me towards 8 Maitland. He had his temporary command post. The remaining constables were herding my guests there when Madge's gravel voice sounded above the crowd.

"Dana, what's going on?" Madge asked. "Where's Debbie?"

I turned around. Clarke was leading her through the side gateway.

"Caught her on the second floor, coming out of the washroom." Clarke tightened his hold on Madge's arm. "She seemed to be in a big hurry."

Chapter Ten

A few seconds later, Friday Evening, August 14, 1998

Dana:

"Bring her here," Fielding said. "I need to talk to her."

"So do I." I scowled up at him.

"Very well, we'll take her next door. You are both mothers of victims, so you can talk to her there, but I have to be present. Then, I'll speak to both of you, separately."

A squeal of tires interrupted us. Two paramedics jumped from an ambulance and ran around to the back. They opened the van's back door and hauled out a stretcher and medical bag and rushed towards us.

"Where's the body?" one of them asked.

"Body?" Madge asked. "What's he talking about? I thought David was kidnapped He isn't dead, is he?"

"No," I replied, but could not continue with paramedics standing under our noses. As if sensing my thoughts, Fielding steered the paramedics away from us. His mouth moved as he pointed to 10 Maitland. As the duo left, I let out the breath stuck inside, put my arm around Madge, and with Fielding, trudged next door. I guided her into the house, past Rita Brooks, who was fussing with everyone, and Randall who seemed to pop up everywhere. I didn't hear a word they said and muttered something about needing a private room for talking to Madge. As Fielding led us to the dining room and closed the door, his cell phone rang. He turned his back on us and mumbled into his cell.

"It's been confirmed," he said to us as he put his cell away.

"What's confirmed?" Madge asked. "What's going on?"

"Madge, let's sit down on the couch over there," I said. "There's something I have to tell you."

"Hey, what's this? And why is he still in here?" She pointed a finger at Fielding. "You both going to give me the third degree? I love, David, too, like he was my own son."

"It's not David, Madge." I tried not to shake while motioning her towards the couch. "Please sit down." She sat. I dropped down beside her and took her hands in mine. "Madge, I'm afraid I've got some bad news about Debbie."

"What? She's gone, too?"

"Not exactly."

"What do you mean 'not exactly?' " Madge glared at me.

"I'm sorry; I'm not doing this very well."

"Just spit it out, Dana."

"I'm sorry, Madge, but Debbie's been murdered."

"What? Lois and I just left her sitting on the balcony drinking some water a little while ago. She can't be dead." Madge dropped my hands, staggered over to the table, plucked a candle from its holder and dropped it flat on the table. She fingered photographs on the china cabinet, turning them face down. She moved to an end table, yanked a plant out of its pot and dumped it on the floor. When she headed for the window, both Fielding and I caught up with her. I put my arms around her and shepherded her back to the couch. Fielding sat in a nearby chair.

She sobbed, big-time heaves. I waited her out, holding her close and occasionally patting her on the back. My eyes did not remain dry. Her heaves petered down to quiet sobs. She looked up.

"Dana, tell me what happened."

I did, omitting the grisly details.

"No, no, no. Not my baby. She can't be dead before me. It's not right."

As she started to heave again, the anger burned inside me. Fielding stood nearby staring at us. He resembled a bull ready to enter the ring.

"Mrs. Sangwell, I need to talk to you right now," he said.

Madge stared right through Fielding.

"Just a minute, Detective Sergeant." I stood up and raised my right hand. "Wait a minute; I'm still talking to Madge. She's in shock."

"I realize this is a bad time for both of you and I'm sorry for your loss, Mrs. Sangwell." Fielding nodded in Madge's direction. The air turned glacial and I shivered. "But I need to talk to you." At my glare, he added, "However, you could go in the kitchen and get a cup of tea. I'm using this dining room to interview everybody, so I will start with you, Ms. Bowman. I have more questions."

Madge staggered up and shuffled over to me. I put an arm around her and looked Fielding right in the eye.

"I'm taking her to the kitchen and getting her settled. Then, I'll be back and you can interview me."

"Very well, send in your Aunt Doris and I'll talk to her, but you're next, and then Mrs Sangwell."

In the kitchen, Aunt Doris started lording it over Madge, with some stiff competition from Lois Chalmers and Rita Brooks. Lois urged a cookie at Madge. Ray Chalmers sat, his face wearing a stunned look. His right hand shook as it picked up a cup. He pulled a flask from his pocket and began pouring its contents into the cup. Bast was not in the room.

"You poor dear," Aunt Doris said to Madge.

I pulled out a chair, helped Madge get seated and sat down beside her.

"More brandy, that's what she needs." Ray shoved the flask towards Madge. "Drink it all; do you a world of good."

"Shut up, Ray," Lois said. She slammed the cookie into his mouth, forcing him to gag.

"It's all right," Madge said. Her eyes appeared glazed.

"Take it easy, Madge," I said. "It isn't easy, especially for you. And the cops won't make it easier. They'll ask you personal and embarrassing questions about Debbie. It's all routine. They have to do it to find her killer."

On cue, Fielding entered the room. "Doris Bowman. I need to talk to you, in the dining room. Where's Marsden?" He thumped out into the hall. "Hey, you, yes you, Constable, get over here." A few seconds later he returned with Marsden. "Marsden, make sure these individuals don't talk to each other. Come with me." He nodded at Aunt Doris.

"Well, I never." Doris put her hands on her hips and scowled. "First I get herded out of George Bowman's home and then I get the third degree." But she left with Fielding.

"Lois, will you put that damn plate of cookies down," I said. "I don't think any of us are hungry now, except perhaps you."

"No talking," Marsden said. He sounded like a little boy pleading for a cookie.

Lois glowered, but she set the plate down in front of Ray. He had stopped gagging, but his face remained red. Lois grabbed the cup from Ray, reached into his jacket pocket and hauling out the flask, shoved it at Marsden and told him to take it out. I turned away in disgust and tried again to tend to Madge. She slumped over in her chair and wouldn't look at me.

"Madge, I'm going to talk to Bast for a few minutes, if I can find him, then I'll take you home. I think you should try to get some sleep. Fielding can wait until morning to interview you; that's okay isn't it, Constable Marsden."

Marsden who appeared to be interested in a spot diagonally up on the ceiling said, "Oh yes, I guess so."

"And, you also know where my brother, Bast is?"

"Helping us out with investigations," Marsden replied.

I knew what that meant.

"I'm not sure I can stay in my apartment alone," Madge murmured in monotones.

"We can get a policewoman to stay with you," Marsden said.

"That won't be necessary; I can go with her," I said.

"No, you can't." Fielding's voice still sounded cold as he re-entered the kitchen "I still need to talk to you, Ms. Bowman—and Mrs. Sangwell."

I turned and glared at him.

"I need to talk to Mrs. Sangwell briefly now. Your Aunt Doris can take Madge home afterwards." Fielding moved closer to Madge. "I know you are in shock but I just have a couple of questions if you would come into the dining room for a few minutes."

"Are you out of your mind, Fielding? Leave it for tomorrow." I tried to move in front of Madge, but Fielding took a step forwards. "Ms. Bowman. All right, you can bring her to the dining room."

"Fine."

Madge walked like a zombie trying to get its legs. Fielding wouldn't let me into the dining room, but I slid the closed door open a little. He kept asking her when she left the balcony and if Debbie was still alive then. Madge's replies were too faint to hear. Finally, he called for me to come in and help bring her out.

"Marsden," Fielding said, back in the kitchen. "Will you get Oliver? I think he's in the living room."

Marsden exited via the hall and returned with Oliver. Fielding led him into the dining room.

"Marsden," I tried to smile. "I have to go back with Madge. She's my friend." I lowered my voice. "Remember our pact at my B and E? Let's make another. I'll go back with Madge. It'll be okay, I have my cell phone."

"Here, here." Aunt Doris shook her head and wagged a finger at me. "You're staying. I'll go and stay with Madge."

"No, I'm going with my friend. Oh, all right. I'll return once she's settled in bed. That okay, with you Madge?"

"Sure." Same monotone.

"Ladies, please, no talking," Marsden said.

"Constable, have some mercy. This woman just lost her daughter." Aunt Doris wrinkled up her gargoyle face and stared at Marsden.

He flinched and shrugged his shoulders. This time I was with Aunt Doris.

"Look, Madge, I can stay the night, if you'd rather ..."

"No, your aunt is right. Just come back with me. I ... I can't face that apartment alone knowing Debbie will never set foot in it again."

"I know." I patted her hand. "You see, Constable Marsden, I have to go with my friend, but I will come back; but before we go, I need to talk to my brother."

"He's in the living room," Marsden said.

"I'll go there if that's all right."

Marsden sighed and nodded.

"Madge, you going to be all right for a few minutes? I'll be right back."

"She'll be fine," Lois said. "I'll make sure of it."

"You better."

"Where's my daughter? I have to see Debbie." Madge leaned forward and grabbed the table like an arthritic old lady bracing herself to move. Once standing, though, she darted over to the counter, opened cupboard doors and peered inside, muttering, "Debbie, Debbie, are you in here?" She knelt down and began patting the floor. "My purse. No, no, no, not Debbie."

I bent down and tried to comfort her. Rita pulled a chair forward, and Lois and I eased Madge into it.

"Pour some more tea, Rita," Lois said. "You sit here, Madge." She frowned at me. Weren't you going to talk to your brother?"

"But, Madge?" I looked at my friend. Her eyes stared at the ceiling. Her right hand gripped the cup and her lips shook.

"Leave her be, for now," Lois said. Her eyes seemed to say "or else" and a shudder slipped through me.

In the living room. Bast and Stringbean sat on opposite sides of the room, separated by more of our guests. Tractor was collecting their fingerprints and footprints. I motioned to Bast but the uniformed cop standing by the door had more upstairs than Marsden.

"Just a minute," he said.

"I just need a few words with my brother."

The room stood silent, with what seemed like a thousand eyes punctuating the stillness. I swayed. Bast and the cop rushed towards me. The room picked up in noise level. Bast reached me first. I lunged out, grabbed his arm and dragged us both into the hall.

"My sister needs some air," Bast said over his shoulder.

The constable said, "a few minutes only."

Bast led me outside onto the Brooks's front veranda. "All right, Dana, what have you got up your sleeve?"

I straightened up. "Could you or Stringbean look outside that basement window for Beechnut?" I burst into tears. "I can't do this. Not with David gone and ..." My body began shaking and swaying a little, this time for real. Bast hugged me.

"I know. It's okay; take it easy. We'll check it out in the morning, although chances are the cops will have found it."

A car crawled up the street and turned into the driveway. I broke away from Bast, rushed towards the car and collided with another uniformed cop.

"Just a minute, ma'am," he said, stopping as the car door opened.

An elderly man, heavy in trunk and bushy in upper lip climbed out.

"I'm Dr. Christopher Farley, the coroner." He tipped his cap, revealing a bald dome. His accompanying smile turned his fierceness to friendliness.

"Dana Bowman, detective, with the agency here." I pointed to 10 Maitland.

"Constable Steadman," the uniform said. "The body is next door, upstairs on the top balcony."

Something seemed to crawl up my spine and stop to rest at heart level.

"Constable, the body is my best friend's daughter."

"Now, Steadman, there's no need to be so callous." Farley patted me on the shoulder. "Are you all right, my dear?"

I was fed up with people inquiring about my health tonight. At least this one had an excuse. He was a doctor and his concern gave me the first smidgen of confidence all evening. I nodded.

After a few more words with Steadman, Farley said, "Okay, Steadman, tell Fielding I'm here. I'll be next door. You, miss, take care." He patted my shoulder again and headed over to No. 10. Steadman led me back to the veranda and walked over to the property division. Bast and I talked in whispers and I kept glancing over at Steadman. He stared at us but appeared unconcerned.

"Do you want me to take Madge home?" Bast asked.

"No, Aunt Doris is coming, too. She said she'd stay."

"Okay, when you're ready to return, call me and I'll come and get you if you like. You shouldn't be driving."

"Fine. But you don't need to pick me up. I can walk. It'll do me good, clear my head." I sucked in air. "See, Bast, I *can* calm down." I forced a smile, but my lips trembled. "I'm okay, Bast, really. We can talk some more later."

Bast walked me back into the house. He returned to the living room and I headed for the kitchen, stopped at the doorway, took oversized breaths and strode in, staring straight at Marsden.

"Aunt Doris is taking Madge home and I'm going with them," I whispered. "I'm not staying. Fielding will just have to question me when I return."

Marsden merely nodded.

"Come on Madge, Aunt Doris, let's go."

Madge stared straight ahead and her lips moved but no sound came out. She grabbed the cup again as if this time she meant to crush it.

"Madge, let's get you home."

"Yes, dear, come on," Aunt Doris said, her voice pitched to soft mode.

"I can get a policewoman." Marsden made a stab at regaining the control he never had.

"No, we're fine. Just make sure Fielding knows I'll be back and don't tell him until he is finished interviewing."

Aunt Doris had managed to get Madge out of her chair and was hanging onto her arm.

"I want to see her; I want to see my daughter."

"Not right now, maybe tomorrow," I said.

"What you need is a good night's sleep," Aunt Doris said.

"Sleep, perchance to dream? No. I need to see my daughter. I need to ... oh God, my baby is dead. I can't believe it." Madge heaved, and Aunt Doris and I led her out to the front door. Steadman blocked our way.

"I'm taking this woman home," Aunt Doris wagged a finger at Steadman.

"I'm just walking them to the car." I steered a protesting Aunt Doris and a meek Madge towards Aunt Doris' car across the street. We climbed in, none of us looking back at Steadman. After some initial fussing with keys, we left. Aunt Doris drove.

Chapter Eleven

Sometime between 11 p.m. and midnight Friday, August 14, 1998

Him:

"Help me. Mom ...mee. I want my Mommee."

The cries woke him up. He tried to sit up, but found a mass of something soft and heavy wrapped around him. He had to get it off; it was smothering him. He couldn't breathe. Sweat covered him from head to toe. Then he pulled it loose and realized two things: he was in bed and he was naked.

Where was Jessie?

"Mom ... mee. Where are you? Momm ... mee" The screams came from somewhere down below.

Then he remembered.

"Hang on, I'm coming."

He picked up the end of the blanket and wiped his face with it, then staggered out of bed. He pulled on a pair of shorts and T-shirt which he found neatly folded on a chair, and dashed out of the room. When he came to the top of the stairs, he stopped, grabbed the banister and hung on all the time he made his slow and even progress down the steps. He couldn't rush down the stairs—that would be bad, bad.

The voice continued its wailing.

"Okay, okay, I'm coming," he shouted as he grabbed a flashlight, opened the basement door and now feeling safer, ran down the stairs into one of the rooms to attend to the boy.

Chapter Twelve

Sometime between 11 p.m. and midnight Friday, August 14, 1998

David:

He had woken up to cold and darkness. Beechnut. Where was Beechnut? He was lying on his back and tried to sit up but his arms were stuck in front of him and his feet were stuck together. Shadows seemed to come at him.

"Mom ... mee," David said. "Mom ... mee. Where are you? Mom ... mee, I'm scared."

No answer. Where was he? Where were Mommy and Uncle Bast? Where was Debbie? They'd been reading *Alice in Wonderland.* Then he had gotten hungry and run downstairs to the kitchen with Debbie after him. It was a game they always played. When he'd heard a noise in the basement he'd run down there and seen one of Mommy's friends playing the game, so he'd chased after ... and then ... he couldn't remember. His head hurt and he felt a little sick. He tried to move his hands again, but couldn't. They were still stuck together.

Where was he? His toes hurt. His teeth hurt and he was so cold.

"Mom ... mee. Mom ... mee." Now he was yelling.

A door burst open and something thudded in.

Oh no, a monster. Coming after him.

"Mom ... mee. Mom ... mee. I'm scared."

He heard a click and a bright light blinded his eyes.

"Pipe down," a voice shouted at him from above, or was it beside him?

"Who are you? I want my mommy. I want Beechnut."

Instead he felt something heavy and sticky cover his mouth. The bright light clicked off and footsteps receded to the doorway, and then he heard a door slam.

In darkness and alone, David began to cry, his sobs muffled by the tape over his mouth.

Chapter Thirteen

Sometime between 11 p.m. and midnight, Friday August 14, 1998

Dana:

Entering Madge's apartment felt worse than attending a wake. The air seemed to breathe "Debbie and David ... David and Debbie." Debbie's three-speed bike leaned against the wall. She used to ride double with David sitting on the handlebars. I looked away and started into the living room. Chalmers's running shoes sprawled on the carpet. Schoolbooks spread out on the coffee table, a jacket flung carelessly over a recliner, CDs sprawled on top of the stereo.

Jacket?

It was one of David's. I leaned up against something. "... temperature is 29 Celsius and the humidex is 37 Celsius," shouted at me. I jumped. Realizing it was the stereo's power button, I pressed it off. Voices came from the hallway.

"I can't go in there," Madge said as I came around the corner. Madge held her face in her hands, and Aunt Doris was muttering at her.

"Madge, you don't have to go in there," I said. "But I need to check out Debbie's room before the cops do, and they'll be here later."

Doris turned and glared at me.

"No you don't, Dana Bowman."

"Aunt Doris, it's my job."

"Your job is to be home waiting for word about David. Your son has been kidnapped, young lady." She pointed a finger and I snatched it.

"Don't you order me around, you old biddy. My son's kidnapping may be connected to Debbie's murder, and I might find some idea why in Debbie's room."

"Stop," Madge said. "Please stop."

I let go of Doris and turned to my friend. "Sorry, Madge; wasn't thinking."

"It's okay. Just do what you have to. Doris can see me to bed."

"Madge, are you sure?"

"Yes, Dana. You can pop in when you're finished."

"All right."

They shuffled off down the hall. Now I faced Debbie's door.

Another door came to mind. When Bast and I were 15, I had knocked and knocked on his door, but he couldn't hear me over his sobbing. Finally, pushing open the door, I had entered another world. Bast, six feet, sat curled up on the floor, rocking on his bum and keening. I had run over to him and touched his shoulder. He lifted his head, revealing racoon eyes, face and arm cuts, and dried blood mixed with tears. Bast's first brush with gay bashing had left me feeling raw, angry and ready to do battle for my younger brother, albeit only 43 minutes younger.

On the other side of Debbie's door, emptiness greeted me, seeping into my bones, my whole body and splitting in two. One part stuck in my brain, but the second part filled my heart. Get a hold of yourself, Dana. Just a quick look around and then you can go home. I shut the door and after staring around, lurched forward, pulling open the closet door.

Inside were the usual teen items. Debbie lived at home while attending Thurston Community College. Denims mixed with T-shirts and a few dressier outfits. Shoes of all sorts lined the floor. Platforms, stilettos, sandals and hey, what was this? A pair of Chalmers's runners, two-toned, the same as the one I had sketched at the Mini-Mall. Brand new runners, the price tag still attached and some tissue paper stuffed inside the right one. I picked up the shoe and shook out the paper. Blank.

The shelf contained cartons filled with Stephen King and Dean Koontz books. I dumped them and rattled each book but nothing fell out.

The bookcase, a three-shelf setup, held a TV, VCR, videos, mostly store-bought movies, ranging in date from the 1950s to early 1990s. Debbie was a movie buff, but I hadn't realized to what extent. In the middle dresser drawer under more T-shirts was an elastic-wrapped packet. I tossed the T-shirts, grabbed my find, and looked closer at maybe six or seven letters. "Jarvis Harwood" and a Thurston address near the college filled the return sticker. Debbie was the addressee. They were postmarked April, May, June, and July, with the last one stamped July 15, 1998. Boyfriend? I didn't even know if Debbie had a steady boyfriend and wondered if Madge knew. The letters went into my bag.

While heading for Madge's room to say goodnight, my cell phone rang.

"Hello."

"Dana, it's Bast. You better get back here. Fielding wants to speak to you right away. I told him you took Madge home and would be right back. And the lights are on all over the second floor of our place, so they must be searching all the bedrooms."

"I'm on my way. Stall them for 15."

I beetled into the bathroom. A faint musty smell assaulted my nose but I ignored it and opened the medicine cabinet. Tylenol, with and without codeine, cough syrup, Q-tips, sunscreen, deodorant, cold cream, red hair dye zoomed before my eyes. I pulled open the two doors below. Toilet paper, facial tissues, soap, Tampax, maxi-pads, Comet, drain cleaner ...

"What are you looking for?" Aunt Doris bellowed from behind.

Grabbing the sink, I swung around and yelled "just doing my ... oh, hell. How's Madge doing?"

"Dana, don't swear. She's settled in bed. You should say 'goodnight' and get back home."

"Be right there."

I reached down for the small plastic-bagged garbage in the wastebasket and noticed the smell was stronger. At the bottom of the garbage bag a used sanitary pad, steeped in dry blood was wadded up inside a bunch of facial tissues. Madge's or Debbie's? I tied the bag shut, removed the cell from my purse and stuffed the bag inside. With cell phone in one hand and a half-zipped purse slung over my other shoulder, I caught up with Aunt Doris and meekly followed her into Madge's bedroom.

Despite the heat, Madge huddled under a sheet and wool blanket. Her face looked grey and her eyes fixed on a point somewhere at right angles to the bedpost.

"Madge."

"It's okay, Dana. I was just thinking of Debbie's graduation last year. She looked so pretty in her long pink dress. White carnations, that's what she wore at her breast. Dana, I can't believe she's gone." She shuddered and began sobbing, great big heaves. "She was still alive when Lois and I left her on the balcony. She said she wanted ... wanted to be alone."

I dropped my belongings, sat on the bed and put my arm around her. "It's okay. I'm here," Her heaves wound down to a hiccup.

"Sorry, Dana. Got to be strong."

"Why? She's your daughter. You have every right. Look, I'll stay here with you, at least until you fall asleep."

"No, hon, you got to get back home. For David."

"All right." I stood up. "But I'm coming back in the morning. Call before then if you need me."

"I will, but Doris is here."

"Well try to get some sleep. Good night."

"Good night, Dana."

I grabbed my bag, left her room, called out "good-bye" to Aunt Doris and returned to the living room for David's jacket. Might as well have some hope. I plunked everything into the basket of Debbie's bike, wheeled the bike out, down the corridor and into the elevator. Outside I climbed aboard, hit third gear and headed home. While riding into the Brooks's driveway, I noticed the CKNT van parked on the street across from 10

Maitland. Camera lights shone on that blond reporter, Charles Haas, interviewing that nasty-faced Detective Harker. Steadman stood beside him. None of them appeared to see me, and wanting to keep it that way, I quickly parked the bike behind Bast's car in the driveway at No. 8, retrieved my bag and tiptoed onto the veranda and inside the front door.

"You two can leave now." Fielding's voice boomed out from the kitchen; chairs scraped on the floor. Ray and Lois stood in the kitchen doorway.

"I can't say it's been charming, but certainly different," Lois shouted back into the kitchen.

Hearing Fielding reply, I hurried outside. Haas was climbing into the CKNT van and neither cop was in sight, so I scooted round to the back of the Brooks's driveway, dumped David's jacket back into the bike basket, entered the backyard and made it to the fence joining 10 Maitland. A hand tapped my back.

"Ms. Bowman, your house is still out of bounds," Fielding said.

I swung around and stared into his cold blue eyes. "Look, I want to find my son."

"The best way to do that is to wait for the kidnapper's call and leave the rest to us. Now, Ms. Bowman, I have a couple more questions. Then you have to go back inside the house." He pointed to 8 Maitland.

He started in on the knife. Had I ever seen it before? When had I seen Ron last? Did he ever visit his son? Did I know where he lived? Besides my ex, did I have any enemies or run-ins with anyone—personal or business?

"Not really. Oh, Lois Marshall—she's the president of the Mini-Mall business owners' association—and my boss, Barney Bevens put me on leave from doing undercover security until Jimmie Halpern was found. Lois called it a conflict of interest. But it wasn't a run-in and although I don't like her, we are not enemies."

"Thank you Ms. Bowman. I'll have this typed up later on today and get you to sign it." He favoured his right temple.

"So you're treating my ideas seriously?"

"Ms. Bowman. I don't fool around where missing children are concerned. As I mentioned, I have one of my own."

"Oh, and I suppose she's safe at home with your wife."

"No ... no, Ms. Bowman. I'm divorced. My ex-wife lives in Vancouver and my daughter is grown up and in Europe."

"Oh."

"Now I suggest you get some rest. Your next-door neighbour will put you and your brother up in spare rooms tonight."

"Fine. Just give me a minute of fresh air."

He nodded and strode over to 10 Maitland. I retrieved David's jacket from the bike.

Upstairs in the Brooks's den, I kicked off my runners, pushed my bag and cell against the wall, dumped David's jacket on the bed, and started to climb in. Blood dripped on the sheet. Crap. My foot. I hopped down the hall into the bathroom to clean the wound and returned to the den. Huddling on top of the bed, I cradled David's jacket and began to rock sideways. I closed my eyes and hoped sleep would come.

Instead the tears arrived.

Later, I seemed to be swirling in water. David floated lifeless a few feet away. Every effort to move forward resulted in me sinking. I jerked up in bed and opened my eyes.

Where was I? A light glowed on beside the bed. Bast sat on the floor, tapping away at his laptop. What was he doing in my room? Wait a minute. This wasn't my room. It was too small and my room didn't contain an ironing board. Then I remembered. Questions swirled in my mind. *Is it all connected to our investigative business? What about Jimmie's kidnapping? And the other two boys? Could David's be connected? But David was kidnapped from home, not a mall.*

Yeah, but the age tallies. And Debbie was present for Jimmie's kidnapping.

What about Debbie's murder?

What if she saw the kidnapping and the killer had to kill her?

I had to check the Internet.

"Bast," I whispered.

Chapter Fourteen

Early morning, Saturday, August 15, 1998

Bast:

Bast sat crouched on the floor writing e-mails. He had to get some information out and back fast. Thank goodness he had stashed his laptop in his car just before the guests started arriving. He could hear his sister breathing in the bed and couldn't begin to imagine what she was dreaming. He hoped she didn't dream. But when he had poked his head in to check on her and found the landline phone there with a different number than the Brooks's main number he couldn't resist dialing up to the Internet. At least they had the same service provider as him so it was no big deal to get in with his account.

An e-mail came in:

From: bean@cover.net

Date and Time: August 15, 1998, 2:05 a.m.

Gave that licence plate number to Marsden. He called it in, but didn't bother to tell Fielding, so that buys us some time. E-mailed my contact at the Ministry of Transport and gave him your e-mail address so he can reply to you directly. Flying to Vancouver later today, but will keep in touch by e-mail.

He heard his sister stir.

"Bast," Dana said. "We need to look up all those recent kidnappings again. See if anything is there about ... about David." Her voice wavered but she clenched her teeth.

"You think there's a connection?"

"I don't know. David wasn't kidnapped from a mall. But what if the kidnapper was here, I mean at our place for the agency opening and he saw David and recognized him from being at the mall ... and ..."

"Maybe, but David was with one or all of us all the time at the Mini-Mall."

"But the kidnapper may not know that, so when he saw David here and remembered him from the mall ...?"

"Possibly. Okay. I'll check." Bast opened Netscape and did a search for "Mall kidnappings Toronto Thurston."

The same two stories from two days ago appeared as well as one about Jimmie. Nothing about last night's. He did another search "David Bowman Thurston" and got a hit. A breaking news story posted on the local CKNT TV station popped up.

"Yeah, here's one." He turned the laptop towards Dana who now crouched beside him on the floor. She had a thin blanket wrapped around her as if she was cold.

"You okay, sis?"

"Yes! Let's read the damn screen."

Together they read:

Cooks Regional Police were called to a suspected kidnapping at the opening of the Thurston-Toronto branch of a Canada wide detective agency. During the opening ceremonies, David Bowman, the six-year-old son of one of the branch's owners, Dana Bowman, went missing. Because a window in the basement was broken, the police are calling it a kidnapping. For more details tune in to CKNT TV*—the heart of Cooks Region, Channel 15 on your TV.*

The link following it led to:

Update to breaking news story

The body of a young woman was found on the attic balcony of 10 Maitland St., the location of The Attic Investigative Agency at its open house in central Thurston a few hours ago. Police won't say who the woman is or whether it is connected to the disappearance of David Bowman, the six-year-old son of Dana Bowman, one of the agency's owners. Stay tuned to CKNT TV*—the heart of Cooks Region, Channel 15 on your TV.*

Both were by-lined Charles Haas. Did that man have to keep popping into his life? After what had happened last year. He couldn't even say to himself what it actually was, probably because he still didn't understand it, and there had been no contact or communication between them for a year. He thought Charles had moved on to Barrie, but obviously that had not worked out. A hand shook his shoulders.

"Huh?"

"Bast, you were miles away."

"Just ruminating." He scrolled down some more on the Yahoo page. "That's it. But I've sent out some e-mails for more information and Stringbean e-mailed and said we should get the licence plate owner info today."

"Oh." Dana thumbed her bangs. "I forgot. I brought something back from Debbie's." Still wrapped in the blanket except for her bare right arm, she dragged that oversized purse she always carted around like it contained her life, turned it upside down and dumped its contents, flinging items out of the way until three piles remained—a packet of what looked like letters wrapped with a thin elastic, a small empty pill bottle in a clear plastic bag, a white garbage bag, maybe a third full, with a peculiar smell.

He leaned over and pulled the bottle from the bag.

"Hmm. No label. Could be anything. Well, it's not suicide. She was stabbed in the back."

"Yeah, but maybe she was on something that affected her judgement. She'd been awful moody lately, looked pale and complained of headaches. Here, wait." She dumped the contents of the garbage bag. Bast twitched his nose at the musty smell of dried blood.

"From the bathroom wastebasket. Oh, hell, I forgot to check for garbage in Debbie's room."

"Don't worry about it. Let's just see what's here." He began removing wadded facial tissue, Q-tips, an empty Tylenol bottle, placing them on the end table.

Dana grabbed the bag from him and tossed out the rolled-up sanitary pad from its covering tissue. A scrap of paper followed, Dana picked it up and Bast peered over her shoulder while she read off the paper's contents."*Sp ... harmacy, ... to, On, ... 445 29-07-1997, Pays: $1. ... Sangwell ...* Hey, that could be 'Deborah Sangwell.' Oh yeah *Mi ... and Repeats: 0.* That's it. Looks like a prescription to me. Can you find the other scraps in all this mess?"

Bast picked through the rest of the garbage bag.

Nothing.

He stroked his beard.

"And there are these letters. Look, Bast, could this Jarvis be a boyfriend?"

"Don't know. Let's see them."

Footsteps pounded up the stairs. Bast grabbed the half prescription slip from Dana's hands and shoved it into his right back pocket. The plastic bag with the prescription bottle followed.

"I'll check this out later in the morning," he said.

He gathered the rest of the garbage collection, tossed it back into its bag and into Dana's purse. He shut down the laptop and packed it away under the bed. When he turned around he saw Dana staring at the packet of letters as if they were a foreign object. Jarvis Harwood, the name on the envelope sounded familiar, maybe from one of the stories he had worked on. He silently cursed himself for being so prolific. But erasing the stories and their sources from his mind had been the only way he could erase the horrors of what he wrote.

"Dana? You all right?" Bast asked.

"Uh ... yeah." She shoved the letters into her bag. That followed his laptop under the bed. Again she stalled.

"Get back into bed," he whispered. "I'm going to see who's out there."

Bast poked his head outside the den door, and when he saw the cop almost at the doorway, he staggered forward and collided with him. Both jumped and Bast feigned astonishment.

"Sorry," Bast said. "Just checking on my sister."

Constable Steadman glared at him. "Back to the room assigned to you." He pointed down the hall.

"Aye, aye ... sir." Bast saluted and continued down the hall.

"My, my, we got our strength back fast," Steadman said from behind.

Bast lunged into the spare bedroom, shutting the door fast. He hoped Steadman didn't snoop in the den and look under the bed.

Chapter Fifteen

A little later, Saturday morning, August 15, 1998

Dana:

The pounding came from the bedroom door.

"M ... M ... Ms. Bowman," Fielding said from outside the door.

Couldn't the man give me a little privacy? I pushed the covers off and realized I was in a strange bed and still wore my party dress. Red for blood. Red. Cut it out, Dana.

"What the hell do you want, Fielding?"

"Are you d ... d ... decent?"

"What?" I scratched my head and yawned.

"Ms. Bowman. I need to talk to you."

"So talk."

"I h ... h ... have a ch ... ch ... change of clothes for you."

"What?" I leaped out of bed, ran to the door and pulled it open.

Fielding leaned against the wall. His face resembled whitewash and red rivers flowed through his eyes. He held a plastic bag, which he slid over my way.

"Your ch ... ch ... change of clothes. C ... Constable Nivens collected them."

"Thanks." I grabbed the bag. "You look like hell. No sleep?"

"Just a migraine. I get them all the time. It'll pass."

"Migraine. Here, come in and sit down on ..." A quick glanced around the room showed an ironing board piled high with clothes standing beside a chest of drawers. A basket of clothing sat in the room's only chair. "... on the bed."

"No, it's okay."

"No, it isn't. Migraines are awful. My mother used to get them, but thankfully I don't. She used to blow in a paper bag, to get rid of the pain, I mean. Maybe there's one here." I started rummaging in the dresser drawers.

"Ms. B ... B ... Bowman. It's all right."

"Here we are." I shook a scarf from a Fashion Shoppe bag and shoved the bag at Fielding. He ignored it. "Put it over your face and blow."

He stared at me, for once speechless, took a deep breath and sputtered.

"Take the damn bag and blow. And go and sit down. I don't want to have to deal with a cop passing out in a bedroom."

A little colour hit his face for a second. He staggered over to the bed, plunked down on the edge, leaned over and blew. I moved towards the doorway, stopped and swung around.

"Look, Fielding, I'm sorry. Guess we're all a little edgy." I sat on the bed beside him and touched his forehead. He flinched and pulled away. "Sorry. Do you want a glass of water?"

"W ... w ... wait. It's the kid. I m ... m ... mean your son. I have a daughter."

"I know. You told me earlier."

"Well, I want you to know, Ms. Bowman."

"Dana."

"D ... Dana, that I'll do my best to get your son back safe and sound."

"I know that, Fielding."

"Don."

"What?"

"M ... my name is Don."

"Okay, Don. Anyway, you have two private detectives in the house to help you out."

"Now, listen here, Ms. Bowman. You let the police handle this. Your job is to answer your cell phone if it rings, so we know what the kidnappers want. Nothing else." He pointed his forefinger under my nose.

I jumped off the bed, started searching for my clothes, saw the plastic bag on the floor and grabbed it, then turned to the man on the bed, the man who was now all cop and nothing else.

"Fielding, while searching my house, you didn't happen to find a pair of black sling-back shoes?"

"Why? Did you lose a pair?"

"Never mind. Won't go with jeans." I headed out the door for the Brooks's bathroom and a shower.

When I returned to the den, Fielding had left. Skipping the Yoga, I grabbed my purse from under the bed, left Bast's laptop, and headed downstairs. Bast sat at the kitchen table, sipping his usual raw-egg concoction. Fielding stood over by one of the kitchen counters and appeared to be ruminating on something in front of him. Rita Brooks fussed at the stove. She looked up and smiled.

"Good morning, Dana," she said. "Did you sleep okay? Here I'll get you some coffee."

"Ms. Bowman," said Fielding. He walked over to the table and pointed to an empty chair. "Sit down."

I slumped into the chair as he glanced at my brother.

"Overture, the dining room. Now. We need to have a chat."

After they left the room, I looked over at the counter where Fielding had held his staring session.

The knife rack.

I thought about the knife handle sticking out of Debbie's back and from there to Lois cutting cheese with Bast's utility knife, the guy with the backpack staring at it, and the knife falling to the floor when I sent my punch glass flying and knocked over the sandwich plate.

How did that knife get from the office floor to Debbie's back?

I clutched the coffee Rita set down on the table and took quick gulps, not caring that it stung my throat. When Rita brought half a grapefruit and a bowl of sugar-coated dry cereal, I shovelled it in by rote. At least it would give me energy to tackle some of the world, my neighbourhood, at least.

Bast and Fielding returned. The latter favoured his right temple but his colour was a few shades darker than its previous whitewash. I mouthed the word "knife" to Bast but he mouthed back "not now." Fielding cleared his throat.

"Ms. Bowman. A word with you in the dining room."

Fielding asked me questions every which way about where I'd seen that knife at the open house.

"The last time I saw that knife or one like it was in Debbie's back."

"And before that?"

"On the office floor."

For some reason I didn't mention the guy staring at the knife.

Back in the kitchen Fielding had more instructions for us.

"We should be finished with all but the attic of your house by 12 noon. You may return then, as long as you stay out of the front of the attic, the balcony and the elevator. It's still not working." Fielding stroked his jaw. "We should have the court order for the wiretap by then or shortly after and will set it up with your business line in your dining room. Detective Harker will be there to operate it, and then you will have to stay put in the house. Meantime, I'd advise you, Ms. Bowman, not to stray far from the house and keep your cell with you."

"What about Jimmie's mother? Has she heard from the kidnapper?"

Fielding stood up and muttered something about "police business."

"Look, my son has been kidnapped, so don't you think I have a right to know if David's kidnapping is connected to Jimmie's?"

"We're keeping an open mind for now. Keep close to home, Ms. Bowman. I'll check in later." He nodded at us and headed out the door.

Bast sat down beside me and whispered that Fielding was only trying to trace the knife's track into Debbie's body.

"He doesn't think you did it?" I asked. "I mean, it is your knife."

"No. I've been ruled out. No fingerprints for one thing."

"Good."

It was then I mentioned the fellow with the backpack and cap staring at the knife.

"I didn't notice him."

"You were too busy going at it with that Haas reporter. Just what is it with you two?"

"Not now, sis."

I shrugged. Too bad we didn't have surveillance tapes in the office, but I could call Bevens and see if anything managed to show up on the mall's tapes during Jimmie's kidnapping. Oh, shit, I was suspended. Maybe Bast could ask Oliver. They seemed to be pals. Better concentrate on asking questions around the neighbourhood, but my butt seemed attached to the chair. What was the time frame for getting back kidnapped kids? A quick glance at my watched showed 10 hours had passed since Debbie's hue and cry. I wanted to be here when the bastard called about David. But this was my neighbourhood, and I intended to milk it. I took a sip of coffee. Lukewarm and murky, like my resolve.

What if I skewered the kidnappers' intentions while nosing around? But doing nothing wouldn't bring David back. I pushed the coffee cup away.

"You okay, Dana?" Bast asked.

Two pairs of eyes fixed on me.

"As well as could be expected. Look, Rita, I need to ask you some questions."

"Sure, anything to help."

Bast slid his chair back and stood up.

"Guess I have a few things to look after, like go to the drug store and those letters you wanted me to mail." Bast held out his hand. "Oh, I'll get my laptop while I'm at it."

"Letters?"

He winked at me. "Yes, those letters you mentioned last night."

"Oh, yes." I flipped open my bag and behind Rita's back, handed him the Jarvis letters.

After he left, Rita pulled up a chair while I rummaged in my bag and removed a small sketchpad and charcoal.

"Now," I began, and started bawling.

"There, there." Rita Brooks leaned over and put an arm around me. "I'll get you some more coffee."

"No I'll be all right." *Sob.* "I just, need to ask you a few questions." Rita passed the tissue box. Yanking out a few, I blew into them and looked up. "I'm okay, now, really, Rita."

"You sure you don't want more coffee?"

"No, I'm fine."

"All right, but you just say the word if you do." Rita took the cup to the sink, then sat back down at the table, folded her hands in her lap and smiled at me.

I started sketching Rita and began the spiel.

"I hope you don't mind if I draw. This is my way of taking notes." When she nodded, I continued. "Rita, I need you to help me find David."

"Of course, dear, but I don't know how. I mean, Randall and I were here all night, but we went to bed early the first time and didn't hear a thing until the police knocked on our door."

"I understand. But you live next door. Now, what time did you and Randall go to bed the first time?"

"Why, same time as usual, 10 o'clock. When you're up in age, the news holds nothing but grief, so we watch a couple of hours of light TV, then go to bed."

"I see," I added a TV with 10 p.m. at the bottom, in the corner and sketched a small outline of a bed. "You do realize that last night was the night of the open house party at my place?"

"Of course, dear. I'm sorry Randall and I couldn't come. As I told you when we got the invitation, I didn't mind the business being next door. This town isn't what it used to be and the police can only do so much."

"Exactly. That's why I want to know if you saw or heard any cars arriving, besides the police ones, say between 9 p.m. and 1 a.m."

"Of course." She started to chuckle. "Oh, I'm sorry, Dana. It's just that Randall heard one car honking its horn and came out to the front door to see. Then he called me and there was this small car trying to squeeze into an even smaller space across the road. It couldn't make it, of course, so it drove into the Robinson driveway and sat there for a bit, which I thought a little odd. The

Robinsons have been away, you know, but maybe they came back."

They were a young couple, new neighbours I wasn't chummy with. Still, my ears perked up.

"Robinson's driveway. What colour car was it?"

"Couldn't say. It was too dark, you see." Rita pushed her bifocals back onto her nose.

"Does Randall remember?"

"I don't know. Wait. I'll get him. He's in the basement playing with his train set."

"Randall ... Randall ... Randall." Her voice receded as she neared the basement doorway. Footsteps were followed by Randall himself.

"Oh, Miss Dana," Randall Brooks had always called me that, even when Ron and I were still married. He was a very reserved person, unlike his overly talkative wife. A former railway conductor, he filled a lot of otherwise empty hours with his train set. Often I would find David downstairs with him watching a long train go through a tunnel or over a bridge.

David.

Randall took my hands.

"I'm sorry; I hope they find David," he said.

"That's what I'm here for." I cleared my throat. "As you know, we've opened the detective agency next door. This isn't exactly what we expected. But I thought it better if I did something. Rita mentioned you saw a car park in Robinson's driveway last night. Do you remember its colour?"

"Well, it was dark, outside, I mean. The car was an old Volkswagen bug, and a bright gaudy colour. With its headlights on, it looked lilac or pink."

"What time was this?"

"9 p.m.," he replied.

"We'd just finished watching reruns of that dreadful sitcom, you know the one about that married couple with the obnoxious kids," Rita said. "Randall thinks it's funny."

Too early.

"But the car didn't stay there for more than a few seconds, Rita," Randall said. "Remember. Just as we were returning from the window, it backed out and tore down the street. And Rita didn't want to miss her program coming up next."

I didn't bother asking what that was. Instead, I sighed.

"Oh dear," Rita said. "All this must be trying for you. Can't you let the police look after it?"

"Yeah, I guess I should just wait until the kidnapper calls." Seeing the horrified look on her face, I stopped. "Sorry."

"Dear me. What am I thinking? Your own son. Of course you have to do something. And his poor babysitter."

"Sorry. I'm a little rattled. Guess I better get going." I stood up. "You sure neither of you saw nor heard anything later?"

"No, sorry, we went to bed at 10 and heard nothing until that police officer knocked on our door and said, didn't ask, he needed our house as a command post, just temporary, he said. Then, of course, we heard a lot. Police and others milling about inside and out."

"Others?"

"Well, I saw your brother," Randall said.

"Where?"

"He was on the back porch. I could see him from the porch light and a tall skinny man about my age, no, maybe a bit younger, joined him. I couldn't hear much what they were saying, something about flowers and a brick wall. Your brother pointed to the side of the house."

"Oh. You didn't happen to see either of them pick something up, like a stuffed toy?"

"Stuffed toy?" Randall wore a puzzled frown. "No, they didn't pick up anything. However, this morning I looked out the window and saw that your flower bed was badly trampled."

"Okay. Thanks for your help. I think I'll see if they'll let me back in the house now."

"If there's anything we can do ...?" Rita started.

"Anything," her husband added.

"Thanks." I headed for the door.

A check with my digital watch showed it was close enough to noon to return home. As I neared my front lawn, a VW bug, fuchsia-coloured, headed my way and stopped two doors down. The driver's door opened. PC Joseph Oliver stepped out. Right behind him a van hit the brakes. The side of the van read *CKNT TV—the heart of Cooks Region.* Oliver broke into a run and pushed me up the veranda stairs just as the CKNT crew charged up the driveway. He opened the front door, shoving us inside, and slammed it shut.

"Fielding," he yelled.

Fielding stepped into the hall from the kitchen. "Ms. Bowman, I was just going to call you. We have our wiretap court order and Harker is in the dining room setting up the wiretap equipment. Oliver?"

"The press are here, outside," said Oliver. He pointed to the door as a repeated knock reverberated throughout the hall.

"Damn," said Fielding. "Stay put, I'll look after this." He opened the front door, shouted a few words, and closed the door behind him. Oliver and I looked at each other.

"I need to talk to you about your car," I said.

"Oh, that. Ha. That's my son's. He bought it second hand and hasn't had time to repaint it. I've had to use it the past couple of days while mine is in the shop for bodywork. The Records Bureau manager doesn't rate a blue and white." Oliver took a quick breath.

"Did you come here to speak to Fielding?"

"No, Ms. Bowman. I'd like to speak with you alone. I'm on early lunch and have to be back at headquarters soon." He pressed nearer, as one conspirator to another. "I've got that licence number for that Toyota you were asking about. I've already e-mailed Bast, but I wanted to tell you in person because of your son being kidnapped." He paused and cleared his throat. "Not that the answer will do much good. Car reported stolen last night at 6:30. Owner of the car with Licence plate number LTD 888 is a Mr. Robert Belcher. Despite that name, a respectable loans officer at the TD. Car stolen from the parking lot outside the TD branch across the street from the Thurston Mini-Mall.

And was found there, again by Mr. Belcher, when he came in to work at 8 a.m. today."

"So, he reported it to the police, again?" I asked.

"Yes."

"Hmm. And I suppose the car's now impounded for prints."

"Yes, but Forensics don't know if it's connected with this case."

"Neither do we, for sure, except it was in the neighbourhood late last night. Look, Oliver, can you do us a favour? Can you find out whose fingerprints are in the car and any other, evidence?" I swallowed hard as I kept picturing a six-year-old boy who couldn't go to sleep at night without a brown stuffed beaver.

"Hmm," Oliver said. "I shouldn't be doing this ... okay; I'll e-mail Bast with the results. Less obvious with the press outside."

He turned to leave.

"Wait a minute." I grabbed his arm. "The VW. Did you park it last night across the street?"

"Huh?" Oliver looked startled. "No. Oh, wait. I used that driveway across the street to turn the car around. Had to park around the corner."

"Okay, and could I have this Belcher's home address?"

"Don't know it offhand. I'll get it to Bast."

"Thanks. Oh, and one more thing." I took a deep breath. "Do you happen to know if anything showed up on that surveillance tape at the Mini-Mall during Jimmie Halpern's kidnapping?"

He stared as if I'd asked him how many peanuts were in a large bag. Then his face softened. "Not sure. But I can check and get back to you or Bast."

"Thanks."

He nodded, and opened the front door to brave the TV crew.

I shuffled into the kitchen just as Bast hurried in from the back. He got comfortable at the desk with his laptop and started hitting keys fast, as if in a speed-induced trance.

"What are you doing, little brother?" I asked.

"Digging up dirt on some of our party guests."

"Hmm I suppose I could do that too. But I prefer to talk to people in person. That way I can see their faces. However, let's see here." I leaned over and started typing.

What can you tell me about Robert Belcher, the TD branch loans officer?

"There, Bast. Dig up something on him."

"Robert Belcher? The TD branch loans officer?"

"Yeah. It's his car, that Toyota that you saw last night, except it was stolen at that time."

"Where did you find that out?"

"Your friend, Oliver, popped by as I returned from next door. Oh, damn." I leaned over and pounded the desk with my right fist. "Bast. Oliver was driving that pink VW last night."

"What VW?"

"The one Rita and Randall saw outside about ... about." I fumbled around. "Where's my sketchpad?"

"Take it easy, sis."

Breathing deeply, I managed to tell him about my interview with Rita and Randall Brooks.

"But the Randalls didn't see the Toyota. Damn. I bet that Toyota is what David was taken away in. I don't care if you say you saw only one person, the driver, a man wearing a baseball cap. David could've been on the floor in back, unconscious or even dead."

"You don't know that."

"No, I guess not." I rubbed my hands through my cropped hair. "Bast, I can't seem to think straight. I can't seem to function."

"Well, that's understandable. You've lost both your son and your best friend's daughter in one evening."

"So you think David's dead." I grabbed his T-shirt.

"No, that's not what I meant. I meant you've had two traumatic experiences within 24 hours, both involving family and friends."

"Ms. Bowman, come into the dining room now so I can explain the wiretap?" Harker stood in the doorway and stared at me. That fellow really had a nasty-looking face.

I followed Harker into the dining room and sat down. A big reel-to-reel tape recorder rested on the table. Harker went into the wiretap spiel, including telling me calls were no longer being forwarded to my cell. Just as he finished, the business phone extension rang, sending me jumping out of my chair. Harker scowled, turned on the tape recorder and motioned me to pick up.

"Dana Bowman?" The caller sounded like he had a cold.

"Yes."

"Now, listen up good, because I'm not going to repeat myself. No cops, just you and your partner, Overture. $50,000 in cash in a nine-by-twelve envelope in two hours at the ice cream stand in Grandview Park. You each buy a chocolate ice cream stick, eat it, then place the sticks and envelope in the trash can under the maple tree about 10 metres from the stand. Go back to your car in the parking lot. Return in 15 minutes to the ice cream stand and David will be there."

"David, is he all right? Can I speak to him?"

"No. He's okay, and will stay okay as long as you follow instructions."

"$50,000? I don't have that much and can't get that in two hours?"

"He's your son."

"How about part cash and part jewellery?"

"Jewellery?"

"Yeah, I suppose you guys could use something valuable. This is an antique gold pocket watch, worth maybe $5,000, and a diamond ring worth around $10,000. We can have the rest in cash, or will, after we visit the bank."

"Yeah, and have the cops tell every fence in Cooks Region and Toronto?"

"I'm not supposed to tell the cops. You told me that."

"Yeah, all right. Just be there. Grandview Park ice cream stand. You got two hours." He hung up.

I turned around. Detective Harker was busy with his cell phone.

"Fielding. Harker here. We got a live one. Ice cream stand at Grandview Park."

I grabbed the phone from his hand.

"No, no. No Cops." I yelled it into the phone. "Did you hear that, Fielding? This guy said 'no cops.' Only Bast and me. You better listen because I'm holding you personally responsible if anything happens to David."

Bast and Detective Harker finally calmed me down. We decided to compromise. Fielding and other plainclothes would position themselves in the park, one even replacing the ice cream stand vendor. Harker would stay at the house and try to find out who had called last on our business line. Bast and I headed to the bank for cash—from Bast's line of credit and the jewellery, our late mother's which I'd kept for sentimental reasons—the dollar value combined was under $2,000. I was banking on the kidnappers not knowing the difference at first glance.

Chapter Sixteen

Mid afternoon, Saturday, August 15, 1998

Dana:

Grandview Park. Two days ago, David and I had spent time swimming and laughing together—normal mother and child routine.

"Take it easy, Dana. We'll get him back." Bast removed his right hand from the steering wheel and patted my shoulder. He slid the car between a convertible and an old clunker.

We took a long hike across the park. Snow Lake shone blue-green, too bright, as if mocking us. Dry grass, some turning brown, crunched under my feet. Damn, they better not have hurt David. I clutched the envelope tighter.

"We're here," Bast said.

The man behind the ice cream stand didn't look like a cop. He must have squeaked by on police height and weight regulations. He also had a longer-than-regulation moustache that could be fake. He said nothing as we bought our chocolate ice cream on sticks. I chewed through the ice cream, almost gagging on the stick. When finished, we trod in silence to the trash can and dumped our sticks. I let the envelope follow. We moved briskly to the car. Couldn't see a thing. Too many trees. The view of the stand disappeared where the park curved around the lake.

"Might as well sit in the car and be comfortable," Bast said. We climbed inside.

Five minutes. I counted the seconds on my digital. Bast drummed his fingertips on the dashboard.

Ten minutes. Bast quit drumming and turned to me.

"Want to hear some music?" he asked.

"Nope."

"Look, Dana, you know I'm a loner. I don't get too close to people. But in the last year I've gotten to know David well. He's a super little fellow. You are, too."

"Thanks." I patted his hand and stole another look at my watch. Thirteen minutes, and I wanted to gag. "Open the window, Bast."

He pressed a button and both front windows slid down. A faint breeze brushed my brow.

Fourteen minutes, and my stomach lurched in time with my heartbeats. It was never like this on stakeout with Stringbean. But it wasn't my child then.

Fifteen minutes. Time was up. We bolted from the car and ran to the ice cream stand. No David. Bast ran to the trashcan. He held up the envelope. I shook the runty cop.

"Where is my son? You screwed it all up by taking the real vendor's place. The kidnapper saw through you and never showed."

Before he had time to answer, Fielding appeared.

"You damn cops. You should've listened to me. I should've listened to him, the kidnapper. I'd have my son back. Damn you." I transferred my shaking to Fielding. He seized my arms.

"Calm down, Ms. Bowman. Sometimes kidnappers just have the victim's family do a dry run, first, to make sure they follow directions and it's safe."

"Yeah right. Well, they'll know it sure isn't safe now with all you cops running around."

He looked taken aback. Maybe the man was starting to realize he wasn't God.

"It's okay, Dana. I'm sure they've left before now," Bast said. He jangled his car keys. I grabbed them and ran.

"Dana."

"Ms. Bowman."

I kept running, ignoring the footsteps behind. At the car, I scrambled to open the door, jumped in and fumbled getting the keys into the ignition.

"Wait." Bast yanked at the passenger door. "Open up."

I pressed the button, and when he climbed in, grabbed the steering wheel, backed the car out and screeched onto the road, then drove around and around the park and down by the lake.

"Let's go home, sis."

"Why? He may still be here somewhere."

Sirens sounded from behind. A couple of blue-and-whites and an unmarked car fanning towards us appeared in the rear-view mirror. I hit the accelerator and sped down the road back into the centre of town.

Chapter Seventeen

Mid-afternoon, Saturday, August 15, 1998

David:

"If I remove the tape will you keep quiet?" the man whispered.

David nodded. He could smell something greasy, like French fries. The bright light from the flashlight hit his eyes, and he shut them; then opened them as the man ripped the tape off his mouth. David tried to hold back but he couldn't help it; it hurt his lips.

"Ow!"

Slap. "I said to keep it quiet."

David nodded again. He was too afraid to speak, even to say he was sorry.

"I brought you some food. Do you like hot dogs and French fries?" The man leaned over and breathed on David. David started coughing which rewarded him with another sharp slap across the cheek.

"Oh for Christ sakes," whispered another voice. "Grow up and for once start acting your age. Can't you see he needs to breathe after having that duct tape over his mouth? And if you're giving him food, he needs his hands free as well."

"Stop acting like you're my mother," the man said.

"Then stop acting like a child. Here, let me."

David heard a whoosh and then the light jumped around as "Mother" grabbed it.

"I'll take care of this. You go upstairs. I'll attend to you after."

David thought he heard the man whisper "tramp," then a door slamming and footsteps thumping up.

"There, there," the voice whispered as "Mother" helped David sit up. "Now let's get this tape off your hand. It's going to hurt at first, but it'll be better if I just pull it off like a bandage and get it over with. Okay?" David nodded. "Mother" placed the light sideways beside David and he saw as well as felt the yank. He bit down on his lip and managed not to cry out this time.

A plate containing French fries and a hot dog was placed on his lap. He touched it hesitantly as if it might bite back, but when he felt a jerk on his shoulder, he picked up a French fry and began to eat. He was surprised that he was hungry and cleaned the plate.

"Mother" ruffled his hair, whispered "good boy," and asked him if he would like to go to the bathroom. David realized that he had to pee. His captor removed the tape from his ankles with a stern warning not to kick or do anything else wrong or she'd hit him. She yanked him up and led him to a wall where she pulled open a door. Inside he saw a sink and a toilet, but only faintly as it had no window and was lit by a nightlight. He tried turning around but his captor grabbed his head and shook it.

"No. This isn't acceptable behaviour. And don't bother to flick the light switch; there's no bulb in the overhead light socket. I'll leave you to do your business in private." She let go of David and he heard the door close behind him.

Chapter Eighteen

A little later, Saturday, August 15, 1998

Dana:

Number 10 Maitland appeared quiet. The CKNT van parked next to the Kitty-Corner Convenience seemed to be the media's only on-site concession. A Cooks Regional Police Mobile Unit now stood in front of the house. A dark sedan pulled out of the driveway across the street. As it passed us, I thought I glimpsed Harker in the driver's seat. Police business, no doubt. Bast signalled me to keep silent and take it slow. I steered the car in front of the brick wall and we stepped out. No eager reporter or cop jumped off the porch. The porch looked too normal with its two white Muskoka chairs and the scatter rug by the front door. My scalp started itching, and I picked up the smell of something dank like sweat. The front door stood open about 30 centimetres; only silence came from inside.

We edged towards the door. Bast nudged it all the way open with his elbow and tiptoed inside. The hallway was empty. A shuffling noise emanated from the living room. We inched towards that doorway and peeked in.

Ronald George Bowman, my ex-husband, lifted cushions from the chesterfield. The rest of the room reeked of ransacking.

"What the hell are you doing here?" I asked. "And what have you done with our son?" Something snapped and I lurched towards him, grabbing his arms and shaking his five-foot-ten frame. "You bastard. Where's David? Come on. Tell me." My hands started to squeeze his neck.

Ron groaned.

"Let him go, Dana." Bast pulled from behind.

On the chesterfield, I sobbed. Ron touched my head.

"You stay away from me, Ron."

He appeared scared, as if caught mid-crime. His blond hair hung every which way, and sweat circled under the arms of his light blue T-shirt.

"D ... Dana?" he said.

"Oh, quit stuttering. I get enough of that from Fielding,"

"Who's Fielding?"

"Detective Sergeant Donald Fielding, Cooks Regional Police. Don't move, young man."

Fielding pointed the regulation Glock .40 calibre. Two backup constables moved cautiously forward, their own Glocks also pointed at Ron.

"Out of the way, Ms. B ... B ... Bowman and Mr. Overture," Fielding said. "You there." He jerked his head at Ron. "Up against the wall. Frisk him," he said to one of the constables. And to the other one, "Check to see where Harker is. He's supposed to be in the dining room."

The sweat spread on the front of Ron's T-shirt.

"He's my husband, I mean ex-husband."

Fielding ignored me. "Read him his rights and take him in and book him for B and E."

"Wait a minute, you can't do that," I said. "Ron, what are you really doing here?"

"Ms. Bowman," Fielding said.

I shut up. One of the constables grabbed the silence to read Ron his rights. When he finished, Ron butted in.

"Dana, what's the name of that lawyer who defended Leila when she took those clothes from that mall you work in?"

"I don't work there anymore. Or didn't you bother to read the sign outside."

"Yes, I saw it. Is that you? Anyway, the lawyer, Dana. He was good."

"Gordon Lambton. But he isn't around here anymore. He's in Toronto."

"Well, can you call him, for me? Oh, do it for yourself. This is your house now."

"W ... w ... will you two c ... c ... cut it out?" Fielding said. "You can visit your, your husband or whatever you c ... c ... call him once we've taken him to Headquarters and booked him."

"All right, I'll call Gordon," I said.

Fielding's first backup led Ron out. Fielding ordered me out of the living room and told the second backup to call Stewart. "And I need to talk to Sebastian? Where is he?"

A grinding sound provided his answer.

"What the ...?" Fielding asked.

"The elevator."

We hurried into the hallway. Bast stood outside the elevator door. Both buttons displayed red, but the elevator numbers showed descending. The elevator shook to a halt and the door slid open.

Bast:

Bast knelt by the man in blue spread out on the elevator floor. As he felt for a pulse, he heard footsteps behind him and turned around to see his sister and Fielding rushing towards him. He felt someone grasp his arm and he swung around. The man in blue lifted his head off the floor.

Marsden.

"Where's Harker?" Fielding asked.

"Huh? What?" Marsden tried to sit up, but fell back with each try. He groaned again as he put a hand to the back of his head.

"What the hell happened in here?" Fielding asked.

Marsden slowly turned his neck around as if it bore a rusty hinge. "Sorry, sir. He whacked me from behind."

"Who? Harker?" Fielding asked.

"No. He went home early, emergency at home. Said another detective was coming to replace him. Ouch."

"Then, who hit you?"

"Don't know, sir. Didn't see him. Could've been a she for all I saw. Well, maybe not ... quite a heavy blow. Ouch. My head."

He started rubbing his forehead and the top of his head. When he brought his hand down, Bast could see it contained blood.

"Here, take it easy," Bast said. Fielding's bulldozer approach was starting to irritate him. Marsden—one of his own—was hurt. "Come on, Fielding, help me get him out and onto a couch."

"No, it's okay," Marsden looked around and scowled.

"You're in the elevator," Fielding said. "Did he hit you in here?"

"No, sir, it's like this. Ouch." Marsden squinted at Fielding and cringed. "I was sitting here ... I mean in the kitchen at the desk when I thought I heard a knock at the side door. I figured it was the press again, so I got up to investigate, walked over to ... well, I got hit on the head. Next thing I know he was bending over me." He pointed to Bast.

"What time was this?" Fielding asked.

"Time? Well, sir, let's see. I'd just checked my watch against that clock up on the wall and it said 2:30 p.m."

Bast looked down at his watch. 3:45 p.m.

"Kind of a long time for Ron as a burglar to be in here, don't you think, Detective Sergeant?" Dana asked.

"Where did this happen, Marsden?" Fielding asked.

"Huh, I mean pardon, sir?" Marsden scrunched up his face and swayed. Bast grabbed hold of him.

"Where were you attacked? Here, in the elevator or by the side door?" Fielding sounded annoyed more than concerned.

"Oh yeah, I remember getting up off the chair and walking towards the hall. Then whack. Sorry, sir, that's all I remember."

"Hmm, so the attack probably took place in the hallway. Had Harker left by then?"

"Yes, he left just after 2:15."

"Which door did he leave by?"

"Oh, front, I guess." Marsden blinked and rubbed his forehead.

"Did you lock the door behind him?"

"No. I presume he locked it as he went out. It has a self lock."

"Never presume anything, Marsden. Now did you actually see him leave?"

"Huh? Oh sorry, sir. No. But I heard him shut the front door."

"And the elevator, did anybody use it?"

"No, sir, you said not to, and it wasn't working. How did I get here?" Marsden frowned and shook his head, stopping as he winced in pain.

Bast looked at Fielding and wished he would show some concern for the injured Marsden.

Fielding rubbed his jaw. "Okay, Overture, Greene. You two stay here and help Marsden. Greene, you call it in and ask for the paramedics. Also call Stewart. Ms. Bowman. You come with me. We're going to check this house, from top to bottom and see if anything else is out of place. By stairs."

Finally, Bast thought. Oliver had told him that Fielding had gone through a divorce and was estranged from his daughter, but did that excuse his cold behaviour to a fellow officer? As he hung onto Marsden who was trying to stand up, he heard Greene call it in.

Dana:

Our silent check revealed nothing else out of order on levels one and two. The basement still contained some glass fragments from last night.

When we hit the Agency floor, even the alarm was silent. Fielding drew his Glock and motioned me to stay put. I scowled at his back and kept a few feet behind. He tapped the agency office door but it stuck. He kicked it in and made an abrupt turnaround. We collided. He grabbed me and tried to push me down the hall. But I saw inside.

I raised my hands and tried to scream but it came out as a weak rattle. My arms fought Fielding and my eyes had to see the truth.

"Better stay back, Ms. Bowman." Fielding's words held a surprising concern mixed with firmness.

"Please. I must see ... David."

"It's not David. Just somebody's idea of a sick joke. All right, I guess the only way is to let you look." He steered me towards the doorway and pulled it open.

A large stuffed doll stared down from a noose in the doorway. Its blond hair was trimmed to David's hairstyle, short bangs in front, curled up at the back. The doll wore David's favourite pair of knee-worn jeans and T-shirt with the face of a beaver. Strapped with hemp to its right arm was the missing stuffed beaver. I jumped back.

Of course it was an effigy. Still, I couldn't move. Could only stare. Stare as Fielding put on latex gloves and cut the rope. Stare as he then gingerly handled only the top of the rope. Stare as he placed it in an evidence bag which he pulled from his pocket and opened. Stare as he did the same with the effigy and the stuffed beaver.

Two arms came from behind and I screamed.

"Dana, take it easy. It's Bast." He guided me down the stairs to my room, helped me onto the bed, pulled a blanket over me, and opened the window to let in some air.

"Leave this to us. You better get some rest."

As he closed the door behind him, the sound of sirens getting closer blasted through the window. The door opened and I jerked up.

"S ... s ... sorry to b ... barge in like this, Ms. Bow ... D ... Dana," Fielding said, "b ... b ... but I wanted to s ... see how you were."

"Well, as you can see I'm resting and, oh God." I tripped out of bed and ran to the bathroom, knelt and heaved. The unwanted chocolate snack and breakfast spilled into the toilet. I flushed it away and staggered to my feet. A cold wet towel touched my face and a huge arm pressed me to an even larger body.

"It's always harder with kids," Fielding said.

I pulled away. Didn't need the mirror to tell me the colour of my face, and didn't care how crimson, white and gill-green mixed it showed.

"You ... you ... it's all your fault." I leaned back against the vanity. "This charade this afternoon. That's what it was, to trick the kidnappers."

"Not exactly. The call you got was genuine. But we now figure the kidnapper wasn't so much interested in the money at the park as in something in this house. And we caught him red-handed." Fielding rubbed his hands together.

"Caught him? Ron? Fielding, you've got the wrong man. Ron wouldn't kidnap his own child. He's never been interested in raising him."

"Don't be so sure. We found a photo of your son in his pocket, and as David looks about five or six in it so it has to be a photo taken after you two split up. The top drawer of the desk in the kitchen was left open with papers sticking out. Don't forget we found him tossing the living room."

"Fielding, you really don't know Ron. When we were married, if he got frustrated about anything he would start tossing things around—cushions, newspapers, magazines, never anything large or heavy. And the desk in the kitchen—it's just a catchall for household bills, receipts, notepads, and I don't see Ron wanting any of our bills. He wasn't exactly quick to pay them when we were married."

He looked taken aback, but shrugged his shoulders. "Well we'll see what we find in his place once the warrant comes through."

"Probably a stack of unpaid bills."

"So, maybe he needed money. Did your ex-husband gamble?"

"No! Are you suggesting he kidnapped David because he needs the money?"

"I'm not saying anything more, but I'm going to question him thoroughly and we'll see what we can charge him with. Vandalism and break and enter for sure as he doesn't own anything in this house anymore."

A bang, followed by loud voices came from outside the bedroom window. We rushed out of the bathroom. Fielding held up his hand.

"Wait," he said. He moved to the window and peered out.

"What is it?"

"Shh. The press have returned. Your brother probably called them."

"Bast is not a crime reporter anymore." I shot over to the window and looked down.

The CKNT-TV van was now parked in front of the Brooks's house. A crew attempted to haul out a camcorder. Bast and that Haas reporter shouted back and forth and it seemed as if their fight was more than just about getting a lousy interview. Bast wore a hot scowl that frightened me; I'd never seen him like this before. Although Haas verbally pummelled my brother with "what's the matter, Overture? Afraid to be on the other side of the interview fence? Afraid of what I'll ask you?" His mouth wore a sneer that made me feel icy inside. This was personal.

Greene appeared, yelling "stop." The other two froze and glared at him. Bast shook his right hand at Haas, nodded, mumbled something, and said, "No comment right now, *Mister* Haas."

"Stay put, Ms. Bowman," Fielding said from beside me. "I'm going down to clear them out."

"I have no intention of talking to them."

Fielding raised his eyebrows. "Good. I suggest you lie down and rest."

Returning to the bed, I climbed under the blanket. After Fielding left, I grabbed the cell phone.

"Hello." Aunt Doris's voice boomed back.

"Aunt Doris, it's Dana. Don't say anything until I finish but they've arrested Ron."

"Arrested Ron? Whatever for?"

"Aunt Doris, I'm trying to tell you. They caught Ron trashing the living room and arrested him for break and enter."

"Break and enter? This house has been in the family for years. He has a right to be in it."

"Aunt Doris, for God's sake, wake up. Bast and I own this house. Now shut up until I tell you what's happened." After taking a deep breath, I slammed right into the last few hours' occurrences. "But I don't believe he kidnapped David. I don't know what he was doing in this house but ... Aunt Doris are you still there?"

"I'm thinking," she replied. A deep sigh came over the line. "I better get Ron a good lawyer. Johnston, the family lawyer is no good for this sort of thing."

"Ron has already asked for Gordon Lambton. He used to practice in Thurston. He's in Toronto now."

"Good, give me his number. I'll call him."

"Ron asked me to."

"Ron asked you? Well, I never."

"Aunt Doris. The main thing is to get Ron a lawyer."

"Right. These cops can't be trusted. Do you know that just after you left last night they were all over the place here? Pulling stuff out of drawers. It was all I could do to keep them away from Madge's room. They finally left at 6 a.m. but were back at 10 a.m. and this time they bothered Madge, asking her all sorts of questions and trashing her room. Wanted to know when she last saw Debbie." She paused and took a deep breath. "And then they took her to the police station to 'identify the body' as they put it."

"Madge, how is she? Can I talk to her?" My hands shook and the phone slipped onto the bed. I picked it up. "Sorry, Aunt Doris."

"... is sleeping, finally. What was that? Dana, are you there?"

"Yes, just dropped the phone."

"Well, as I was saying, Madge is finally getting some sleep. If you call back around suppertime she may be up. Now you call that lawyer. Now."

She hung up. I leaned over, opened my night table drawer and started rummaging inside for the telephone address book. No luck. Probably in my bag. Where was my bag? It had been slung over my arm in the bank but there was no recollection of it afterwards.

"Damn." Glancing around the room, I found it resting on the bureau, so stumbled over and hauled out the directory for the number.

"I'm sorry. The number you have called cannot be reached at this time. Please hang up and try again."

I threw the phone down on the bed.

"I can't do this." My hands shook, and my breath charged through my chest like running racoons. Heaving in air, I tried again. After a few rings, someone picked up.

"Gordon Lambton here."

Chapter Nineteen

Late afternoon, Saturday, August 15, 1998

Dana:

"Hello Gordon."

"Dana, is that you?"

"Yes."

"How are you doing?"

"Okay, I guess."

What does one say to an ex-lover who left you for a kleptomaniac?

Gordon Lambton was my first and last lover after Ron. Gordon is the classic rich, married lawyer, although our meeting didn't quite fit the classic bar pickup. Madge, Lois, Debbie and I went out to celebrate my 37th birthday two years ago at The China House, which refers to its dishware, not its food. I clowned around, moving Lois to more than a chuckle. The China House has these dainty basket chairs, and even though my weight barely hits 100 pounds, the chairs were made for dolls and not the china kind. Anyway, I flayed my arms around, rocked back and forth, when as they say "whoops," the chair and I fell backward and met the carpet. A pair of strong masculine arms lifted me up. You might say Gordon did the physical pickup and I the emotional one. We still had our affair going strong when Ron's girlfriend, Leila, pulled her kleptomaniac stunt in the Mini-Mall. I didn't even ask Gordon to defend her. Saw it on the TV news. Next thing I knew, Gordon was defending her *pro bono*. And he got the charges dropped.

"Dana, you all right?" Gordon asked.

I swallowed twice and cleared my throat.

"As good as can be expected."

"Hey I heard about your little boy and that woman's body found in your place."

"That woman was my best friend's daughter."

"Sorry, Dana. I really am. If I can help in any way."

"As a matter of fact, you can. Ron, remember him? My ex? Leila's ex? Well, he's just been arrested. The cops caught him ransacking this place. Maybe they even think he kidnapped David. Anyway, they arrested him for break and enter."

"Hey, hold it, Dana. Calm down."

"Calm down? Listen Mr. Bigshot Lawyer, my son's father has been arrested and you tell me to calm down." I hit near record high pitch, ready to crash the chandelier.

"Hey, hey, just a minute, Dana. Sounds like you're upset. You and Ron back together?"

"Oh, grow up, Gordon. Ron needs a lawyer and asked for you."

"Oh. Well, in that case, where is he being held?"

I could hear him rustling papers and knew Gordon had switched to business mode, so gave him the information he wanted.

"Okay, Dana, I'll get over to Ron right away. Talk to you later. We really must get together sometime."

"Yeah, sure when pigs fly."

"Pardon?"

"Guess I better say, goodbye."

"Right Dana, be in touch."

"Oink," I said into the disconnected receiver.

The cell rang.

Oliver. After asking how I was doing, he got down to business.

"Those surveillance tapes in the mall. You were right. They weren't working all Wednesday. Nothing showed, and ..."

"And what?"

He cleared his throat. "About Debbie. I thought I better tell you, and you can tell her mother before Fielding or one of his minions gets to her first."

"Tell Madge what?" My brain seemed filled with fog. David had been kidnapped. Debbie was dead. Stabbed. The cops had arrested Ron—wrongly. What more could there be now?

"I just spoke to Dr. Farley," Oliver said. "He found evidence Debbie had been pregnant—maybe six weeks—and recently miscarried or aborted, probably the latter."

"What? Debbie, pregnant? I find that hard to believe. She was the typical teenager, first year in college, earning extra money babysitting. She ..." A packet of letters with the name Jarvis Harwood broke the already diminishing fog in my mind. "Typical teenager? What am I saying? Typical teenagers do get pregnant. Christ. How am I going to tell Madge? Madge is ..." I shut up then, realizing I was talking to a cop. But what could I tell Madge? Madge who marched in front of the hospital and carried placards. She had always said that her daughter had been brought up right and she would never get pregnant without first getting married. It was only those other poor kids who got stuck, didn't know what to do and tried to take the easy way out—abortion. I buried my head in my hands and moaned. "My God, this will kill Madge. Okay, Oliver, thanks for telling me."

I closed the cell and moved towards the door. Fielding was calling upstairs to Stewart and Tractor. A quick look outside the window showed that the CKNT van was back but parked down the street. Haas stood smoking outside the van. He looked my way and I ducked back inside the room. Whirling around, I snatched my bag, shoved the cell inside, slung it over my shoulder and stopped ...

What if the kidnappers called again?

I called Bast's cell and caught him just leaving the office. I told him to forward the business line to my cell, then ran down the hall to David's room.

Taking a deep breath, I pushed open the door, and darted inside, running straight to the window. Closed. I shook and pulled the handles and with a squeak that could probably be heard inside and outside, it jerked up. When it reached halfway, I unfastened the screen at the bottom, pushed it out, slithered onto the sill and looked down into the backyard. Nobody stared back.

Good. I threw my bag into the yard and reached for the corner drainpipe, missing it by a few inches. Damn. Wiggling some more, I took a deep breath and lunged for the drainpipe.

Climbing wasn't my strongest point but after landing on my rear end, I grabbed my purse, ran to the back of the yard in between trees and scrambled over the fence into the neighbour's property.

These neighbours weren't familiar. I cut through their backyard and driveway, and at the street, took a shortcut to Madge's apartment. Aunt Doris blocked the doorway.

"It's not suppertime. She's still sleeping. Did you get Ron a lawyer?" She shot out the words like a human BB gun.

"Aunt Doris. I have more news of Debbie's death. I must speak to Madge now."

"She already knows Debbie is dead. What's the matter with you Dana? Go back home and wait for David's return."

"Aunt Doris, Fielding or one of his cohorts will be back, and it would be better if I spoke to Madge first."

We eyeballed each other.

"It's important, Doris. She may get a shock and it's better if it comes from me, her friend, than a cop."

"Very well." She shrugged and stood aside.

Madge sat in the living room, her eyes staring at the ceiling. I sat down beside her on the chesterfield and held her hands. It felt like touching ice.

"How goes it Madge?"

"Oh, I was just thinking how Debbie looked last September as she headed off for college. Jeans and a T-shirt and I thought she should be in a dress." Madge addressed the ceiling.

"Madge, there's something ... something else I have to tell you ... about Debbie."

"She was raring to go, first time away from home."

"Madge." I shook her. She continued her observation of the ceiling. "Madge. Did Debbie have a boyfriend?"

She jerked her hands away and glared. "What?"

"Did Debbie have ... did Debbie date anyone special while she was in college?"

"Oh, Debbie always had many dates all through her teen years, but no one special. 'Mum,' she said, 'I'm going to get my education first, get established in my career; then I'll get serious about some man.' "

"Well, she must've gotten serious about someone in the last few months."

"What?"

I grabbed Madge's hands again. This time the ice rattled and her eyes pleaded.

"Madge. I've just had a call from PC Oliver. You know the skinny cop from last night?"

Her hands rattled harder. "Get to the point."

"Oliver just talked to Dr. Farley, the coroner. He found evidence Debbie had been pregnant and probably abort ..."

Fingernails stabbed into my palms.

"Not true. Not true. You're lying."

"No, Madge. I'm sorry. I'm not."

"No, no, not my baby. She's only 19." Madge yanked her hands away, clutched the arm of the chesterfield and jumped up. "You're a liar, Dana Bowman. I thought you were my friend."

"I'm sorry, Madge. I wish it wasn't true. Maybe she was raped. She wasn't acting like herself the past few weeks and ..."

"How dare you? My baby."

"I'm sorry, Madge. That part I don't know. I shouldn't have said it."

"No, you shouldn't have. Lies."

"Madge, did Debbie know a Jarvis Harwood?"

"Lies, Lies." Madge picked up in tempo and volume.

"It's okay, I'm sorry." I reached for her but she stepped back.

"More lies."

"Here, here, what's all this?" Aunt Doris stood beside Madge and stared at me.

"I'm sorry," I said.

"You better be, Dana Bowman. Bothering a woman in her grief like that." Aunt Doris waggled a finger, scowled with her gargoyle face and put her arm around a weeping Madge.

"I'm sorry. I'm sorry."

"Get out of here, Dana Bowman. You're no friend of mine." Madge's whimpers turned to heaves.

"There, there," Aunt Doris murmured. "You, Dana, had better leave. I'll look after Madge." She led Madge out of the room, all the time murmuring "It's all right. She's going. Come along and get some rest."

The calm after this storm left me stymied. My throat felt as if it had choked on a thunderbolt and my brain felt singed by lighting. Swallowing my new loss, I seized my bag and slithered out the door. In the past 24 hours I'd lost two friends, an aunt and my son. To get some of them back, I had better increase my detecting. Taking a deep breath, I strode out the back door of Madge's apartment building. The next stop was the Robinson place across from 10 Maitland. Maybe they had returned last night and had seen the baseball-capped guy in the Toyota.

Chapter Twenty

Suppertime, Saturday, August 15, 1998

Him:

He was lying in bed asleep when he felt someone shake him awake.

"Jessie." He rubbed his eyes.

"Over here, hon."

He looked to the side of his bed and saw her standing in the moonlight—Jessie, in a tight mini-skirt and halter top, which she began removing piece-by-piece until she stood naked before him. She began gyrating. As she moved closer to the bed, he could feel the blood rush through to his groin. She was leaning over him, touching him, when he suddenly felt hard whacks on his bottom and someone screaming ...

He was bent over, staring at the red tiles on the kitchen floor, his pants tangled around his ankles. His bottom felt like fire, and he realized the screams were coming from his mouth. The wallops slowed down until they stopped.

"Now, get up, you little bastard."

He tried, but almost tripped on his pants.

"Pull them up, you stupid bastard."

His heart beat as if it would take off right out of his chest. Hands shaking, he pulled up his pants, then almost fell over trying to stand up. He grabbed the back of a chair, turned slowly around, and stared at his tormentor. Jessie, fully dressed in a track suit and runners, held a small wooden paddle by her side. She glared at him with eyes that looked both vacant and evil. Those eyes mesmerized him and he couldn't move his own eyes away. He felt guilty, scared and something else that filled him with so much rage he thought his head would explode ...

He sat in front of Jessie's dresser and stared in the mirror.

Those first two boys were no good. Sorry, Jessie. You deserve better or should that be worse? They wouldn't do you justice. He chuckled at the use of that last word, then felt a hard slap on his back.

"Sorry, Jessie." He said it out loud as he turned around.

No one was there.

He finished combing his hair and scrutinized his face. The pimple had disappeared. Good. He stood up. Time for the second Toronto boy to die. They needed to know that this boy too was wrong; he was damaged goods. He strode over to his backpack and hauled out the knife. He fondled it from the end of the handle to its tip, careful that his fingers didn't touch the sharp serrated edge. He grabbed the handle, and with the knife pointed straight out in front of him, he charged downstairs into the first bedroom and tried to ignore the boy's screams as he slashed his throat just like he had done to the first boy. When all was quiet, he took the knife into the bathroom next door. He could see an older woman bending over the toilet, retching. He backed out of the room and slammed the door.

You're supposed to be dead, Mother. You can't leave me outside all alone. You can't ... He was suddenly aware of the knife in his hand. Better finish up this business. He took a deep breath and pushed the bathroom door open.

No one was inside.

He stepped into the room, bent down over the tub, turned on the taps and began rinsing the blood from the knife. As the blood flowed down the drain, a sense of relief flowed, like a bad mistake had been righted. Some of that relief dissipated when he returned to the bedroom. He would have to dispose of the body. He turned on the overhead light—a night light wouldn't do to clean up—and stared down. It looked worse than he had anticipated.

"I had to do it, Jessie. This one wasn't right either, for you, for us."

As he pulled a blanket from the bed, he found his hands were shaking. He hated being cursed this way and he also wished he was cursed more so he could choose the right boy at once. He thought of the little boy who was the son of the private detective and frowned. He hoped he would be right the next time.

He pushed the second boy's body into the blanket. He wondered if he would need to pick up more bleach at the supermarket. He hated all this leftover mess, but once he took out this trash, a good clean-up would make it all right.

Chapter Twenty-one

Suppertime, Saturday, August 15, 1998

Dana:

Opening the gate from the laneway behind the Robinson property, I looked around. The two-car driveway stood empty and the place appeared deserted. I headed to the rear of the house, giving their swimming pool a nodding glance, and climbed up the wooden deck stairs. Raps on the door brought no response, so I moved to the nearest window and peered inside at a kitchen, very modern, quiet and empty.

"What do you think you're doing?" a high-pitched voice blasted from behind.

Swinging, I dropped my bag.

"I knocked on the door, then tried ..."

"Tried to get in the window?" The woman glaring at me looked about late-twenties and had blond hair hanging down to her waist.

"No. I was trying to get someone's attention, that is, if someone was home."

"Well, obviously there wasn't until now." Her eyes inspected me from head to toe.

"Sorry. We've obviously got off to the wrong start. I'm Dana Bowman from across the street at number 10." I held out my right hand. The woman removed her right hand from her hip and shook my hand.

"Cherry Robinson, your new neighbour." She smiled. "You must be the woman whose little boy was kidnapped."

"Yes. You know? I thought you were away."

"Yeah, Ken and I were away on our boat, but we just got back this morning and found police and TV cameras all over the street. Of course, we asked what's going on. Some cop talked to

Ken and me, but we know nothing because we were away." She pushed a strand of hair from her forehead. "Someone was murdered, too, at your place?"

"Yes, my son's babysitter, Debbie. She was a friend, too."

"Oh yes, I think I've seen her with your little boy out the front of our place a few times. That's a real shame. Have they caught the killer yet?"

"Not really. Well they picked up David's father, my ex, snooping around here earlier this afternoon. Hey, you didn't happen to see anything going on at the front of number 10 today?"

"No, I've been out since noon."

"What about your husband?"

"Ken? Oh no, I don't think so. He got a call soon after we got back and he had to go in to work."

"I see. What does your husband do?"

"He's a doctor."

"Does he practice in town? I can't recall seeing a sign for Dr. Ken Robinson."

"No, in Toronto."

"I see. Well, sorry to have bothered you."

"No problem."

"Maybe I'll come by sometime, to visit. I mean we are neighbours. I'll just knock on the front door next time."

"Sure, no problem."

I scooted out to the driveway. Cherry Robinson's vehicle, red and sporty, was not Bast's four-door sedan from last night.

Someone tapped me on the shoulder. I jumped and swung around. Cherry Robinson held my bag.

"Oh, thanks." I grabbed it and charged down the driveway, colliding with a moving mass. A microphone pushed up against my chin and a video camera loomed overhead.

"Dana Bowman. Charles Haas. CKNT News. Have you found out anything more about your son's kidnapping?"

A camera clicked, and a smaller microphone joined the first.

"John Scott Duluthe, *Cooks Region Sentinel.* What happened at your house earlier this afternoon? Was someone arrested?"

My eyes swept from the 30-something CKNT reporter to the nerdy young man holding a camcorder behind him to the newspaper reporter in my face. I took a step back and imitated Cherry Robinson's stance.

"Listen you blockheads. My son has been kidnapped, my best friend murdered, and you swarm around me like a pack of vultures."

"We're only doing our jobs," Duluthe said. "Come here." He motioned with his right hand. "Your brother and I worked for the same paper. Now, I have his beat."

"If you think that gives you licence for an exclusive, forget it."

"Didn't you get a ransom call earlier today?" Haas butted in.

"How did you find that out? Oh." I covered my mouth with my left hand.

"Maybe your brother talked to me," Haas said.

"Right. Okay, I'll give you a statement. The police have made an arrest, my ex-husband, Ron Bowman. But he didn't do it. Fielding is all wrong. So go and investigate that one. Just leave me alone."

They exited faster than a fire sale crowd. I crossed the street to 10 Maitland. An unfamiliar uniform tried to give me the third degree on the front porch until Bast stuck his head out the door and said, "It's okay, Constable Ryan. She's my sister Dana; she lives here." He waved me in as if something would spoil if I didn't move pronto.

Ryan nodded. "Fine. Just stay in the house but out of the office, living room and elevator. Fielding's orders."

I followed Bast into the kitchen. While he busied himself with boiling water for tea and coffee, I closed the door to the hallway.

"All right, Bast, what do you know that's so urgent?"

Chapter Twenty-two

Suppertime, Saturday, August 15, 1998

Bast:

Bast hit the "play" button on his tape recorder while Dana sat across from him at the kitchen table.

"This is Sebastian Francis Overture of the Attic Investigative Agency. It is 4 p.m., Saturday, August 15 and I'm just arriving at 355 Grandview Place, the home of Robert Belcher, loans officer, of the TD Bank, in Thurston. The missing Toyota is parked in the driveway."*Woof, woof. Woof.* "Hey down boy." *Woof. Woof.* "Hey, mis ..." *Scratch, thud.*

As the tape played out, Bast thought back to what was definitely not his best interview. Should have asked Belcher more about that cell phone. And talked more to the boy before entering the house. But he had been forced to dodge the big Lab jumping up at him. That was when the boy, about 11, had run up to them and Bast had turned his recorder back on.

"Brute Caesar, come here," the boy said. "Sorry, mister, he's really friendly."

"I see, young man. Is your father in?"

"Yes, and who are you?"

"Sebastian Overture. I'm a private investigator looking into the theft of your father's car."

"A real private eye, oh neat-o. Come on in. Brute Caesar calm down. Sit. Sorry about that. He won't hurt you."

Bast hadn't been too sure about that. But he had smiled at Brute Caesar, then sitting, wagging his tail and panting. Bast had followed the boy towards the house, a monster back-split on a sparse parcel of land, although part of a swimming pool poked out from the back as a man who looked to be in his early 40s opened the gate and walked towards them. He wore sunglasses and a thin smile which somewhat belied the knee-length shorts and golf T-shirt. Another boy, a few years younger than the first one, had followed him, and after instructions from the man to stay put outside with Brute Caesar, Mr. Belcher had introduced himself and invited Bast inside.

Once seated in the living room, Bast had got down to business.

"I'd like to hear your version, Mr. Belcher, of what happened with your car. Don't mind the tape recorder. That's for accuracy."

"My boss, Mr. Blake, called me up. He's rather conservative, no scandal with the bank. He said a private investigator was coming over. So, my question is why? I told the police everything." Belcher turned his nose up and Bast felt the chill from his attitude.

"Well, there is a little bit more. Can I be frank with you? You see, sir, your car was seen going by the Attic Investigative Agency place, on Maitland St. last night just after a little boy was kidnapped. I realize it was probably the thief who was driving then, but we need all the information we can get to find that little boy."

"Mr Overture, it was like this. I left work last night at 6:30 p.m., a little later than usual; it had been a busy day, and my car was gone. At first I thought Anne, that's my wife, had taken it to go shopping or pick up one of the boys. Then I remembered her car was back from the garage. I checked the rest of the parking lot to see if maybe I'd parked it somewhere besides my reserved spot. Not there. I'd left my cell phone in the car at lunch, so had to run back inside to call the police."

"Did you have your car keys on you?"

"What? Yes, but I keep a spare in the glove compartment. I've lost sets of keys before."

"Then what happened, sir?"

"A policeman in uniform arrived and took down all the information, you know, make and model, licence number ..."

"LTD 888?"

"Yes, that's right. Anyway, Anne was just coming in with the kids. Gave her quite a shock. She thought I was being arrested. She was upset when she found out about the car and more upset at this morning's return of my car."

Bast remembered that Belcher had looked down at the floor.

"And the cell phone, Mr. Belcher? Was it returned?"

"No."

"What about last night? Did you or your wife go out?"

"No, after the officer left, we all stayed in. Anne had a casserole in the oven and we sat down to eat. After dinner, I played pool with Timothy and Ethan in the rec room downstairs. After the boys went to bed, Anne did a little sewing while I read the newspaper. Oh, we were both in the den. We turned the TV on for the 11 p.m. news but there was nothing on it about the Toyota. So we shut it off and went to bed. And ..."

"And you were all in the house until the morning?"

"Yes. But with the bank being open Saturdays, I had to go in. Anne was taking the boys to a soccer game; Ethan plays. With one car, I rode along with them, and she dropped me off at the bank. It was then we saw it. Or rather Anne did. She just shrieked and the boys got excited and started yelling and pointing. My car was sitting in its usual parking spot. I called the police immediately. They came and towed the car away to check for fingerprints, or whatever they do. Anne was pretty hysterical by then, and the boys were over-excited, so one of the tellers drove us all home. I took a cab in later and returned home with Anne's car."

"When did the police return the Toyota?"

"Funny you should ask. They brought it back not half an hour before you arrived, although my cell phone is still missing. Said they didn't find any fingerprints except mine, Anne's and a few of the boys. Like I said, Anne does most of the chauffeuring for our boys and what, Mr. Overture, is it? Whatever is wrong ...?"

"It's just that I really had hoped the police would find something in your car."

"I wish they had. With two sons of my own, I know how you feel."

"Do you? David is my nephew."

"Oh, I thought ..."

That had ended the interview. But on his way out, Bast had noticed a new and very heavy-looking dead bolt on the front door. He had pulled out his cell and called Oliver to see if Belcher was on the B and E list.

"Was he?" Dana asked, interrupting his thoughts.

"Yes, complete with dead raccoon in the swimming pool."

She wrinkled her nose, and told me about her visit to the Robinsons and the encounter with the press.

"I'll kill that Haas. He always did want my job." He didn't realize he was shouting until he saw the startled look on Dana's face. "Sorry, but he's too aggressive. You know, it mightn't be a bad idea to go on TV and plead with the kidnappers."

"Yeah, sure, little brother. And have all the crazies calling. No way."

"Come on, it might help get David home."

"No way." She banged on the table. "You of all people should know that's not a good move. For Christ's sake, you used to be a reporter."

"And that's why I'm telling you to go on TV." Bast grabbed her hand. "You, David and I—we're all the family that's left."

"There's Great Aunt Doris."

"I meant blood family. Ever since Dad died ..."

"Dad? He's been dead nearly 10 years. And you hated him."

Bast removed his hand and cradled his head. "Yeah, well, he was family and ..."

"Come off it Bast. He scared the shit out of you. He wanted a strong athletic boy and a demure daughter. Instead he got us, two mixed-up frats."

"Whose fault was that?"

"What do you mean little brother?"

"Will you quit calling me 'little brother?' Just because you're 43 minutes older than me."

"Oh, so that's what this is all about. You're mad because I came out of mother's womb before you did. Typical male." She stood up, placed hands on hips and scowled.

He glared back down, red-faced with beard and chin shaking.

"I'm not your typical male," he said. "You above all people should know that."

"Right, and I suppose you think I'm not your typical female."

"You're short." Bast sneered.

"Oh, for Christ's sake." She threw up her hands and stomped around the table. "This isn't going to solve anything. Go back to your computer and cell phone, and detect. I'm going out."

"Where are you going?"

"I don't know. But not on TV like you suggested. I just need to get out of here for awhile. Don't worry; I'll take my cell." She searched the kitchen for her purse and hurried out of the room, with Bast following just as she collided with Constable Ryan.

"Whoa! Take it easy." Ryan put out a hand to steady her, but she skirted around him.

"Have to get out of here. My son's been kidnapped, may be dead for all I know." She continued barrelling forward into another collision.

"Whoa!" said the British voice.

"Not you too, Fielding. I'm not a horse. My son ..."

"It's okay, D ... Ms Bowman." He looked over at Ryan. "I'll take care of Ms Bowman. You stay in the living room. You." Fielding pointed to Dana. "You n ... n ... need a break."

"A break? Yeah, I need a break in luck to find David."

"That's n ... not what I meant ..."

"Oh, so you're going to take me away to some exotic place like Hawaii?" she snarled. "Aren't I supposed to stay put in case the kidnappers call? Oh, you took the wiretap machine away because you think you caught your kidnapper. Give me a real break, Fielding, and get off my back."

"N ... n ... no, D ... Dana; you misunderstand. I want to take you sailing."

"Sailing?" Her jaw dropped.

"Yeah, in a boat," Bast said. "On water. I've heard it's very relaxing."

Dana whirled around. "What? You, with him?" She pointed at Fielding and scratched her head.

"No, Dana. But you do need something to take your mind off all this, just temporarily. If you don't, you might crack and that won't do if you want to help get David back."

"I'm not breaking." She whirled around, glared at Fielding, then back to Bast. "You stop ordering me around. I'm pulling age." She smiled and turned to Fielding. "Well, if I have permission to leave, fine. I'll go sailing with you tomorrow. Pick me up at noon."

Bast stroked his beard and looked at Fielding. That went easier than expected. Sailing should calm his sister.

He forgot that sailing didn't always go smoothly.

Chapter Twenty-three

Sometime after noon, Sunday, August 16, 1998

Dana:

Fielding followed me out the front door. A brown four-sedan screaming *unmarked cop car* sat by the curb. He opened the passenger door and I climbed in and belted up.

"Okay, Fielding, what's with this sailing?" I asked as we headed towards Snow Lake.

"I have a sloop docked at Snow Harbour and I f ... f ... find taking her out h ... helps relax me. Have you ever been sailing?"

"No."

He turned into the parking lot at Snow Lake. A line of boats, anchored to the dock, swayed slowly on the rim of the lake. It did look peaceful. Until Fielding's car came to a stop and I climbed out of the car and made the mistake of looking to the right at the tail end of Grandview Park. Squinting, I could almost see the ice cream stand. A hand touched my shoulder and I jumped.

"Sorry, but you looked a little peaked."

"Fielding, you bastard," I shouted. "You just wanted to bring me back here to go over yesterday or maybe you found something left by the kidnappers."

"No, s ... s ... sorry, Dana, I really do have a sailboat." He hauled out a cooler from the backseat.

"Great. A drinking party."

"N ... n ... no, s ... sandwiches, f ... fruit and iced tea. Come." He took my arm and led me to the dock. We clomped along the wooden dock until we reached halfway. "There. She's 23 metres long." He pointed to a small yellow boat. I walked closer and glanced at the writing on the side.

"*Feverfew*? Why name a boat after a herb?"

"Because of my migraines. Feverfew is ..."

"... supposed to prevent migraines." We finished the sentence together.

"But obviously it doesn't work for you," I said.

"No." He set the cooler down in the boat and pulled out a paper bag.

"For migraines?" I asked.

"No, barf bag."

"Great. First you feed me; then you provide a means to dispose of dinner. Very considerate."

Fielding's face showed up instant sunburn.

"N ... n ... no. Sorry, bad joke. But some people get seasick, when the waters get choppy, even in a sailboat." He glanced up at the sky. "Not much chance of that right now. Just a light breeze. Enough to keep us moving, nice and peaceful like." He climbed into the boat. It swayed a little. "You can come aboard." He held out a hand.

I ignored it and plunked my right foot onto the boat. The boat swayed some more. Lifting a leg, I staggered towards Fielding. He grabbed my arms and the boat rocked. We stood in silence, staring at each other. I looked away, focusing on a narrow blue tarp wrapped around a rod, at the life jackets, at the motor.

"Motor." I lurched towards the motor attached to one end of the sailboat. "Gas it up."

"No, that's just there in case of an emergency, in case I get called away on police business. But, we're going sailing and before we do anything else, we're putting on lifejackets."

"Why?"

"Because, it is very easy to fall off a sailboat into the water. It happens to even experienced sailors."

"Oh, and you're experienced?" The sunburn returned to Fielding's face. "In sailing."

"Y ... y ... yes. Some friends and I do a l ... lot of sailing in the s ... summer. They have a boat docked further up the lake. We even race a little."

I rubbed my hands together. "That sounds exciting."

"Not for us, n ... not today. Here, put on a lifejacket." He handed me one which I donned. Fielding put on the other one and shoved the cooler under the front. "Please sit down while I hoist the sail."

"Need any help?"

"No." He looked into my face. "Fine, but you'll have to obey orders if you want to crew."

"Aye-aye, sir." I saluted.

Fielding turned away and moved into what resembled a cockpit, lowered the centreboard and removed the tarp, exposing two sails.

"Here, store the tier below deck."

"Huh?"

Fielding pointed to where the cooler rested. Taking hold of the tier, I folded it and placed it below deck.

"Maybe I'll just watch this time." I sat down on one of the benches.

Fielding's deft actions in preparing the sails fascinated me. Occasionally, he handed me something and said, "Hold this." When he appeared to be ready to raise the sails, I stood up.

"Let me help put up the sails."

"It's called 'hoisting the sail.' "

"Okay, let me help hoist the sail."

"Very well. But first you need to learn a little sea lingo."

I nodded and listened as he explained about the boom, mast, mainsail and jib. The sails hoisted with no mishap. Big and small, they fluttered on either side of the mast like angel wings. I sat down on the bench—no the thwart, Fielding corrected me. He continued lecturing as he removed the anchor. Using what he called a tiller, he steered the boat out of the harbour. He sat down opposite me while keeping a hand on the tiller.

"So, Fielding, tell me how you became a cop?" I asked.

"Don, call me Don."

"All right. Don, why did you become a cop?"

"Why or how?" Fielding smiled, smoothing out his stern police face. "Well, I joined the Metro Toronto Police Force as a cadet right out of high school. Why? I didn't want to continue to live at home and needed to work. Toronto was recruiting for police and it seemed a good way to earn some money. I got into the traffic area and found myself interested in tracking down jerks that break the rules of the road. I ..."

"Why, did some road hog run you off the road?"

"No. I don't like people breaking the law. It makes for anarchy. You must understand some of that, D ... Dana, with the line of work you're in."

"Yeah, but I don't go by the good old police book."

"So I gathered. Anyway, after several years in traffic, I got transferred to Morality, then Break and Enter in downtown Toronto, got promoted a few times and got myself transferred 12 years ago to Cooks Regional."

"You didn't want to stay in Toronto?"

"No, the crime was getting to me, and Sandra, that's my daughter, was a teenager and she, well she had tried hash a few times and the crowd she hung around with were into the hard stuff, so I thought the best thing was to move her out of the situation."

"What about her mother?"

"She came too. But we drifted apart. I think she missed living in the city. She packed it in and moved back to England. We finally divorced when she wanted to get married again."

"But you were born in England, too?"

"Yes, just outside of London. Mum and Dad divorced, so Mum and I moved to Vancouver to her brother's. Lived there for awhile until she met a language professor from U. of T. and we moved to Toronto and lived with him until I finished high school."

The boat swayed. Fielding leaned over and pulled on the tiller.

"Hungry?" he asked.

I nodded.

"Get out the cooler."

Pulling out the cooler, I opened it, and handed out sandwiches. I bit into one. Ham, cheese and tomato. Delicious. It had been a long time since my last meal. Fielding opened two cans of iced tea. We gazed at the water. The waves were minimal, and seemed to drift the sloop along. We sailed around for hours, and for the first time in days, the roller coaster inside me halted. Now the sun sagged toward the water line, emitting pink and blue visuals. I inhaled and sighed.

"A loonie for your thoughts," Fielding said.

"Just a loonie? We have toonies now." Smiling, I looked into deep blue eyes. They matched the water.

"Okay, Dana, I've told you my story. Now how did you get into detective work?"

"What, no short female?"

A wisp of sunburn crossed Fielding's face. "N ... n ... no, I m ... m ... mean, well, why did you choose detective work?"

"It sort of chose me. I started as a secretary for Laurence and Orley and later they let me help with some of their investigations. You must know all that from Bast."

"Your brother and I never saw eye-to-eye."

"Why's that?"

"Just differences of opinion."

"About what? Come on, tell me."

"Well, he's left and I'm right."

I let that one slide, for now.

"So, you also paint?" Fielding asked.

"Just sketch, mostly people. I like to catch their main characteristic, what makes them tick. Often that's not their most flattering. Bast does it, or did it with words, I do it with pictures."

"And now the two of you try to catch crooks," Fielding said.

I looked up at him. He was smiling. I smiled back.

A loud whir nearly sent me flying off the bench. Fielding removed his cell phone from the cooler.

"Fielding here," he said into its mouthpiece.

"What? Where? All right. I'm not far from there. No, on my boat. I'll be there shortly." He pushed in the antenna and stuffed the phone in his pant pocket.

"What was that call all about? Have they found David? Tell me." I leaned over and grabbed the front of his lifejacket. He pushed me away.

"I'll need some help lowering the sails," he said.

"That's it? Come on, Fielding, what the hell was that call about?"

"Police business."

"Police business, my ass. I'm coming with you, so I'm going to find out anyway."

"No you're not. I'm dropping you off at Snow Harbour."

"The hell you are. Fielding, you're hiding something from me. Now spit it up."

He did. And what he said made me want to regurgitate the sandwich and tea. Instead I gulped air and saliva. He pointed to the motor and I leaned over, pulling the line hard. It sputtered to life, and we were off in the opposite direction from Snow Harbour.

Chapter Twenty-four

Sunday evening, August 16, 1998

Him:

He couldn't seem to get the blood off. He had lost track how many times within the last 24 hours he had stepped into the shower, letting the water run over him, and looked down at the bathtub, thinking he was clean. When he shut the water off and raised his hands, he kept seeing blood. He could hear Jessie's voice screaming at him about being a bad boy and cowered in the corner of the tub. He didn't want the paddle again, although he knew he deserved it.

"Sorry, Jessie," he said more times than he could count. "It had to be done. The boy wasn't right for me, for you; neither was that first one. They weren't evil enough or not even evil. Please don't hurt me. I'll get it right the next time. This boy is okay; this ... what? Hey, please don't hit me."

He heard a loud wailing—like a chorus—and realized it came from downstairs. He shut off the shower, stepped out of the tub, grabbed a towel and began drying himself. The screaming from below continued. Shit. He'd told the boy that he had to be quiet. He even figured he'd been listening to him so had removed the duct tape from his mouth.

"Coming, coming" he said as he grabbed his terrycloth robe, slid into matching flip-flops and headed out the door. Out of the corner of his eye he thought he saw Jessie in mini-skirt and halter.

"No, not now." He hurled it out.

He started running downstairs; then stopped. No he had to be careful; had to take it slow. He forced himself to walk down the stairs to the main floor. When he reached the basement stairs the wailing hit his ears with the force of an amplifier.

"Coming, coming," he said, racing down to the basement to deal with the situation. When he opened the door, the boy lying on the bed stared up at him. No sound came from his closed mouth.

What the ...?

He heard a rustling from behind and swung around.

Jessie stood, paddle in hand. She began to cackle as she moved towards him.

Chapter Twenty-five

Sunday evening, August 16, 1998

Dana:

The boat continued its fast run, its loud putt-putt drowning out the waves. Fielding had taken over the steering. I sat on the thwart, head crouched down in my hands. Please God, don't let it be David. Not like this.

The boat jerked and I looked up. To the left, the sun's top quarter shone deep pink against a mottled sky. In front, the tunnelled light from Fielding's boat showed land creeping closer. Fielding cut the motor and we drifted into an unfamiliar dock where a small rowboat was anchored. Six figures stood on the dock. Two wore uniforms; one interviewed a man in plainclothes. Another plainclothes flashed a camera at the ground behind; another stood near a man wearing a big straw hat. Dr. Farley? I willed them to move so I could see beyond them. But they kept their positions. I leaned over the boat and strained my neck but still couldn't see. Fielding pulled me back as I began shuddering. He pointed to the thwart and muttered "sit," but I shook my head and kept an unsteady stand. He returned to the boat business and after anchoring it, helped me out of the lifejacket and reached for my hand. I absentmindedly took it and let him lead me onto the dock. Now one of the uniforms and "Straw Hat Man" were bent over a mound in the sand. My gut heaved. Something squeezed my hand, and I realized I was still locking mitts with Fielding, so yanked my hand away and heaved again.

"You all right?" Fielding asked.

I covered my mouth and managed to squeak out, "Yes, just give me a sec." Straightening up, I took several deep breaths and swallowed. "Well, what are you waiting for? Christmas?"

Fielding shrugged and strode towards the others. I followed. My eyes picked out Stewart from the group. He nodded, crouched down and aimed his camera at the mound.

"Just a minute, Dana." Fielding raised his right hand and moved towards the others for a confab, leaving me a street's width behind.

Stewart's flash bounced pieces of the scene before my eyes. With "Straw Hat Man" and Stewart bobbing around, it resembled a Halloween horror turned rancid. I clutched my stomach.

Fielding must have spoken to them, because "Straw Hat Man" stood up and squinted my way. It was Dr. Farley. He took a few steps, but stopped when Fielding touched his arm. The two whispered. Both turned and strode towards me.

The waves picked up speed behind and their sloshing became a crescendo inside my head. Fielding's and Dr. Farley's mouths moved, but I seemed to be rendered deaf, so covered my ears.

"What? What?" The only sound was those damn waves.

Fielding grabbed my arms and shook me. The waves inside ebbed.

"... shock," Dr. Farley was saying.

"What?" I asked.

"Can you hear me?" Dr. Farley asked.

"Yes."

"Good."

"I'm okay. Let's get on with this." I pulled away from Fielding.

"First," Dr. Farley said, "I have to prepare you for what you are going to see. He was caught in a fishing line hook belonging to that man over there and it got hauled onto shore." He pointed to the sixth man standing off a bit to the side. "The throat was cut pretty badly and already the fish have begun nibbling on the face. It could be worse if the body had been in the water longer. I'm estimating overnight and today so around 20 hours or so, but I won't know for sure until I do an autopsy."

"Wait." Fielding held up a hand towards Dr. Farley and turned to me. "Are you sure D ... uh, Ms. Bowman, you want to see it?"

"It could be David. Couldn't it Dr. Farley?"

"It's the body of a male child, age six or seven."

I sucked in air. "I have to look." Fielding reached for my arm. "Alone. Okay, you can both come along."

The three of us moved in silence. Those damned waves started thrashing around inside my whole body. Please God, not like this. When we were up against the dark mound, Dr. Farley pointed a flashlight at it, and it became a person, a child hidden under a blanket. Fielding crouched and removed the blanket.

"But he's naked." I screamed, digging fingernails into my scalp and continuing on like an echo.

"Easy, Dana," Fielding said.

The waves continued to whip around inside, forcing me to wobble. Instinctively I grabbed Fielding's arm, took a deep breath and forced myself to look down. After a few more breaths, I dug fingernails into Fielding's arm as my eyes moved over the body. A fish hook was caught in the nose. The head was almost ripped off the neck and a few fish nips appeared on the left cheek and right arm. But it was the eyes—staring stark scared up at me as if pleading for his life. Hazel eyes. Hair knotted, wet and dirty showed only traces of red. I removed my hand from Fielding's arm, crouched down and reached over to close the eyes, then drew back.

"It's not David. David has blond hair and the eyes aren't his."

I stumbled up and ran at random into the darkness. Footsteps and words followed behind me, but I continued running as if David's life depended on it, until I tripped and collapsed in the sand.

"Put your hands between your knees." The voice sounded as if coming from underwater.

I did as told. The waves inside my head quietened down. Looking up, I covered my eyes.

"Kill the lights. For Christ's sake, kill the damn lights." White lights danced inside my eyes.

The light veered right. I opened my eyes and rubbed them as if that would rub all the badness away. Dr. Farley and Fielding were on their knees and both held onto my arms. I sat in the sand, legs spread out in a V and could feel the colour return to my face and multiply to sunburn alert.

"She's okay." Dr. Farley shone the flashlight into my face.

They helped me up. Near the dock, one uniform covered the body while the other joined us.

"Your son is on the police computer as 'kidnapped' so that was picked up and they called me," said Fielding.

"I see. Who is this poor little boy then?"

"Could be one of the other missing boys. We don't know at this point." Fielding sounded deflated. "Once Dr. Farley completes his autopsy we may have a better idea. He could have been dumped anywhere in the lake and drifted downstream. Come on, let's get you home."

I looked at the lake and sighed.

"No, not that way. In a squad car." He took my arm. "Michaels, you can drive Ms Bowman home. Bursey, you can stay here. Dr. Farley, I want a copy of this autopsy ASAP. Ditto Stewart with the photos."

Just in case. Fielding didn't need to add the words. Maybe this poor little boy, whoever he was, tied in with David.

The slamming of car doors woke me from my meandering. Charles Haas and his lackey toting the video camera sped towards us.

"Let's go." Fielding pulled me into a run. I yanked my arm free but kept on running with Michaels joining us. Fielding had his cell out and yelled into it, "Bast, a squad car is taking Dana home ..." When he finished talking, he said he had to stay. "You'll be all right?"

I nodded. He reached as if to touch my arm, but didn't and walked away. Michaels started the car just as Haas and his crew came back into view.

Three quarters of an hour later, we pulled up to my driveway. No press yet, only Bast, who charged down the veranda steps.

"Dana, I'm sorry. Are you all right?" He held me in his arms. "Jeez, sis, if I'd have known, I'd have gone."

"I've seen dead bodies before, Bast," I replied.

"But not children."

"How would you know? You haven't been too much a part of my life until the last year or so."

He pulled away.

"Look, it's not David. David has shorter hair and the eye colour is wrong. So can we just leave it alone? The important thing is to find David." I glared at him. "Well, don't just stand there, don't ..." I burst into tears.

Bast moved closer.

"No, no. I just need to be left alone."

He didn't budge.

"Is something wrong with you? Am I missing something?"

"I hate to tell you this, but you're not going to be alone yet."

"What do you mean?"

Bast growled. "There's a visitor inside."

"Visitor? Who?" I looked onto the street. "I don't see any cars here, just yours and mine in the driveway."

"He parked around the corner."

"He? Just what is going on?" I ran towards the veranda.

"Wait," Bast said.

I didn't, but kept charging up the stairs, yanked the front door open and almost fell inside the hall.

"Is that you, Dana," a familiar voice greeted me from the end of the hall. "The police were reluctant to let me into the living room, so I've been making the officer on duty nervous."

Gordon Lambton stepped into the hallway from the kitchen and strode towards me.

Chapter Twenty-six

Later Sunday evening, August 16, 1998

David:

He was learning fast. Say nothing, and no tape on his mouth. Stay put except when "Rude Man" or "Mother" took him to the bathroom or let him sit up to eat, and his hands and legs didn't get taped. His eyes were getting used to the dark room and after his first trip to the bathroom, they had left the bathroom door open so the nightlight shone from it. He didn't think the room he was in had any windows, and the smell like old dirty socks made him feel dizzy. The cold air went right to his bones. The room was nothing like the basement at Mr. Brooks.'

He thought of the trains choo-chooing around, and wished he were there. Even the basement at his house was better than this one, although with Mommy not letting him go down there the last little while, he couldn't be sure. When he had followed that friend of Mommy's downstairs at Mommy's party, he hadn't looked around the basement. Over by the window something hard had hit his head and the next thing he knew he was down here.

He didn't know how long he'd been here or where here was or what they were going to do with him. Every time the door opened he thought this was it, but then it was just "Mother" bringing some food or "Rude Man" checking on him. He could tell it was him from his loud creepy voice. "Mother" was the one who usually took him to the bathroom and made sure he washed his hands and face. But if he dawdled or tried to look at her she slapped his behind hard and called him a bad boy. So he hurried and quit trying to look around.

Once they hadn't closed the door tight behind them and he had heard loud whispering. He thought "Rude Man" had said something about killing him now and he thought "Mother" had replied "wait." Then the door had closed tight.

What were they waiting for? Money? Mommy and Uncle Bast didn't have much money. He'd heard them talking a few times about needing more money for the house. Uncle Bast kept talking about something called a line of credit. David imagined a clothesline with this "credit" sitting on the end, although he didn't know what a credit was.

His toes felt cold; his hands were cold, and he started to shake. He thought of Mr. Brooks and playing with his train set. He could even hear the "woo-woo" of the train and wished it would come to this basement so he could climb aboard and go home.

Chapter Twenty-seven

Late Sunday night, August 16, into early morning, August 17, 1998

Dana:

Bast led us out to the back porch. Once seated, Gordon went right into business mode. I ignored his Tom Cruise face and stared at my feet.

"Well, Dana, Ron's bail hearing is tomorrow morning at 10 o'clock at the Thurston Courthouse. He has no previous arrests, so he should get off on bail. I'm going to try to get him off on his own recognizance because frankly, Dana, he has no collateral. He's broke."

"What about the cottage?" I asked.

"He sold it last year."

"What?" I looked up and found Bast staring at Gordon and Gordon looking straight at me. I looked down fast. "But, Gordon, surely he bought something else then?"

"No. He owed a lot of money and used it to pay off debts."

"Debts? The guy was a bit of a skinflint when we were married. What is it? Expensive girlfriends? Leila?" I smirked at Gordon.

Gordon shifted his eyes away. Bast continued glaring at Gordon and kept silent.

"That's confidential, Dana," Gordon said. "All I can tell you is he made, shall we say, several unwise investments and had to pay them off. Now he's broke. Which brings me to my next question."

"You want us to pay your fees," Bast spoke. I looked over at him. His mouth curled up in a sneer and his hands clutched the arms of the patio chair.

"Not exactly," Gordon replied. "I've spoken to Doris Bowman and she'll look after my fees. It's collateral for his bail that I need."

"Doris can look after that," Bast said.

"No, she can't. But she said and I quote, 'You can get your collateral from George Howard Bowman's house, the one Dana and her brother, the queer, live in.' "

Bast jumped to his feet. His chair toppled backward.

"Listen here, Lambton, neither my sister nor I are paying anything for that scum she married. She's not married to him anymore."

"All right, all right." Gordon raised his right hand. "Let's not get all hot and bothered about this. You do believe Ron is innocent."

"Of kidnapping David, yes," I replied.

Bast remained silent and continued to scowl at Gordon.

"What about you Gordon?" I asked. "Do you believe your client is innocent?"

"Of David's kidnapping, yes. Anyway, it looks like that charge might be dropped if his alibi checks out."

"And what of breaking into this house, with a cop present?" I asked.

"He says the door was open and he didn't see any cop and that's all I can tell you without breaking the seal of confidentiality."

"Fine." Bast spit out the words. "We will be in court tomorrow for the bail hearing."

"That's not necessary. Doris Bowman will be there." Gordon nodded at him.

"Madge, what about Madge?" I asked. "She shouldn't be left alone."

"She won't be," Gordon said. "A neighbour will stay with her."

"Fine. Now, if you'll excuse us Mr. Lambton. My sister has had a hard day."

"Of course, I'll be in touch."

Gordon left via the side of the house. When I heard the gate swing shut, I turned to Bast.

"What the hell was all that about?"

"What do you mean?"

"Come on, you know. Why did you keep glaring at him? You've never met him before."

"Wrong."

"Oh, I suppose you could've met him in court in your crime reporting days."

"That too."

"Oh, for Christ's sake, why is everybody acting so dense today?"

"Look, I know about your relationship with Gordon."

"What business is that of yours? Anyway, it's over."

"I know." Bast averted his eyes.

I walked over to him and stared straight up. "Okay, Bast, let's have it. Where did you meet him before?"

"I didn't actually meet him. Just saw him, in a bar in downtown Toronto."

"So Gordon was in a bar."

"No, sis, you misunderstood. I saw him in a gay bar."

"That's crap, Bast. Gordon is straight."

"Maybe, but I know what I saw."

"What you saw? Just what was Gordon doing?"

"He wasn't picking up a man. In fact, from where I sat, I could see him talking to a woman, wearing a floppy hat. She either had short hair or it was shoved under the hat. They sat opposite each other in a booth. I don't know who the woman was as she had her back to me. Lambton was facing me and he looked worried. I couldn't hear what they were saying, but at one point the woman handed an envelope over to Gordon. He looked in it before putting it in his jacket pocket. I think the envelope was filled with money."

"Did you see the money?"

"No, but the envelope was fat and I thought I saw part of a hundred sticking out of it."

"So Gordon was conducting business."

"In a gay bar with a woman when he's supposed to be straight? Let me tell you something. I was following a story on some crooked deal and Lambton was defending one of the companies. I saw him in court that morning and followed him afterwards because I thought there was something off about the way he was conducting his defence."

"Who was the client?" I asked.

"Some small entrepreneur, caught up in the ruckus. I forget his name. My point is I don't trust Gordon Lambton and I don't think you should either."

"I never did. Now, about that story, what happened to it?"

"It was never published. For some reason the editor killed the story. But I got paid my kill fee for it."

"Okay then, could you get your hands on the court report for this case?"

"I don't remember the name."

"Yeah, but you can remember the date, approximately?"

"I guess so. I can check my notes."

"All right, then you can find it."

"I guess so. But why would you want to see that?"

"Won't know until I see it. But there are so many loose ends in this business, I'd like to eliminate some."

"Fine, I'll check tomorrow."

"Thanks. Well, I think I'll go up to bed."

"Want something to eat? I can bring you up a sandwich."

"No, maybe, no, I'm not hungry."

I headed upstairs to my room, but not to bed. After prowling around a bit, I headed down the stairs to the kitchen.

Bast sat at the table making a sandwich. The cop was nowhere in sight. I helped myself to a glass of water from the tap at the sink, strode over to the table and sat down.

"Change your mind about eating?" Bast asked.

"No. Bast, did you get that empty prescription bottle analyzed?"

Bast looked up. "I've taken it around to a few pharmacists in town. All say it's a prescription bottle but not one of theirs. One said it looked like it might've come from that speciality pharmacy in Toronto, Sprinkle. You know the one there was all that fuss about last year because the pharmacy is associated with a medical centre—Sonbaker—that was supposed to be involved in some research projects connected to abortions. But I think it went sour."

"Hmm. I might have read about it in the paper."

"Well, anyway, I thought I'd check it out tomorrow after I check on Jarvis Harwood. But first I want to make sure he's still at that address." Bast hauled out an envelope from his back jeans pocket. "And I can't help thinking that his name sounds familiar."

"Maybe somebody you interviewed for one of your crime stories."

"Possibly. Although the return address on the envelope doesn't sound like somewhere I went to interview a subject. Oh before I forget, the seal's off part of the attic, the stairs, the office and enough of the reception area to get in the office. Think I'll try to get some work done on the desktop."

Bast swallowed the last of his sandwich, stood up and headed upstairs. I finished the glass of water and followed him. When we reached the attic, I saw what Bast meant by partially blocked off. The yellow police seal was across the office door to the balcony. Steadman stood inside the seal, staring at the balcony door and muttering "that's right sir," into his cell.

"Just going into the office to do some work," Bast said.

Steadman nodded and continued his cell conversation. Bast and I entered the office. He headed for the computer and I headed for the big shelving units. I pulled out my sketch pad and charcoal pencil, sat in one of the chairs and began to sketch.

Madge, Doris, Ron, Lois, Ray, Oliver, Fielding, Cherry Robinson, even Gordon, sprouting horns, made it to my sketchpad. But not David, not my son. I stared at each picture and sighed. From the desk came the click of Bast's fingers hitting the computer keys and the occasional beep from the computer. One of these people could open the book. I closed my eyes and began visualizing each one sneaking out onto the balcony and killing Debbie, and down in the basement luring David out of the house.

But it can't be the same person who did both. He left from the basement with David and he couldn't have gone back in the front without Aunt Doris or me seeing him.

Nothing fit. I opened my eyes and found myself staring at Cherry Robinson's sketch.

"She reminds me of someone," I said.

"What's that?" Bast swivelled around in his chair.

"Cherry Robinson, she looks familiar, yet I only met her today."

Bast glanced at the sketch. "Never met her."

"She's been living across the street for a few months. Too bad she and her husband were out of town Friday night. You find anything on the computer?"

"Yeah, Jarvis Harwood's e-mail address. Still can't remember interviewing him for a story, though. So I just e-mailed him something general about wanting to interview him for a follow-up to a story I'd written and could I stop by his place. I also asked for his address and if he was still attending Thurston Community College."

"So?" I asked.

"So," Bast replied, as he looked at his computer screen. "There's a reply coming in now from Jarvis Harwood."

I joined Bast at the computer as he clicked on the letter. It opened and I read:

"Are you the Sebastian Overture who wrote that story in the *Toronto Daily Herald* about adults who lost their parents to tragedy at an early age? Sorry I wasn't available to talk to you about my friend Cam whose mother died from an accident when he was seven. But I see from the story you did talk to him. To answer your question, I'm going into my second and last year of Early Childhood Education. My goal is to eventually own a day-care centre, but first I suppose I will have to pay my dues working as a day-care provider in someone else's centre. Come by tomorrow morning just before noon to talk to me." His address followed.

Bast clicked open another e-mail. From Oliver. The ransom call on my cell was traced to a B. Belcher at 755 Grandview.

"Kidnapper must've kept the phone; phone still not found," Oliver had written.

I took another look at the sketch of Cherry Robinson and scratched my head. "Who the hell does she remind me of?" I threw the sketch onto the floor. "I'm going for a walk."

Leaving Bast at his computer, I headed downstairs and out the door. At Main St., I prowled up and down. My legs and mind had no destination. A few cars whizzed by. The motor of one seemed to linger.

"D ... D ... Dana." Fielding leaned outside of the passenger window. "I was just coming back from the crime scene at the beach. I'll get *The Feverfew* tomorrow. Oh, s ... sorry. I c ... can give you a ride home."

"No. Oh, don't worry. Cell phone's here." I patted my bag.

"How about going for a cup of coffee."

"Fielding, I don't need coffee. I'm revved up, ready to go into action. Ready to grab the killer, the kidnapper. But, hell, I don't know where I'm revved up to go or who I'm going after." I threw up my hands, sending my bag to the ground.

"Get in the car." Fielding leaned over and opened the door. "And don't forget your purse."

I shoved my bag onto the floor and climbed into the passenger seat. Fielding drove to the outskirts of Thurston and into a driveway of a modest-looking bungalow.

"M ... my place," was all he said as he opened the front door. "Sit here in the living room and I'll get you a brandy."

"I don't want a drink."

"T ... tea?"

"Fine." For some reason it felt as if I was on a bad date.

Fielding headed to the kitchen.

The whole living room was filled with books, on wall-lined shelves, on end tables, even on the floor. I stumbled towards the light, a floor lamp beside the couch, pushed the books off, and sagged into it. I blinked and looked closer at my surroundings.

Not all books. A few trophies stood on a mantle over a real fireplace.

"I ... If ... if you're c ... c ... cold, I can light a fire," Fielding said as he brought in a tray of steaming tea and set it on the coffee table in front of me.

"In August?" I asked, sinking further into the couch as Fielding sat down beside me. For some reason I was aware of how close. *Bad date*, I kept thinking. "You do a lot of reading?" I took another look at the books on the shelves.

Fielding launched into a discussion about his book collection. It seemed he had everything from Sherlock Holmes to Carl Jung and serial killers. When he got into the profilers in the FBI south of the border and how they classified serial killers as organized and disorganized—Ted Bundy was organized—my interest perked up to the point where I began asking questions and giving my opinion.

"So, Don, you're saying that because Mommy was a drunk or Daddy molested or beat him that makes someone a serial killer?"

"Of course not always. But you can bet that in many cases, something in the serial killer's childhood affected him. And often in childhood they exhibit violence towards animals—killing cats for instance."

"Raccoons, too." I thought of the raccoons killed with the break and enters. "Come on, Don."

Fielding held up his hand. "However, there is usually a trigger in the serial killer's life later on that starts him killing."

"Don, do you think those boys in the malls were kidnapped by a serial killer?" When he didn't reply at first, I jumped in with the inevitable. "Do you think David was kidnapped by a serial killer? Or do you still thing my ex is responsible? Do you ..."

He placed his hand over mine. "D ... Dana, I don't know about the serial killer, but can't rule out the possibility, especially if another little boy turns up dead."

"So, you're not charging Ron with kidnapping and murder?"

"No, and not for the boy we just found. You heard Dr. Farley give the approximate time of death. Your ex has an airtight alibi for that ... jail, where he still is, waiting bail."

"Don, let me finish my third question. Do you think David's kidnapping is connected to the three boys taken in the mall washrooms? No, don't answer it yet. David's circumstances are somewhat different and this time the 'caregiver' was murdered and maybe because she saw something. Look at it this way; in the other three instances, the mothers or caregiver were in a washroom stall and inconvenienced at the time, but with David, Debbie wasn't, and David wasn't kidnapped from a mall washroom but from his own home."

"Wait a minute, Dana." Fielding held up his other hand. "Don't forget Debbie was there for one of the other kidnappings."

"So, you think they are connected to David's kidnapping."

"I'm not saying that; I have to keep an open mind. You're too close to it. David is your son."

"Well, what do you think you are doing here now but getting close to it?"

Fielding seemed taken aback.

"Look, this is a big mistake." I stood up.

"I know." Fielding rubbed his jaw. "Technically, you could be classified as a suspect, although you've been cleared at this point."

"Then, why did you bring me back here."

"You were in no shape to be out and some other police officer might have arrested you."

"Arrested me? For what? Vagrancy? I thought that went off the books years ago."

"No, well, you, you, you were acting a little odd."

"Oh, I get it. I'm wacko and would've been hauled off to the loony bin at the hospital."

"No, D ... Dana, I don't think you are nuts. You've been through a lot in the last few days, more than most people."

"So, what do you care?"

"Care, I c ... c ... care about ... about ... what ... what happens to you."

"After a few days? Right." I shrugged my shoulders. "We're both nuts."

Grabbing my bag from an end table, I headed for the front door. Fielding was right behind me. He hesitated; then placed a hand on my shoulder. I looked away. "If you n ... n ... need anything,"

"Yeah, right." I removed his arm. He opened the door and as I stepped outside, some life seemed to ignite inside. "Well, goodnight."

"Goodnight," he repeated.

As he closed the door I thought a phone rang inside, but when I stared inside the door's window, he still stood there, looking at me. Shaking my head, I turned and stepped into a brisk walk.

Wandering around Thurston at two on a Monday morning was a relatively quiet venture. A few dogs barked. Traffic appeared non-existent. The place seemed devoid of people except for me. At Maitland, a police cruiser nosed by but didn't stop. I turned my eyes from the road and walked straight into someone. A hand stifled my mouth mid-scream.

"Sh, if I let go, don't scream or talk," Bast said.

I nodded and he let go.

"What's the matter?"

"Sh." He held up his right hand. "I thought I heard something in the bush in front of the house next door."

"The Brooks place?"

"No, other side." He pointed.

"Probably a squirrel or a racoon."

Raccoon? We both saw the figure slither out from the bush and start to run. We charged after him. Of course Bast, 14 inches taller, caught up to him, with me panting up a minute or so later. He had a firm hold on a short thin man, who held a blob in his right hand. The smell of blood came from the hand. Bast shone a small flashlight at it.

Battered dead racoon. Bast directed the flashlight up.

Ray Chalmers's face cringed back at us.

Chapter Twenty-eight

Monday morning, August 17, 1998

Bast:

The press caught them coming and going at the courthouse.

"Get that mic away from me," Bast shouted at Charles Haas. He heard Dana's intake of breath behind him and he could feel his face turn hot. Why did Haas have to come back to Cooks Region now?

"No comment," Dana said as Bast turned around.

His sister looked like hell boiled over—bags under her eyes from too little sleep. He'd heard her moving around in her room earlier this morning long after Ray's arrest. What did he expect—smooth smiley face with her son still missing? Suddenly, he felt ashamed for trying to keep his little digression with Haas last year under wraps. Seemed minor compared to his kidnapped nephew.

He took Dana's arm and led her into the courthouse. At least the press had been banned from Ron's and Ray's bail hearings.

Once inside the courtroom, they had more than Haas to deal with. Aunt Doris stuck her gargoyle face into Dana's.

"Looks like you've been up all night," Aunt Doris said. Her voice held a smidgeon of gloat.

He expected Dana to lunge at her but it was him, Bast, who had the urge.

"Not worth it," Dana whispered.

As they moved towards the front, Lois turned around and shot a deep evil look at them.

"Mother Hen defending her chick," Dana whispered.

"Chick is right but they are husband and wife."

"More like mistress and slave," Dana said.

"Hmm," Bast said, as they took their seats.

Gordon arrived. Bast noticed his sister staring down at her feet. Gordon ignored her and went directly to his place on the other side. A few seconds later a fellow with "big city lawyer" written all over him strode into the courtroom. "Big City" joined Lois, and the two went into deep conversation. Ron and Ray made their separate appearances. Ron was charged with one count each of Break and Enter and Vandalism at 10 Maitland. No kidnapping charge. Ray faced 10 counts of Break and Enter and six counts of cruelty to animals. Bast hoped Ray Chalmers would get the book. Although he wasn't a fan of raccoons, he didn't believe in killing them.

Both men got bail, $75,000 for Ray and $50,000 for Ron. Lois put up Ray's bail. Bast reluctantly agreed with his sister to put up collateral on their house for Ron's bail but he thought Ron should also get the book thrown at him. Now, the house had a mortgage and a lien.

"Where's Ron going to stay?" Dana asked Gordon. "He can't stay with us."

"It's all taken care of. Don't worry," Gordon looked at Aunt Doris.

"How is Madge doing?" Dana asked Doris. "I'd like to see her."

"Not on your life," Doris sneered at her and turned to Ron. Ron shrugged his shoulders.

They all left the courtroom in an uneasy group. Outside the door, Haas shoved a tape recorder in Dana's face and shouted, "Ms. Bowman, how do you feel about your ex-husband breaking into your matrimonial home? Did he have anything to do with kidnapping his son?"

Bast leaned forward and pushed the microphone out of the way.

"You leave my sister alone or I'll ..."

"You'll what, Mister Overture. You better not mess with me, or we'll have to revisit last year."

"Are you threatening me, Haas?"

Haas smirked.

Bast snarled. Too bad, he thought, and paled as Haas shoved the microphone in his face.

"One more thing, Mister Overture." Haas smirked. "The racoon robber got away with $75,000 bail. What do you think of that, Mister Overture? I understand you used to cover this beat as a crime reporter."

This time Dana snarled at Haas. "You want a statement? Okay, I'll give you one. *No comment. Now leave us alone Mister Haas.*" She touched her brother's arm and he pulled away from Haas. "Let's get out of here, Bast." As they left, she asked, "What the hell was that last year stuff all about Bast?"

"Just some work thing. Professional jealousy over a story that got out of line. Haas didn't take it very well." He hoped Dana would accept that and when she said nothing, he was relieved. He couldn't go into it now with Dana. Maybe never. "Look, Dana." Bast tried to keep his voice even as they walked down the corridor. "I'm heading down to Toronto to check out that pharmacy. What about you?"

"I'm going to talk to Lois and Ray, preferably separately, and go over to see Madge. Oh, Ron will be there. Damn. I suppose I'll have to talk to him."

"Mightn't hurt to find out what he's been up to lately, before he hit Thurston," Bast said. "Yesterday, at the house I got the impression he wanted to talk to you."

"Hmm," was her only reply. She waved to Bast as she followed Lois and Ray out the door.

Dana:

"Lois," I said. "We need to talk."

"What about?" she replied. A spot of red lipstick stuck to her front left tooth and purple circles shaded under her eyes. She scratched behind her ear. "Obviously you and your brother caught my husband red-handed. Can't talk now anyway. We do have a couple of businesses to run."

She clicked her heels and gave Ray a shove. Ray's face registered pure fright. I shrugged my shoulders and walked in the opposite direction. I headed out a side door to the parking lot, got in the car and drove straight to the Mini-Mall.

Lois's van was still warm in the parking lot. I entered the mall and headed for The Fashion Shoppe. Lois was nowhere in sight and the cashier was someone new. I strolled inside, pretended to look at some jewellery and made for the cashier.

"Hi, I'm looking for Lois Chalmers."

"Sorry, she's not in right now," the pert girl replied. "Can I help you?" Everything on her was black, from makeup to clothes.

"No, I need to speak to Mrs. Chalmers. Do you know when she'll be back?"

"I'm not sure. She had to go to court. Can I give her a message?"

"No. I'll come back later."

My next stop was Chalmers Shoe Store.

Neither Ray nor Lois was in sight, but scuffling noises came from the back room. A muffled voice mumbled what sounded like "ouch," followed by a female voice shouting "shut up, you miserable weasel." A loud thud followed. I hastened towards the back room but an arm blocked my way.

"It's okay, Ma'am. The owners sometimes get a little loud when discussing business."

I shrugged, left Chalmers's and peeked into the store next door. It seemed to be undergoing much renovation as ladders, scaffolding and white dust filled the area. A sign stating *Sprinkle Pharmacy opening September 8* flapped from the top of the storefront window. I nearly missed Lois as she charged from the shoe store, but there was no mistaking the click of her heels and her resolute walk as she hurried away. I moved outside the new store and strode towards her.

"Lois, wait up. We need to talk."

She swung around. "I told you. I have a business to run."

"Back there?" I pointed to the shoe store.

"Going to the bank, as if it's any of your business." Her eyes gleamed, and a slight smirk appeared.

"Money talks for you, Lois, doesn't it?"

"Money keeps the business going."

"And Ray too?"

"Don't you dare speak about Ray that way?"

"Well, you had to spend $75,000 to bail him out."

"He is my husband." She sounded almost defensive.

"Sounds more like a liability. Did you know he was the racoon killer? Did you put him up to it? And then there is David."

"That's enough, Dana Bowman. I had nothing to do with David's disappearance. I was upstairs at your agency opening, not in the basement. Remember you are on hiatus from your undercover security position here and I have the say whether we'll hire your Attic Investigative Agency."

"Mr. Bevens may see that differently, Lois." My turn to smirk.

"We'll see about that. Now, I really must get to the bank. You'd do well to mind your own business. Let the police find your son."

Christ. She sounded just like Aunt Doris. But I let her leave ... for now. Ray was a much easier mark.

Back at the shoe store, I ignored the clerk's protestations and moved towards the backroom.

Ray Chalmers stopped me from going in. But he resembled death run over. The tissue he wiped his mouth with couldn't quite catch all the blood dripping from the corner. His left eyelid swelled up and the forehead above was already en route to shinersville. His thin, oily black hair further accentuated his pale face, which bleached even further when he saw it was me.

"Hey, just the man I wanted to see." I grabbed his arm. "How about we go for a coffee? You look like you could use one. I'm sure your clerk can look after this store on his own for awhile."

A grunt was Ray's only reply. I steered him towards the door and addressed the clerk. "It's okay; Lois said he should take a break after all the court business. She said you could hold the store for awhile."

"But, I ..." he said.

Ray waved his free arm at him.

"It's all right." He almost gagged on the words.

Once outside I manoeuvred him towards the Food Court.

"Sit," I said as we reached the first empty table. "We're going to have a nice chat, just you and me and hey, it's even in a public place, so you don't need to have any fear of me."

Ray settled down.

"Now, I gather I can trust you to stay put while I get us some coffee."

Ray shrugged.

"Pardon, I didn't catch that."

"Yes," he whispered.

I patted his left shoulder and he cringed. "Good boy."

"Now," I said, once we were settled with coffees, "what did you do with my son?"

"No, I had nothing to do with that." Ray whined.

"Aw, come on, Bast and I caught you red-handed last night. And the cops found a few pieces of jewellery in your pocket. Very careless of you and that from a previous robbery."

"I was going to fence it."

"Yeah, right." Leaning forward, I placed my arms on the table as if to grab his shirt. "Now, one more time and you better give me the right answer. *What did you do with my son?*"

"Nothing," he replied.

I stood up and reached towards him. He shrank back further into his seat.

"Don't lie to me. You stole Belcher's car and used it to kidnap David."

"Is everything all right," a young man's voice asked. A security guard, whom I didn't recognize, stood beside the table.

"Everything's fine. Daddy and I were just having a family chat."

"Okay," the security guard said and left us alone.

I sat down and glared at Ray. "This time the truth. What did you do with David?"

"Nothing." Ray held up both hands. "Please, Dana. It's the truth. I did break into those other places, even that Belcher's, but I didn't steal his car. And why would I break into your place, any time? I couldn't do that. You used to work for us, I mean my wife, doing security for the Mini-Mall business association so I ..." He shrugged.

"Just racoons," I said.

"Well, they are dirty creatures who get in your way."

"Is that why you maimed them?"

"Sort of. The first place I broke into as I was leaving, a racoon knocked over a garbage can blocking my way and I tripped over it. The little varmint kept poking its ugly mug into the spilled garbage and I got real mad. I grabbed a broom from against the wall and started hitting it with its handle. When I found I'd killed it, I got scared, so decided to make it look like some crazed animal hater had done it."

"And what about the other B and Es? You can't tell me there was a racoon conveniently at each place you broke into."

He shrugged.

"Well?" I asked.

He shrugged again. I pretended to get up from my seat. He cringed, put up his hands and said, "Look Dana, I know how it looks. But I didn't break into your house and steal your kid. Look that night I was upstairs like nearly everybody else in town for your damn agency opening."

"True. Okay, fine, for now. But, tell me, why were you robbing those houses?"

"Lois doesn't give me a big enough allowance."

I didn't know whether to believe him or not, especially considering the scene back at the shoe store.

I left the Mini-Mall and drove to Madge's. A cop car sat in the building's parking lot. In the elevator I mulled over what to say to my friend, after getting past the dragon lady. Then there was Ron.

Madge's door hung open and forbidding. Aunt Doris and a uniformed cop rushed towards me. Aunt Doris, of course, reached me first. She grasped my left arm with unsteady fingers; her eyes blinked and darted like a worrying ferret.

"Madge has disappeared," she finally managed to say. "It's all my fault." She began to cry.

Chapter Twenty-nine

Noon, Monday, August 17, 1998

Him:

He stared at the TV screen as the CNKT reporter—that Haas fellow—bleated on about the second little boy's body being found. The boy has a name. Idiot. Oh, he's speculating about it being connected to the first little boy whose body was found. Johnny Corvette. Aaron King. That's right. The world needs to know the names of the boys who weren't bad enough.

Wait a minute. That English detective with the jaw was speaking now. Something about keeping an open mind and hope about finding the other two little boys alive.

Not if he had anything to do with it.

Two boys. That included the detective's son. Did that mean he was the boy bad enough to remove this curse on him and sort out the mess between Jessie and him?

Was David Bowman the one?

Panic roared through him. He began to shudder. Was he getting mixed up about which boy was the most evil? Maybe it didn't matter which one. Maybe it was supposed to be both boys.

He wished Jessie was here right now so he could ask her.

Was that a sound upstairs? He ran out into the hall and looked up. He thought he could see Jessie at the top of the stairs starting to do her striptease and he could feel something boil inside him.

He didn't know if it was sex or anger. He only knew he had to do something about it NOW.

Chapter Thirty

Noon, Monday, August 17, 1998

Dana:

Footsteps thudded from the kitchen area. Ron appeared behind Doris and put his arm around her, murmuring words of comfort.

"You do get around, Ms. Bowman," said Constable Ryan.

"I'm Madge's friend and I'd like to know what happened."

"Mrs. Lister across the hall was here for an hour or so," Ron said. "But she says Madge sent her home, said she wanted to take a nap and would be fine until Aunt Doris got back. So she went home. Guess Madge sneaked out then."

"That's enough," Ryan said. "Now you two make yourself scarce while I interview Ms. Bowman." When I scowled at him, he added, "Or we could go down to headquarters."

We sat down and faced each other across the dining room table. I tried to ignore Aunt Doris and Ron in the living room.

"Why aren't you out looking for Madge?" I asked.

"I've called it in."

"What if she was kidnapped?"

"Now, Ms. Bowman." He scowled. "I need to know when you last saw Madge Sangwell."

"Yesterday afternoon." I detailed the disagreement-with-Madge episode. "After that I just walked around."

"Tell me, Ms. Bowman. Were you upset enough to retaliate when Madge Sangwell threw you out?"

"What? You think I had something to do with her disappearance?" I stood up "You're way off base, Constable Ryan. Madge was my friend and I'm feeling guilty, not resentful, that she threw me out. Hell, I even feel a little stupid that I couldn't help her. That's why I came over here, to talk to her even though she did throw me out."

"All right. Take it easy. Now, where were you this morning from 10 a.m. on?"

"In court. Ask him." I pointed to Ron. "I was at his and Ray Chalmers's bail hearings, then I went to the Mini-Mall and talked to Ray Chalmers. It was in the food court. Ask one of the security guards who talked to us at one point. Then I came here."

Ryan scribbled in his notepad.

"Is that all?" I asked. "I have to go look for my friend."

"One more question. Where do you think your friend is?"

"I don't know. That's why I have to go look."

"Ms. Bowman, leave it to the police."

"Oh screw you police. Still two missing boys, three murders and two B and E arrests, only one of which, I think, is valid. Not much of a record is it Ryan?"

"And yours is any better?"

I bit that one and turned to go. Ryan stood up to follow.

"Ms. Bowman, leave it to the police," he said.

"Why don't we both go and look?"

"I can't leave here now. But there are officers out looking."

A knock sounded at the door. Ryan shouted, "Who is it?"

"Detective Harker. Fielding asked me to come here."

Ryan opened the door. Harker stepped in and the two moved over to the window to confer. I caught "take over here for now," from Harker. I didn't listen for any more, but eased towards the door and slipped out into the hall. As the elevator door opened, feet ran towards me. I dashed inside and through the closing doors could see Ryan's distorted face yelling at me. He would probably take the stairs, so I moved fast out the door downstairs to my car and headed for Main St., driving north, unsure of my destination. First, the cop on my tail had to go. He wove in and out between cars and was catching up. No sirens whined yet.

I sped past the north boundary of Thurston and increased the speed, turned off and led Ryan a merry chase along dirt roads, finally losing him by squeaking through at a railway crossing seconds before the barrier came down. Then I returned to Thurston, spending the next half-hour driving around town in circles and trying to figure out where Madge could have gone. In a sudden panic I sped towards Snow Lake, parked the car at an angle and ran to the beach. The lifeguards hadn't seen anyone of her description, but Madge wouldn't do anything foolish, at least until Debbie was buried. Or would she? I kicked some stones and returned to the car. More aimless driving around followed with more random thoughts. I flicked on the radio.

The 2 p.m. news follows but first a word from our sponsor.

Two p.m.? What day was this? Monday? I shut the radio off, turned the car around, probably giving the guy behind me a heart attack, and sped to Thurston General Hospital.

The Thurston Women Against Abortion League, better known as TWAAL, paraded on the sidewalk outside the hospital entrance. A few carried placards. Some appeared to chant; from inside the car it was difficult to hear the words. I stopped the car and took a closer look.

The women appeared to span the ages from the toddler clutching her mommy's hand to a grandmotherly type shaking a placard depicting a dead foetus. Opening the car door, I swallowed my opinions to talk to them about Madge. The grandmotherly type turned my way.

Rita Brooks. Her eyes stared past me as if she was in a trance. A shiver slid down my back. Grandma from next door had turned into a stranger. I stepped from the car and something whooshed by, nearly knocking me over. My hands began shaking. Clutching the edge of the car door, I swung around.

The woman flung herself against the protesters, grasped one at random and shook her. A loud keening erupted and the woman turned sideways.

Madge.

I charged towards them and grabbed her while she shoved and yelled like a vibrating inferno, sending me falling backwards but someone propped me up.

"We better get her home," Rita Brooks said, coming around in front. Her face now wore grandmotherly concern.

"Murderers. You killed my daughter. You killed my Debbie." Madge shrieked at the other women, paralyzing them momentarily into silence. Then their vocal chords returned, spewing out at Madge.

"Quiet." I yelled into the cacophony.

Silence and a glare from Madge answered my command. She put her head in her hands and started crying. Rita and I each put an arm around her.

"There, there," Rita said.

Madge started shaking and keening. "My baby, my baby, no, no, no."

"You people better go home now," I said through clenched teeth.

"We got business here," said a woman waving a placard of a dead foetus. My stomach churned.

"Let's move it, ladies," a male voice shouted.

Ryan had caught up.

We glowered at each other. He raised his baton and moved towards the swarming women. Rita and I dragged Madge, now a whimpering dead weight, into my car.

"Thank you, Rita," I said.

"That's okay, dearie. I'll follow you in my car and help you with Madge back at her place."

I nodded, climbed in, shut the door and turned to Madge huddled up against the passenger window.

"I'm sorry, for everything, Madge."

She whimpered. A horn honked behind us, so I started the car and drove off.

The parking lot behind Madge's apartment building contained two cars. No reporters. No cops. No one. Good. Rita and I propped up Madge between us and dragged her into the elevator and over to her apartment door. Rita knocked.

The door opened. Harker peeked out over its chain.

"Fine," he said. "I'll take over from here."

"Do you know what happened?" I frowned.

"Yes, Ryan called."

"We have to help her in," Rita said.

"That won't be necessary." After opening the chain, Harker put a proprietary arm around Madge, effectively pushing us away.

"What's going on here? Where's Aunt Doris?"

"She's inside. You're not allowed back in here. Fielding's orders." He glared at me. The man really needed major facelift surgery. I wanted to smack his face.

"The hell with Fielding. Madge is my best friend."

I moved forward, but Harker's body blocked me. He gave the door a shove with his free arm.

Rita and I looked at each other. Rita shrugged her shoulders. I muttered "Christ" under my breath, then "sorry."

"That's okay. You're under a lot of stress and worry." Her eyes looked beyond my shoulder and she seemed to mouth the words by rote. "I'm sure the officer is only following orders. What Madge needs now is some rest." She paused and adjusted her skirt. "I guess I better be getting back home." She opened her purse and pulled out keys and gave me a superficial smile.

"Wait a minute, Rita, about the demonstration in front of the hospital ... I didn't know you were involved in TWAAL."

"What about it?"

"Rita, considering the accusations Madge just threw out at the group, doesn't it occur to you that maybe one of your members might be involved?"

"No!" Rita glowered like a madwoman and I stepped back. What did I really know about my next door neighbour?

"Okay, Rita, that was badly put. Perhaps knowing who the members are—besides you and Madge—they could be eliminated as suspects in Debbie's murder. And really, this is something that Detective Sergeant Fielding should know."

"No, not the police."

"Then Bast and I."

"No." She turned and headed towards the elevator.

I took the stairs to the ground level, climbed into my car and drove home. My mouth and throat felt drier than dead grass in the summer heat.

Bast had better have some good news.

Chapter Thirty-one

Just past noon, Monday, August 17, 1998

Bast:

Driving over to the Thurston College campus area in the east end, Bast ruminated on the story Harwood had referred to in his e-mail. Cam was Cameron Fontaine, one of the four young adults he had interviewed for that story. He remembered Cameron would only talk to him on the phone and wouldn't even tell him the name of the childhood friend who had always been there for him. Bast had obtained it from the college housing office, but then the friend hadn't been available for an interview, so he had talked to one of Fontaine's professors. No wonder he couldn't remember Harwood's name. He wondered if Fontaine would be there today. He might be able to tell him something about Harwood's relationship with Debbie.

Harwood lived on the second floor of a typical older home converted to apartments for college students. It was located on Barker Ave. a couple of blocks down the road from the main college entrance. The inside smelled of incense and grease, the latter growing stronger as Bast climbed the stairs to Harwood's apartment.

When Harwood opened the door, Bast shook the hand of the slightly built man with dark hair and glasses who stood in the doorway.

"I guess you're here with some follow-up as you called it about Cam. He's not here right now but I'll be glad to fill you in where I can."

Bast entered a small narrow hallway littered with shoes, a tennis racket and books. The living room wasn't much tidier.

"Sorry." Harwood moved newspapers off a chair. "Cam usually keeps the place tidy. I'm the sloppy one. Sort of a Felix

Unger and Oscar Madison situation. Well, have a seat. Would you like a coffee?"

Bast nodded and when Harwood went into the kitchen, he wandered over to the mantle where a few photographs stood. He stared at a picture of two teenage boys—one obviously a slightly younger Harwood in black-rimmed glasses and a taller blond fellow neatly dressed in jeans and a black T-shirt. Harwood's jeans were torn at the left knee and his white T-shirt half hung out at the waist. Harwood gave a big grin at the camera while Cameron's lips were stuck together like he was holding in his emotions.

"Oh, that was taken just after Cam's sister died," Harwood said from behind. Bast turned around just as Harwood set the coffee mugs down amongst the magazines and empty take-out trays on the coffee table. "She practically raised him, you know. Well, I guess you would know; you wrote about him in your story. I think your story helped him finally come to grips with her death, because right after it was published in the *Toronto Daily Herald* Cam was finally able to return to the family home—it's been closed since we came here to college. He's been up there, sorting stuff out to sell it. Is that what you want to follow up on?"

"Not quite." Bast sat down on the chair and Harwood sat across from him on the couch. "First of all I'm no longer a crime reporter. My twin sister Dana and I just opened The Attic Investigative Agency in Thurston, but you probably know about that from the news. Dana and I are looking into the events of that evening and I'm here about these letters you wrote to the late Debbie Sangwell, your girlfriend."

"Where did you get those?" Jarvis' voice had risen a few notches and he looked ready to bolt.

"They were found at Debbie's place and ... I wouldn't move if I were you ..."

He sat back and put his head in his hands. "Oh, God. I didn't kill her. I wasn't even there. We broke up a few months ago."

"But not before you got her pregnant."

"Oh God."

"That is a good motive for murder for someone who didn't want the baby and told its mother-to-be to abort it. Told Debbie, who couldn't have an abortion because her mother was against abortion."

"You don't know what it was like. I loved Debbie and she loved me but her damn mother was against birth control and had instilled that in Debbie. She, Debbie I mean, wouldn't even let me use a condom. Do you know how difficult the rhythm method is?"

"I can imagine," Bast said. "But if you've read the news stories, you also will have read that a little boy, my sister's son David, was kidnapped the same evening an hour or so before Debbie was murdered. So her murder probably ties in with the kidnapping."

"Debbie would never harm a child."

"I know that. She babysat David. No, my interest is in this information you told Debbie in your last letter to her, about this Sprinkle Pharmacy in Toronto and some procedure about going to the pharmacy counter and stating you had a problem for a Mr. Ke and she would be directed to him and all would be well. My question, Mr. Harwood, is what did Mr. Ke do? What did he give Debbie?"

"Give Debbie? Then you know."

"Know what, Mr. Harwood? Look up at me when I'm speaking." When Harwood complied, Bast stared at him hard, right in the eyes.

"They'll kill me if I tell."

"Tell what, Mr. Harwood?"

"About Sprinkle; about Mr Ke, about the pills."

Chapter Thirty-two

Late afternoon, Monday, August 17, 1998

Dana:

"And he didn't really know very much after all," Bast said after telling me about his visit to Jarvis Harwood's. "Basically he had heard that girls 'in trouble' as he put it, could get help at Sprinkle's by asking for this Mr. Ke. He said one of his friends told him so, but when I asked him which friend, he said he couldn't remember. Then I asked him if it was Cameron, and he said 'no way.' "

"Who's Cameron?" I asked.

"Cameron Fontaine." And then Bast told me about the story he wrote for the *Toronto Daily Herald* about four young adults—two men and two women—who had survived childhood traumas. Cameron had lost both a mother and a sister—not at the same time—to tragic accidents—both falls—the mother at a bar and the sister at home. There was no father on the scene.

All this was very interesting, but Cameron didn't seem connected to Debbie and this Sprinkle Pharmacy and those pills. The latter two must tie in with Debbie's murder and probably David's disappearance. More and more I was beginning to realize that David probably saw something or someone he shouldn't have and that's why he was kidnapped, and like Debbie, possibly—I couldn't finish the thought.

But there was also the serial killer. Maybe he kidnapped David. But all the other little boys were taken from a mall. Suddenly I remembered the young man with the backpack staring at the knife when Lois was slicing cheese.

And I didn't see him after David was gone.

"Dana, you all right?" Bast asked. "You seem far away."

"Bast, do you remember a young man carrying a black backpack in the office at the reception. It was when Lois was cutting cheese?"

Bast stroked his beard. "No, I don't think so. Why?"

"Just that he seemed to be fascinated with the knife Lois was using. And he didn't seem to be around after David ... you know ..."

"I know, but I think a few people managed to sneak out in the confusion when Debbie charged into the office just then. He could have been one of them."

"I suppose so." I ran fingers through my hair. "Okay. Can I see those letters? I haven't even read them yet."

He handed me the letters and I opened the first in the pile and began reading. They contained an abundance of "I can't wait to see you," some rehashing of their actual dates—Harwood wasn't exactly a creative scribe. The third letter was basically a "Dear Jane" letter where Harwood pulled the typical male cop-out when his girlfriend became pregnant—he wasn't ready for a permanent relationship with commitments. However, it was in the fourth and last letter, dated July 30, that I found a reference to what Bast heard from Harwood's mouth. And something more.

Do not tell anyone about Mr. Ke. I'm told he is not what he may seem and he has powerful cohorts in various places who want this product kept secret. I'm told it will help you. Don't forget—Sprinkle. Right now you have to go down to Toronto for it. Do it when I'm not there.

Sprinkle—that was the name of the pharmacy moving in next door to Chalmers Shoe Store. My mind went back to the conversation I'd overhead between Ray and Lois.

"What is Harwood doing this summer? Taking more classes or working?" I looked up at Bast who was busy with his laptop.

"Huh? Oh, that's interesting. He was a clerk until the end of July at that Sprinkle Pharmacy in Toronto, you know the one connected to the owner who runs that Sonar Medical Research Clinic attached?"

"Same date as his last letter to Debbie. Looks like he was running scared."

"My other piece of news is this empty bottle you found in the waste basket at Debbie's and Madge's." Bast hauled it out of his back pocket and brought it over. "After talking to Harwood, I drove to Toronto. One of the pharmacists at Sprinkle definitely identified it as one of theirs. See. It has that peculiar shape of wider at the brim than the bottom. However, he couldn't or wouldn't tell me whom it was made out to, even when I showed him the scrap of prescription paper. Said it was one of theirs. Then he clammed up."

I fingered the paper. "It certainly has Madge's address on it. But was it Madge's or Debbie's prescription and for what?"

"I'd like to know that too. I'd also like to know what you have there. Suppressing evidence, D ... D ... Ms. Bowman? And you, Bast should know better." Fielding stood in the doorway from the hall. He moved over to us and held out his right hand. "I'll take those."

Bast handed over the empty prescription bottle. I glanced again at the prescription paper and gave it to Fielding. He pointed to the letters and I passed them over.

"I should have you two charged with obstructing justice, but I'll let it go if I get a detailed explanation of where you found these and what else you know about them."

Fielding interviewed me first, ending with a lecture on suppressing evidence.

Our cell phones started ringing.

"Yes," I said.

"Dana Bowman? It's Oliver. I have some information you should have."

"Yes, hang on a minute." I turned to Fielding. "This is a private conversation. It is not any kidnappers."

Fielding nodded and kept talking into his cell. I moved out to the back porch, closing the door behind.

"All right, I'm alone, now."

"I shouldn't be telling you all this, but some of it will be released to the press. I just had another look at the autopsy report for Debbie. The murder weapon was a kitchen utility knife. But there weren't any fingerprints on the handle—it was wiped clean. The blade had a few shreds of cheese embedded on it."

"Okay, thanks Oliver. I have to go now." I closed my cell and stared straight ahead.

Ron Bowman was climbing over the fence from the Brooks yard into my backyard and he appeared dishevelled and hot.

Chapter Thirty-three

Late afternoon, Monday, August 17, 1998

Bast:

Fielding returned from the hallway and shoved his cell into his jacket pocket.

"Bad news?" Bast asked.

He didn't reply. Maybe he'd tell Dana. There was some kind of attraction between them, and it made him sick. He wished he hadn't pushed them into going sailing together. He'd just thought it would show Dana how overbearing Fielding was and steer her away from him. Dana would have to find out for herself.

"All right Mr. Overture," Fielding said. "Let's get down to business. Where did you get the prescription bottle and paper?"

"I didn't get either. Dana found them."

"I see. Where did she say she found them?"

"On the balcony here, the second floor balcony, but only the bottle."

"And when was that?"

"Just after we found the body."

"And where do you think that bottle came from?"

"A drugstore."

"Which drugstore would that be Mr. Overture?"

"Not one around here."

"Where then, Overture?"

"Toronto, perhaps."

"Perhaps. Come, come, Mr. Overture, be more specific."

"Sprinkle."

"Sprinkle? How did you know that?"

"I didn't for sure until I went there. But it looked like one of theirs, the shape of the bottle, you know."

"No, I don't know. How did you know?"

"One of the pharmacists up here thought so."

"So you checked it out?"

"Yes, I checked it out and the pharmacist at Sprinkle confirmed it."

"And did he confirm who the prescription was made out to?"

"No, that's confidential."

"That's confidential, what do you mean by that? You're not telling me or he's not telling you?"

"He wouldn't tell me."

"Okay, now. This piece of prescription paper, who found that?"

"Dana did."

"Did you see her find it?"

"No, she told me."

"And you believed her?"

"Yeah, she's my sister."

"What did she tell you about this piece of paper?"

"Said she found it in the bathroom garbage at Madge's. Look, Dana brought back the whole plastic bag of garbage from Madge's bathroom."

"Oh, and what else was in that bag?"

"Nothing of importance."

"Nothing? Come, come, Overture, you should know that anything can be of importance. Now, where is that bag?"

"I don't know."

"You don't know. Mr. Overture, you say you saw your sister with a whole bag of garbage she claims was from Madge Sangwell's bathroom and you don't know where it is."

"That's right.

"Well, where do you think it is?"

"Maybe the Brooks's garbage, unless they've collected it for pickup."

"Why would it be in the Brooks's garbage? You said your sister found it in Madge Sangwell's wastebasket."

"Because we were at the Brooks—where you put us right after Debbie's murder. And Dana brought it back there." He glared at Fielding, but the latter's face showed only hardness. Bast tried not to flinch.

"Did you see what else was in that garbage bag?"

"Nothing of importance."

"Mr. Overture, we've been through this before. What was in that bag?"

"Okay, okay, some facial tissue, and a used sanitary pad."

"Hmm. I see. And what about these letters? Who is this Jarvis Harwood who sent letters to Debbie Sangwell? Her boyfriend? Baby's father? I also read autopsy reports."

Bast sighed. This time he gave Fielding all the pertinent information about Jarvis and Debbie, and a printed copy of his story on the four childhood trauma survivors.

"Very well, Overture. That's all for now. I'll have a statement typed up and you can come in tomorrow to sign it." Fielding closed his notebook and left.

Bast returned to his research on the laptop. He was looking for the killed story about that company Gordon Lambton represented a year or so ago. Only the story's sidebar showed up. The Lambton-represented company was named, Donnelier, a subsidiary of a holding company, Ontario #435798. The company principals were an L.M. Cole and a K. R. Robinson. He hadn't a clue who Cole was but Robinson? Wasn't that the name of the young couple across the street, Cherry and Ken? He tried to contain his excitement and read on. Donnelier had been charged with fraud April 14, 1997, court date June 11, 1997, remanded to Sept. 23, 1997, then stayed. There was a brief quote from one of the arresting officers, a Detective Guy Shoane. "We're not finished with this one," he had said. "Detective Paul Harker and I agree there is more to this than meets the eye."

Harker? That was the name of the detective operating the wiretap, the officer who skipped out early for some sudden family emergency, leaving Marsden in his place and then Marsden was clobbered. And also the detective investigating Jimmie Halpern's mall kidnapping.

Bast almost tripped over his chair as he stood and charged up the two flights of stairs to the attic office. He had to find his interview notes and his copy of the court documents.

Chapter Thirty-four

Late afternoon Monday, August 17, 1998

Dana:

Standing in the backyard, Ron looked like hell gone haywire. I ran to join him and pushed him back under a tree.

"What?" he asked.

"Fielding is inside. What the hell are you doing here?"

"I came to tell you that I had nothing to do with your friend's murder or our son's kidnapping."

"Our son?" I shrieked the words, sending spittle into the air. "When have you ever acted like a father?"

"I guess I deserve that." He lowered his head. "Anyway I want to make up for it."

"Right, you're suddenly going to be a part of David's life."

"Yeah, well, when this is all over."

"That figures. Typical Ron, let someone else handle the problems, then enter the picture." I leaned forward. "That's not why you're here, is it?"

"Yeah, well." His mouth twitched.

"Yeah, well, what?" I glared at him.

"I thought, I mean, well ..." He frowned. "I just wanted to thank you for getting Gordon Lambton to represent me."

"That's it?"

"Well, you and me. We were once married. Maybe ..." Ron began laughing, a jittery laugh, high pitched and loud.

"Lower your voice, Ron. Do you want Fielding to come out and find us under a tree together? There is no 'you and me.' You killed that when you ran off when David was a toddler and took up with Leila although I never knew the correct order of that—maybe the affair came before the desertion." Spittle shot out, hitting him on the chin. He stepped back, catching his hair in a tree branch.

"Okay, I deserve that I guess. But the affair, as you call it, ended when Leila moved on."

"Right. To Gordon."

"Yes, we both had a similar experience here. And I only heard from Leila once since then. She called. It was nothing personal. She just wanted some advice about a problem where she was working at this place Sprinkle and ..."

"Sprinkle? The drugstore attached to a medical centre in Toronto?" A sinking feeling coupled with anticipation raced through me. I grabbed his T-shirt and shook him, getting a whiff of underarm sweat. "What did Leila tell you? I know you. You dance around the subject—throwing out differing tidbits. Now, get to it."

"All right, Leila sounded very upset and wasn't making much sense. Kept going round and round about something not quite right at Sprinkle. When I finally got her calmed down a bit, she said she'd been fired because she'd been caught by the pharmacist pulling one of her kleptomaniac stunts. But she'd taken something 'odd' as she said. Bottles of pills, which I told her wasn't unusual for a drug store. She said they weren't labelled, and even the big bottles and containers with the core supply of some common drug are always labelled."

"What kind of pills, Ron? Did she say what they looked like?"

"I didn't ask. I was still miffed at her dumping me for well, my lawyer. But looking back I realize she sounded frightened." He shrugged his shoulders. "Dana, I swear that's all I know. I never heard from her again."

"Do you have a home address for her?"

"No, sorry." He averted his eyes and wiped his hands on his jeans. "I guess I better get back to Madge's. It got kind of messy around there when she returned home, so I decided I needed some fresh air."

"And made a beeline for here?"

"Yeah, well, we did have some good times together, Dana." He reached his hand out to me and I drew back.

"That's history. Thanks for the information. I better get inside before Fielding discovers I'm gone. You better return to Madge's. Bye."

I slid out from under the tree and found myself face-to-face with Rita Brooks. She stood on the other side of the fence, staring at a point high up in the air. In her right hand she held a piece of paper. When she saw me she started waving it.

"I had second thoughts," she said. "You can have a quick look at the list of the TWAAL members and you'll see none of them are the type of people who would murder a 19-year-old girl." Her eyes had a far-away look, perhaps that of a fanatic. My back felt like a snake was crawling up it, and I shook my head as if to chase the serpent away.

"Thanks, Rita." My hand shook as I took the paper. As I started folding it, her hand seized mine, sending the paper to the ground over on her side. Rita bent over, snatched the list and gave it back.

"Now. Look at it now, right here." Her voice trembled and her eyes showed terror. What the hell didn't she want me to know?

"Rita, that's ridiculous."

"No. Now. How do I know you won't copy them over or give them to that English detective?"

"I won't. Promise."

"Oh, all right, but I want the list back in an hour."

"Why? Does the paper disintegrate then?"

Her look of terror had morphed into a snarl.

"Okay, Rita. I was out of line. One hour it is."

She nodded and returned to her house. While walking to the back porch, I began checking the list of names. A few surprised me; some were unfamiliar.

"Interesting reading?" Fielding asked.

Crap. How long had he been out here?

"Not really. Just some stuff I have to do."

"A list of names? Give it over here." Fielding held out his hand and I shoved the paper behind my back.

"Client confidentiality."

"What? I saw Rita Brooks hand you that paper, and if it has anything to do with Ms Sangwell's murder or your son's kidnapping, you have to hand it over."

"No, I don't. Rita is a neighbour and a friend and what's between us is none of your damn business."

"Not in a murder and kidnapping." He moved his hand closer. "I looked the other way with the prescription bottle and letters, but I'm not doing so now. Unless you want to be arrested for obstructing justice, I suggest you hand it over now."

"Oh, very well, Detective Sergeant Fielding. But it's on you to tell Rita Brooks why and how her li ... piece of paper got in your hands." I thrust the paper at him and stomped up the porch steps.

At least the paper contained no heading—just a bunch of names and phone numbers. Still, I felt like a traitor, a role that seemed to follow me around the last few days. Upstairs in the office, I typed remembered names on the desktop computer. Bast came in, so I brought him up to speed with Ron, Leila, Fielding and Rita's list.

"Move over. I can do this faster than you." He opened the browser and started searching the names. He clicked on one.

I stared at the screen, mouth open as I read.

Chapter Thirty-five

Near suppertime, Monday, August 17, 1998

Him:

He still wasn't sure if Jimmie or David was the right evil boy.

"You're the bad boy."

He swivelled around. Jessie stood before him in her track suit, wooden paddle in her hand.

"You're the bad boy," she said again. "You ruined our lives."

"No, you ruined mine."

Where did that come from? He'd never stood up to Jessie before.

"None of your lip." Jessie moved closer.

He turned around, pelted out of the living room and up the stairs until he was in his room. Then he shut the door and turned the key in the lock. Not that a key would do any good. Jessie always managed to get in. He just never knew if it would be the tart or the mother until she stood in his bedroom and ...

It had gone quiet out there. He turned the key and slid the door open.

"Jessie? Jessie, where are you?"

Silence.

He tiptoed to her room and peeked in.

No one.

He noticed her hair brush sticking out over the dresser, so he strode in, sat down and nudged the brush in so it was evenly lined up with the comb and hand mirror. He stared at the face in the mirror and wondered who the grown man looking back at him was. He jumped up, ran downstairs, grabbed his backpack, and exited the house.

He needed some fresh air. Sometimes Jessie could make things stifling.

Chapter Thirty-six

Near Suppertime, Monday, August 17, 1998

Dana:

I re-read the newspaper story Bast had found online. Leila had been killed in a hit-and-run last September. Simple accident? The details were sparse.

I decided to call Fielding. Leila's death didn't occur in Fielding's jurisdiction, and he owed me something after my agreement to go sailing with him, and especially for what we saw afterwards on the beach. For good measure I threw in the evidence Bast and I had handed over. Taking a deep breath, I tried to shove the picture of the dead boy out of my mind.

Leila and Debbie were both dead and the link between them seemed to be Sprinkle. How did all that connect to David's kidnapping? The closeness in time to Debbie's murder and David's kidnapping made me think they were linked. Was Sprinkle the connection there too? What about the three mall kidnappings? How the hell did they fit in? Debbie was only around for Jimmie's kidnapping and David's. I ran my fingers through my cropped hair. I was running in circles. Calm down, Dana. First things first. Picking up my cell, I called Fielding.

We met at Timmy's in the Mini-Mall, both of us trying to avoid looking directly at each other. At least this coffee was in public.

Fielding rustled papers in a file folder and pulled out a newspaper clipping. "Technically I shouldn't be discussing this with you, but since it happened in Toronto and the victim was someone you caught stealing in Thurston's Mini-Mall, I'm going to bend the rules a little as a professional courtesy."

I raised my eyebrows at the word "victim."

"So, you don't think it was an accident either, Fielding?"

He didn't bother to correct me on his name, but just stared at the clipping. I reached across the table for it. Our hands jumped back when they touched. The story was an update to the one Bast had found online.

"She was run over twice and according to the skid marks, by the same car." He now held what looked like a report and skimmed it. "This is a copy of a Toronto Police Force report and I can't let you see it, but in summary, Leila Smythe was pretty banged up when she died."

"So you think someone ran her over on purpose." A chill slid down my spine.

"Don't know."

"Come on Fielding."

He kept staring at the report.

"Anything about Sprinkle in there?"

"I can't say any more." He started to return the papers to the file. "What else do you and that brother of yours know about Sprinkle that you haven't told me?"

"That is *our* business—client confidentiality." I shrugged.

"What client?"

A stare was my answer.

"Now Ms. Bowman I've given you and your brother some leeway here because it is your son who was kidnapped."

"Madge," I said. "Who the hell else would our client be? Debbie's ghost?" I blinked back the tears that threatened to spew out.

"Well, you don't seem to be having much communication with *your client* in the past few days."

Did the man not miss anything?

"Yeah, well. I suppose she ... both she and I ... could be expected to be a little off with what has happened in our families."

"I guess I deserved that. All right. I'll let you see the accident photos. Have to warn you—they are grisly." He handed them over, and I jerked back from them. But it wasn't Leila's bloodied broken body that got to me.

What if something like that happened to David?

"Fielding, level with me. Do you think all these things are connected? The four kidnappings, Debbie's murder and now it looks like maybe Leila's? And Sprinkle, and don't forget the break and enter in my basement."

"That B and E was separate and before David's kidnapping and Debbie's murder," Fielding said. "And as you already know, that B and E was part of the series of break and enters by Ray Chalmers, and the knife, or rather knives, in that case were Chalmers's hunting knives."

"Yeah, are all the rest connected?"

"Ms. Bowman, let the police do their work. And D ... Dana, that might make it easier on you." He put his hand out towards mine.

I ignored it and stood up. "Christ. All I want are some answers to get my son back. It's been days and I feel like we are running around in circles. Somewhere in all this mess is David, my son. I'd like him back, preferably alive, Detective Sergeant Donald Fielding, and I'm not about to sit around anymore and try to pull information out of you that for some reason you won't give me. And don't you dare say 'police business' or I'll ram your badge up your ... your ... nose." I grabbed my purse, knocking over my coffee, not caring where it splashed, and tried to ignore Fielding calling after me. When his chair scraped and footsteps followed, I scurried into the mall proper and around a corner, hiding in the Ladies until realizing it was the same Ladies where Jimmie had been kidnapped. Right now I wasn't interested in searching for clues on that. Right now I only wanted my son back. I ran out to the parking lot and drove home in a rage.

Chapter Thirty-seven

Monday night, August 17 into Tuesday, August 18, 1998

Dana:

At home, I brushed past Bast, charged upstairs and flung off my clothes, throwing them in a wad on the floor. In the shower, I huddled against the stall and let the water mix with my tears and cascade down. It all seemed so hopeless. What chance did I or even Fielding have to get David back alive? My mind jumped to what life without David would be, and my heart hurt. This could not happen; this could not be. It took three tries for me to stand up tall. Finally I shut off the water, stepped out, towel-dried, pulled on panties and a nightshirt, crawled into bed, and fell asleep in minutes.

I was back on that damn beach with Fielding and Dr. Farley, focusing on the covered lump at our feet. Farley pulled back the cover to reveal David's lifeless body. His eyes stared, not at me, but straight up in terror. His body seemed to slip towards the lake and I screamed "Stop. Help." But Fielding and Dr. Farley stood as if turned into statues. I ran after David's body as it disappeared into the water.

"David," I yelled.

David's body jerked up to a standing position; I lost my balance and fell into the lake, screaming as I went under. Hands grasped my shoulders and shook me.

I bolted up and stared at Bast and down at the bed.

"Dana, are you all right?"

"Huh?" I rubbed my eyes. Dry. So was rest of my face. "What? David, the lake."

"It's okay. You had a bad dream." Bast put his arms around me and I clung, sobbing.

"No, Bast, not a dream. It was real." I told him about my meeting with Fielding and our discussion about Leila's death and Sprinkle. "He didn't come right out and say it, but I know he thinks it might be a serial killer. Bast, what if a serial killer has David? What if ...?"

"Sh. We'll find him." He cleared his throat.

"What? You're hiding something from me. What is it?" I grabbed his arm.

"Just something I found out about that case Lambton defended."

When he finished his update, I scratched my head.

"Robinson, Robinson . Wait, that's the name of the new couple across the street, the ones away when everything happened here. I met the wife ... Cherry. Her husband's name is Ken."

"K.R. Robinson," Bast said.

"Right and he's a doctor in Toronto. But who the hell is L.M. Cole?"

"I'm still hunting out my notes from those interviews I did for that story—guess they got misplaced when I moved my stuff up to the agency office. Meantime I e-mailed a few sources for more information on the two of them and Donnelier and its holding company. Nothing yet. Perhaps by morning. Right now you need to get some sleep."

"Yeah, so I can have more nightmares."

"No. Look, I'll get you a cup of hot milk."

It helped. I fell asleep soon afterwards. No more nightmares. No dreams at all.

The trouble was, in the morning, my body didn't want to budge out of bed, and my mind still stumbled around in fog. Something plunked down near me. Rubbing my eyes, I looked up at Bast sitting at the edge of the bed.

"How are you feeling?"

"Washed out."

"No wonder, after the past few days, Reason I came in, besides to see how you are doing, Trillium called. They'll be here tomorrow finally to fix the elevator. They think it's some malfunction in the operating setup and the seal is off the balcony now."

My cell rang.

"Hello, Dana Bowman here," I said in a hollow voice.

"Dana Bowman. It's Ken Robinson, your new neighbour from across the street. Cherry said she met you the other day. I was just calling to express my sympathy for what happened at your place and to say, I hope you get your son back soon."

"Yes, thank you." I motioned to Bast. "Yes, Mr. Robinson, just the man I wanted to see."

"Call me Ken, and what did you want to see me about?"

I almost blabbed "Sprinkle" but instead said, "Cherry tells me you're a doctor."

"Ye ... es."

"I need some medical advice, not my personal health; I'd book an appointment for that with my family doctor. But something's come up in this investigation and I need some medical expertise. My family doctor is of the old school so I thought of you."

"What ... do you ... need ... to know?"

"Why don't I drop over in about an hour and we can talk about it?"

"I'd rather come over to your office. Cherry is in the middle of a housecleaning binge here and it's a bit confusing. I could come over in say, an hour?"

"Fine. See you at ..." I glanced at my digital. It read 12:15 p.m. "1:15?"

"Yeah, okay, 1:15."

I hung up the receiver and jumped out of bed, clutching Bast as my head whirled. Bast steadied me and I took a deep breath.

"You need some food inside you," Bast said. "I'll make you a sandwich and some coffee."

While I munched and drank, Bast talked.

"I'm still doing a background check on Rita Brooks's anti-abortion list. But I've got an inkling why she started THWAAL. The Brooks don't have any children, but did you know that Rita Brooks gave birth to a stillborn child?"

I dropped the sandwich.

"What?" I picked up the mug of Java. "Where did you find that out?"

"From the horse's mouth ... almost. While you were sleeping this morning, I paid Randall Brooks a visit and we got talking. You know for someone who supposedly hides out in the basement with his trains, he doesn't miss too much. He told me about Rita and how losing one child like that and not being able to have another one affected her. I think he wanted me to understand why she started THWAAL."

Half an hour later the two of us sat in the agency office waiting for Ken Robinson's arrival. Bast told the cop on duty to make himself scarce as we had agency business to conduct and didn't want to intimidate potential clients.

Ten minutes later, footsteps sounded on the stairs. A man with freckles and red hair straggling down his neck stepped in. He removed his Blue Jays cap and sunglasses, revealing a thinning scalp and blinking eyes. Bast stared at him.

"Dana Bowman."

"Ken Robinson." His handshake felt limp and clammy.

We sat in a triangle. Robinson began his spiel. He appeared to address the computer on the desk.

"Before you ask me your medical question, I'd like you to know that I run a medical clinic in downtown Toronto. It's a family-based clinic with some research in that area, so whatever knowledge I have, it's in that area." He punctuated each phrase with a nod of his head.

"What is the name of your clinic?" Bast asked.

"What?" The eyes looked at Bast, now. "Oh, it's just called Sonbaker Medical Clinic."

"Most of these clinics have a pharmacy attached for the patients' convenience? Do you?" I asked.

"Yes," he replied. The eyes had returned to the computer.

"Which chain of pharmacies is that?" I smiled.

"It isn't; I mean it's an independent pharmacy."

"Oh, I see." I sugared up my smile. "That wouldn't be Sprinkle Pharmacy would it?"

Robinson almost leaped out of his chair, but instead dug his fingers into the chair's arms. His face registered red and his eyes blinked 130 kilometres an hour.

"Sprinkle it is, but contrary to those news reports, I don't personally own it."

"Then who does?" Bast asked.

"A company, a corporation."

"And you don't own any shares in it. You're not one of the principals?"

"No, of course not." He glanced at me and smiled. "Now, you had some medical question you wanted to ask me."

"Yes, and it's not exactly connected to the investigation. It's about this friend who's five weeks pregnant and very nervous. Can't keep anything down. She doesn't want the baby and she doesn't want a surgical abortion."

"Can't help you there. She should see a gynaecologist."

"What about a morning after pill?" Bast asked.

"Nope. Can't help you there either. Tell her to see a gynaecologist." Robinson clenched his teeth, stood up and cleared his throat. "Well, if you'll excuse me, I have to get going. I dropped Cherry off at the Mini-Mall to get some cleaning supplies, so have to pick her up. My car is in for repairs, so we're sharing hers."

"One more question," Bast said. "This corporation you said owns Sprinkle. I believe one of its shareholders is an L.M. Cole."

"Yes, yes." He jumped up. "Gotta go. Sorry."

We shook his hand. Still clammy and his eye-blinking rate had skyrocketed.

"He's not telling all," Bast whispered to me as we heard his footsteps going down the stairs. "And I can prove it."

Bast turned on the desk computer, clicked on Netscape and on the bookmarks. A news story appeared.

Toronto Daily Herald.
Lifestyle Section
June 30, 1998

Morning-after pill alternative to surgical abortion

I read scanned through the introduction, then read:

RU-486, chemical name Mifepristone, in conjunction with the hormone Prostaglandin or Misoprostol causes the foetus to contract, then expel from the uterus. A pregnant woman can take Mifepristone up to nine weeks after conception, although studies show it is more effective taken by the fourth week.

Since 1989, Mifepristone has been used as an alternative to surgical abortion in France, the United Kingdom from 1991 and Sweden 1992. China has produced Mifepristone domestically since 1992 and because of RU-486's high cost, a black market developed in Chinese cities earlier this year.

I skipped down.

RU-486 is used with a second drug, Misoprostol, which is legally prescribed for preventing ulcers caused by NSAID drug-use.

The two drugs are, taken three to four days apart. The pills cause the uterus to contract. Bleeding then occurs, followed by a miscarriage. If a woman changes her mind between the two drugs, she risks giving birth to abnormalities.

Information followed about how pro-life groups and politics with drug manufacturing companies were keeping RU-486 banned on this side of the Atlantic, including in Canada.

"And you think Robinson has something to do with this RU-486 drug?" I asked.

"Maybe." Bast stroked his beard. "Debbie was pregnant and Leila worked at Sprinkle, was fired for snatching packets of questionable drugs and died in what may or may not be a hit-and-run accident afterwards. Debbie was probably scared her mother would find out she was pregnant. And there was that pill bottle found in Debbie's garbage. Look, when I was covering that court case where Donnelier was charged with fraud, there were allegations, no proof that Donnelier was trafficking in banned drugs."

"And Robinson was in court, then?" I asked.

"Yeah, I think so." Bast rubbed his beard. "I remember a skinny fellow with thinning red hair sitting on the defendant side beside Lambton in court. He had a moustache and the hair was longer then, down to the shoulders. He never testified and as he had his back to me I didn't get a look at his face except when he turned around and it was only a glimpse."

"And you think he's trafficking in illegal drugs?"

"It's possible."

"Bast, what does that have to do with Debbie's murder? From what Oliver told me, she was six weeks pregnant, so she could've taken a morning after pill. Anyway, I presume that's what was in that bottle from Sprinkle a.k.a. Dr. Robinson. What happened to this other pill, this Misoprostol, that is taken a few days later? Bast, she probably took it—maybe even the day she died. Where's the bottle for that?"

"Madge," said Bast. "Remember, one of the uniforms found her in the washroom by the elevator after Debbie was killed. Maybe she flushed its contents down the toilet. And I don't think she was searched right away, so she could have carried the empty bottle out with her."

"She was a little concerned about her purse at Rita's."

Chapter Thirty-eight

Mid-afternoon, Tuesday, August 18, 1998

Him:

"What the hell do you think you are doing, Jessie?"

He found her leaning in the open window on the passenger side of a strange car parked behind the Mini-Mall. Her white shorts rode up her bum and he could just imagine the front of her red halter top. Probably talking to a man. Tart! Hooker! When she turned around, he could see he was right about the halter top. She said something to the man in the car, smiled, waved and started towards the mall's back entrance. He followed her and as they walked in the back empty corridor he pulled out a jacket and his knife from his backpack, covering the latter with the former, and grabbed her before they hit the main mall area. He shoved his spare hand over her mouth and told her to keep quiet or he would stab her. Then he removed his hand, steered her outside and into his car and drove them home.

"My name's not Jessie. My name is ..."

"Shut up, Jessie, you tart. You whore. Well, I'll make you pay. You will have your last little dance, last little fling and then you'll be sorry."

He pushed her towards the basement stairs, manoeuvred her down and then dragged her screaming into the room the two dead boys had occupied. He slammed the door behind her and left her howling inside.

Tramp. Tart. He would make her pay and at the same time save her. He would make the bad boy pay and save him. Then he might finally have peace from this curse.

Which boy is the bad boy? The question popped into his head.

No. No. Don't do this to me. He had made his choice. It was the right choice.

He put both hands up hard against the sides of his head and ran down the small narrow hallway to the room at the end.

Chapter Thirty-nine

Suppertime, Tuesday, August 18, 1998

Bast:

He thinks it might be a serial killer. Bast, what if a serial killer has David?

As Bast drove along Snow Lake Road, he thought about Dana's words from this morning. The Donnelier story, Robinson and all the anti-abortion issues had pushed the conversation with her from his mind. Now, with the window open and a bit of a breeze coming in, he seemed to focus better. Too bad he couldn't dredge up the connection he had started to make before Robinson's phone call. Was it something Harwood had said, not something connected with Debbie but his childhood, no, not Harwood's childhood but his friend, the one he had interviewed by phone for that story—Cameron Fontaine. No, wait a minute. It wasn't something he had heard—it was something he had seen. Think, Bast. Think. His head started to swim. He pulled off to the side of the road and took a deep breath.

It was that photograph—the one of Cameron and Jarvis when they were 17. His mind did a leap and finally another picture, a moving picture jumped to the forefront.

He was in the Mini-Mall, trying to calm down a screaming Debbie, and out of the corner of his eye he saw a young man in a white T-shirt walking towards them. He had caught only a glimpse of him because Debbie had jerked, and as he had pulled tighter he had the distinct impression of someone banging against them.

But his other impression now was more important.

He was sure that the young man in the mall and the 17-year-old standing beside Jarvis Harwood were the same person. And he remembered the look on that young man's face—the same as in the photograph with Harwood. Coincidence? Or what? He didn't believe in coincidence.

He pulled out his cell and started to punch in Dana's number. No, better not. What if he were wrong and he got his sister going and going she would—right to Cameron Fontaine's door and put herself and possibly David into danger? But David was already in danger.

Like Dana, he had seen some of Fielding's books on serial killers, but in his office, when Fielding wasn't in it, of course. Fielding would have some idea what made serial killers tick, and if Fontaine with his traumatic past of both a mother and sister dying tragically before he became an adult could qualify ... He called Harwood and got the Fontaine family address.

He steeled himself and called Fielding's number and told him the rest of what he knew and suspected about Cameron Fontaine. Then he turned the car around and headed for the same address as he had told Fielding.

Chapter Forty

Just after suppertime, Tuesday, August 18, 1998

Dana:

I drove around and around in downtown Thurston and made several passes by Madge's street. But I couldn't face her.

Later.

Back home in the office, I picked up a newspaper clipping of one of Bast's stories left on the desk and began reading. The story had been published in Saturday's *Toronto Daily Herald,* July 18, 1998 and was by-lined Sebastian Overture. It was the one Bast had mentioned about those four young adults who had traumatic childhoods caused by family deaths—one of those where-and- how-are-they-now tales. My eyes and ears perked up at the information that Cameron Fontaine was from Thurston. I didn't recall Bast mentioning that—just that Fontaine was a friend of Jarvis Harwood and that his mother and sister died from falls down stairs. Then I remembered Fielding saying, *there is usually a trigger in the serial killer's life later on that starts him killing.*

The chills started spreading up my spine and the newspaper rattled in my hands.

What if Bast's story was Cameron's trigger point? But how would that send him on a kidnapping and killing spree of little boys? True, his mother had died when he was seven and his older sister, then 20, had raised him until her death when Cameron was 17. I would think that Cameron would go after women, not little boys. Unless he somehow connected these boys to himself. Another reading of Bast's story made me realize that Cameron was the only one of the four subjects interviewed who came across wanting. Something about him was missing. Did Bast fail to notice or did he exclude it? Or maybe Cameron hadn't told him. Whatever wasn't there just might tell us why and perhaps save David's life.

Jimmie's too.

I had to talk to Bast and Fielding. Fielding's cell went to voice mail but Bast picked up. He hemmed and hawed about where he was but when I said "Cameron Fontaine," he relented.

Dusk, Tuesday, August 18, 1998

Dana:

"We are going to do exactly as Fielding ordered," Bast said, as I climbed into the passenger side of his car. We were parked in the driveway across the street from the Fontaine house, waiting for Fielding and company to arrive.

To take my mind off David being inside, I stared at the house—an old two-storey probably built in the 1950s. The house sat close to the street and leaned to the right. The veranda seemed to sag. A light shone from a narrow front window on the second floor and another fainter light showed in a basement window. I pushed the car door open. Bast yanked me back.

"No. Wait for Fielding."

"But there's a light in the basement. Don't kidnappers hide their victims in the basement?"

"Wait for Fielding."

"But David could be down there."

Then a cavalcade of cars came quickly, but quietly, along the street. They parked in front of the house, along both sides of the street. The police tactical team poured out. Fielding, wearing a Cooks Regional Police vest, climbed out of the first car by the driveway and started moving his arms around, probably giving orders to the others. Some headed for the back. They had their guns pointed forward and all wore helmets and vests. Fielding raised his hand in a "wait" signal and strode down the driveway and over to Bast's car.

"Now, I want you two to stay put here while we go inside."

We both nodded, but as soon as Fielding left and the police started moving inside, Bast and I looked at each other. Without a word we exited the car. Once we couldn't see any of the officers outside, we quickly ran onto the Fontaine property.

Chapter Forty-one

Dusk, Tuesday, August 18, 1998

Him:

He felt like the director of a play trying to get them into position. Jessie balked at stripping but after a few swigs of red wine and a few points of the knife at her throat, she had at least stopped denying who she was. He smiled at her. She smiled back. He steered her towards the top of the stairs.

"Stay there, sweet Jessie and keep drinking," he said, handing her the bottle.

She just continued smiling at him. Her eyes were glazed. Good.

He went to his bedroom where he had dragged the boy up from the basement while Jessie drank. The boy had not said anything, didn't even cry. Good. He was obeying him. Now he looked at the boy and said, "Okay, your turn now." The boy still didn't talk and followed him into the corridor.

"Stand over there." He pointed to the end of the hall away from the stairway exit where Jessie now leaned against the wall. The boy did as he was told. "Face me; don't look out the window. Look down the hall at Jessie. Now when she starts dancing and removing her clothes, you run down towards her. AND YOU PUSH HER DOWN THE STAIRS."

The boy said nothing, just stared at him.

He looked over at Jessie. She was out of it. He moved halfway toward her and then gave her his orders.

"Okay, Jessie start dancing; start removing your clothes."

He stood back against the wall, looking at Jessie and the boy. He had to get it right this time. He hoped he had the right boy, even though the kidnapping circumstances were slightly different than the first two. He looked at Jessie who had started to dance in a circle, wiggling her hips, the bottle still in her hand. No that wasn't right.

"Jessie, put the bottle down," he said.

She kept dancing.

"Jessie."

She smiled, gyrated back to the wall, slithered down, and placed the bottle beside her on the floor, almost losing her balance as she tried to slide up.

"Oopsie," she said, grabbing the top of the banister. Standing, she began gyrating and fiddled with the top button on her halter top.

He turned towards the boy and whispered, "Now."

The boy didn't move.

"Now." He pulled the knife from his backpack on the floor and pointed it at the boy. "I don't want to have to use this."

The boy charged forward and he followed right behind. He had to save his sister and punish himself and his sister. As the boy neared Jessie, he reached out with his free hand to grab him to push him down the stairs.

"Cameron Fontaine. Police. Stop. Put the knife down."

The British voice reverberated in his ears and the room seemed to swirl. Jessie's face leered at him and the boy—where was the boy? He tripped but stopped himself. No that wasn't right. The boy was supposed to fall—he had to be punished for killing his sister. No that wasn't right. ***He*** *had killed his sister and* ***he*** *had to be punished. Wait. The thoughts and pictures—mother with a whisky bottle in her hand, Jessie stripping, Jessie in sweats holding a paddle over him—whirled around. He clutched the banister and felt his legs wobble as hands grabbed him from behind, knocked something out of his hand and moved his hands behind him. He heard something snap and feet rushing past and words shouting at him.*

"Cameron Fontaine you are under arrest for the murder of Johnny Corvette and Aaron King and the kidnapping of ..."

He didn't hear the rest as he blacked out.

Chapter Forty-two

Dusk and after, Tuesday, August 18, 1998

Dana:

I dug my fingernails into Bast's arm as we stood at the bottom of the Fontaine veranda. At the top, Constable Ryan stepped out from behind an old two-seater swing and glared at us. From inside, Fielding's voice shouting "Cameron Fontaine" and the rush of police had me lunging up the veranda stairs. Ryan grabbed my arm but after I pretended to go limp, removed his hand. I dodged around him to the door and opened it. As I stepped in, hands grabbed me from behind and steered me back outside.

"Let go of me. I have to get my son." I swung around. Bast held onto my arm and Ryan stood scowling beside him.

"Take it easy, Dana. The police will take care of it."

"For Christ's sake Bast, he's my son."

"And my nephew. Look. We don't know what's happening inside. But there are enough police to do what they have to."

"Yeah, like cart out David's dead body." I tried to yank free, but Bast held on tightly. From the corner of my eye I saw Ryan take out his handcuffs. "You, Mr. Cop over there. Are you planning to arrest me for trying to save my son?"

"Dana, please." Bast turned to the constable. "My sister is upset. Don't make it worse."

As Bast led me down the veranda stairs, I continued twisting and turning. Had they been able to save David? What about Jimmie? David *had* to be alive and so did Jimmie.

The front door opened and Bast and I stepped away from the veranda. He lightened his hold on my arm but this time I couldn't move. Two uniforms dragged out a young man. He moved as if his feet were paralyzed and his blond hair hung over his lowered face.

"Wait," Bast said. He removed his fingers and walked over to the trio. "Lift his head please." They complied. "Yes, that's the young man who bumped into Debbie Sangwell and me at the Mini-Mall when Jimmie Halpern was kidnapped."

I moved a little closer.

David. What about David?

I didn't realize I had spoken aloud until one of the uniforms said, "Wait for Fielding."

The two resumed dragging Fontaine towards a police cruiser. As they passed by, the blond man raised his head and turned towards me. His eyes were vacant. But I recognized him. And felt my breath stop and start up again fast, too fast.

It was the young man at our agency opening who had stared at the utility knife. The knife that had killed Debbie Sangwell.

The door opened again and another uniform came out with a boy. Fielding followed.

"But that's not David," I said. "Where's David?" I ran towards the front door. Fielding blocked my way. "Dana, you don't want to go in there."

"Why? Did that bastard kill David?"

Fielding's answer was drowned by approaching sirens. We both swung around. Two paramedics climbed from an ambulance, hauled out a gurney from the back and hurried inside the house. I was right behind but large hands stopped me.

"David? No. Let go. I have to go in and get to David."

Fielding tightened his arms around me. "Sh. David's not in there. A woman fell and bumped her head on the floor at the top of the stairs. Fortunately, Jimmie Halpern stopped her from falling down the stairs."

"Oh." My heart dropped below my stomach.

The front doors opened again and Fielding steered me out of the way. A young woman with blond hair and cuts to her face lay on the gurney. She moaned softly. She looked familiar, so I leaned closer.

"That's Cherry Robinson," I said. "What's she doing here?"

Later, at police headquarters, where we all had to give statements and answer questions, I found out that not long after he left The Attic Agency, Ken Robinson had reported his wife missing from the Mini-Mall. He'd dropped her off; she'd gone inside and hadn't come back out. He had told police once she was on a mission she was never distracted. She needed floor polish to finish her housecleaning. I told Fielding that tallied with what Robinson had told us when he left our agency and that generated more questions.

Fontaine had spilled all his beans if that's what you would call his ramblings about his sister's triple behaviour. Fielding let Bast and I observe the interview through the obligatory two-way glass. No doubt he'd broken a few rules there. Round and round went Fielding's questions and Fontaine's answers. Every time Fielding asked "What about David Bowman? Did you kidnap him from his home? Where is he?" Fontaine looked up at him and said. "I don't know what you're talking about."

"Did you kill Debbie Sangwell?" Fielding asked.

"What?"

Clearly Fontaine had a horrific childhood—no father present from before birth, single mother who was an alcoholic working as a prostitute to try to put food on the table for two children. She couldn't cope because she constantly yelled at them, mainly Jessie, calling Jessie "no better than she was—the daughter of a tart." Fontaine had shouted that part out loud and clear. It had made me recoil, and I was glad the glass separated us. Jessie was his half sister from an earlier liaison of his mother's. When mother died, Jessie took over her role, but she got mixed up, seeing herself as a mother, older sister, and tart.

"The fucking bitch was a whore, dancing around, taking her clothes off in front of me." Cameron was tearing at his hair when he said this. "Then she'd hit me on the bare backside with a hard wooden paddle, and then she ... she ... well, I'm glad she's dead ... down the stairs. Thump. Goodbye Jessie the tart. What a loud thump she made ... lying at the bottom of the stairs. Dead. Dead.

Good. Good." He started to bawl. "Jessie, I didn't mean it but I couldn't take any more ..."

"Did your sister sexually assault you, Cameron?" Fielding asked.

"What? What?"

"Where is David Bowman? We know you have him somewhere. Where is he?"

"I don't know. I didn't kidnap him; it wasn't me. Jesus, I can't do this anymore." He started banging his head on the table. The detective sitting quietly taking notes had to help Fielding restrain him. The two detectives led him out of the interview room.

"He's been sent to the psychiatric ward of Thurston General for assessment," Fielding said later as we sat in the police cafeteria drinking coffee and tea. "But now I'm sure he had nothing to do with David's kidnapping and Debbie's murder."

"Gee, too bad you didn't realize this sooner." I glared at Fielding but knew the onus was also on me.

"We'll find him," Fielding said.

"And we'll help."

"No, Dana," Fielding said. "Leave it to us."

Talking to Madge now rose to the top of the priority list.

Chapter Forty-three

Close to midnight, Tuesday, August. 18, 1998

Dana:

The door flew open at Madge's apartment. Ken Robinson shot out, knocking me down.

"You," he said as he helped me to my feet.

"Yeah, me. Why aren't you over at Thurston General visiting your injured wife?"

He stared, turned and ran. I shrugged and stepped inside.

"Madge? Aunt Doris? Ron?"

A rustling sound from Debbie's bedroom drew me to its closed door. Once inside, I found Madge and Aunt Doris tearing the room apart. Aunt Doris heaved clothes at random and Madge flipped through dresser drawers.

"What the hell is going on?" I asked. "And where's Ron?"

Both women stopped. Aunt Doris's face registered shock, Madge's pure terror.

"What was Dr. Robinson doing in here? Certainly not giving you a sedative, Madge."

"My baby, my baby." Madge started to whine. "I must find it. I must find it."

"Find what?" I asked. "Oh. If it's those first pills you're looking for, they're gone. I did find the empty bottle. Fielding has it now." I jumped back, raised hands in front to ward off Madge's attack, and leaned forward to grab her arms. "Take it easy."

"They say my baby was aborting."

"Your friend, Detective Sergeant Fielding paid us a visit last night," Aunt Doris said. "He showed us the doctor's report, what she died from, and asked us about those pills." She curled up her nose.

"Lies, lies," Madge said.

I put my arm around her shoulders. She pulled back.

"Not quite." I said.

"What do you mean by that, Dana?" Aunt Doris said.

My heart and pulse were in a fast race. "Let's go into the living room and sit down."

"I prefer to stand," said Aunt Doris.

"Me, too," said Madge.

"Very well. But let's go into the living room."

We trooped out of Debbie's room and into the living room. We stood like three suspicious warriors. I clenched my hands together, took a deep breath and plunged right in.

"We think Debbie was taking an illegal drug to make her abort. She also had to take a second drug, not illegal. We think you found this second drug, Madge, or at least some of it, and flushed it down the toilet just after you last talked to Debbie."

Madge grabbed the arm of the nearby chair and twisted herself into it. She leaned forward, head in hands. "Yes, at least I think I found it in your second floor bathroom, Dana. It was marked as Debbie's Tylenol Codeine prescription, but the pills had no Tylenol name on them and they were the wrong shape and colour. I think I put the empty container in my purse, meaning to ask Debbie later, but then ..." Madge put her hands to her face. Aunt Doris led her to the chesterfield and the two sat down. I remained standing.

"Is it still there, Madge?" I asked.

"What?"

"Oh, leave her alone, Dana," Aunt Doris said.

"The bottle, Madge, is it still in your purse?"

"Here, look." She dumped the purse's contents on the floor.

No pill bottle. And a quick rummage through the pile didn't find it or a prescription label.

"Wait a minute," Madge said. "That English detective looked through my purse the first time he was here."

Fielding, you bastard. After all the kerfuffle about bottle number one, he knew all the time.

"That Dr. Robinson asked the same question," Aunt Doris said.

"What?"

"That doctor, you must have met him outside. He left just as you came."

"Did he take anything?"

"No," said Aunt Doris. "I got tired of his badgering, so I told him to leave because Detective Sergeant Fielding was due here any minute."

"Oh, and is he?"

"Not that I know of," replied Aunt Doris. "But Ron will be—he went out for a walk."

"My baby, my baby is dead, thanks to those pills," said Madge. She began crying.

"Madge, she was murdered," I said.

Madge's sobs rose to heaves. She started thrashing around on the chair. My feet seemed to become a permanent floor attachment. I tried to speak but only managed a squeak. Aunt Doris helped Madge up and led her to her bedroom. My body still remained in the same spot.

In my mind, David whirled into view, spinning around, and with each turn grew smaller until he curled into foetus size. Blood flowed from his tiny body. I pitched over, knocking my face on the hardwood floor, then looked up and saw Madge's furniture, the drapes and the soundless TV picture. A continuous rapping seemed to bounce off the wall behind me. I staggered into an upright position and tried to stop my arms from shaking. The rapping continued and I realized it was the apartment door, so stumbled over and pulled it open, leaning against it for support.

Detective Harker stood in the hallway. He wore his nastiest face.

I started blathering about Robinson bothering Madge and reached the pill bottle when I stopped and put a hand up to my mouth.

"What pill bottle?" Harker asked. "Here, I better come in." He took out his notepad. "Okay, start talking." He looked up and grimaced.

"Don't you cops speak to each other?"

"What? Look here. I'm the one asking the questions."

"Don't pull rank on me. Anyway, Bast and I already told Fielding and *he* has the pill bottle." Without explaining which bottle, I swung around and stomped into the hallway.

I didn't remember driving home, but remembered sitting at the kitchen table, burying my face in my hands. Someone must have transferred me to the bed because I lay flat, gazing up at the ceiling. My thoughts registered zero and my eyes remained open, staring into nothingness.

Chapter Forty-four

Just before dawn, Wednesday, August 19, 1998

Bast:

Bast sat at his office desk. After getting Dana settled in her bed, he couldn't sleep, so made an early start to the day, carrying coffee to his desk. Now his eyes glared at the computer screen. He was certain that Oliver's e-mail message half an hour ago was key to Debbie's death and David's kidnapping. He had also finally found the draft of his story on the Donnelier court case. Both confirmed Ken Robinson was a shareholder in Donnelier. The former also cleared up the matter of L.M. Cole's identity. From there it wasn't a stretch about Cherry Robinson either. Dana was right. Cherry did look like someone else they knew—L.M. Cole.

So where did all this get them? He had sure been wrong about Cameron Fontaine. True, two more deaths were averted but not Debbie's and what about David? More and more he thought Debbie was dead not just because of seeing David's kidnapping, but because of what she knew about Sprinkle, and David had seen someone or something he shouldn't have.

He scratched his head. The sweat started creeping in at the roots of his hair and beard.

It all seemed to come down to Dr. Robinson, Sprinkle and that Donnelier Company. He re-read Oliver's e-mail. He should compare notes with Dana but not now. She was in no shape. Maybe he should call Fielding about L.M. Cole. Or maybe not. He didn't want to get Oliver in trouble. He would think about it. The picture of his sister lying catatonic on her bed upstairs convinced him he had to do something now. He jumped up, not bothering to close the e-mail and the story draft, and headed for the hospital.

He hoped he would beat Fielding there.

Chapter Forty-five

Early Wednesday morning, August. 19, 1998

David:

David was scared. He was all alone. Where was everybody? It was *too* quiet.

"I want to go home." He said in his head. "Mother" hadn't been in his room for a long time. "Rude Man" had shown up ages ago with a hot dog and chips and taken him to the bathroom. He had pushed him towards his bed and put the tape back on his ankles and wrists. It was too tight. After his usual "keep quiet or I'll tape your mouth," "Rude Man" had left, but without the dirty plate. The smell of it was making him feel sick.

Funny, he was now calling this basement room "his room." With all those footsteps up and down the stairs he knew he was in a basement. It smelled damp, like the basement at home, except he could smell something else, like something rotting. Like a dead raccoon. Was there a dead racoon here in the room? The dead racoon he'd found under the tree? He suddenly felt sicker. No, the police took that racoon away.

What was that? Was that footsteps coming down the stairs? He held his breath. Maybe it was "Mother."

The door opened and a light shone on him. He blinked and closed his eyes. If he didn't see it, maybe it would go away.

"There you are little boy. It's about time we moved you out of here." The person grabbed his shoulders from behind and he flinched. He couldn't help it. "Hold still you little nuisance while I get this on you." He felt something go around his head and cover his eyes—tight. It hurt.

This wasn't "Mother" or "Rude Man." This was a big bad monster. He wanted to scream, especially when he felt the tape tugged off his ankles. But he remembered "Rude Man's" threats and stopped in time.

Despite the raspy whisper, David was sure it was one of Mommy's friends. As the monster dragged him out the door, he tried really really hard to remember which friend.

Chapter Forty-six

Early Wednesday morning, August 19, 1998

Dana:

The ringing jolted me up. At first, I felt disoriented until I saw a pale face staring back from the mirror. My face. It was suddenly quiet, too quiet.

"Bast," I called out.

More silence and then the damn ringing started up again. It seemed to come from the table beside the bed. After it went through another stop-start cycle, I reached across the bed and picked up the cell phone.

"Hello."

"D ... D ... Dana, you sound a little far away. Are you okay?"

"Fielding? Just a little tired."

"Is your brother there? I just missed his call. He left a message to call him back. Do you know what he wanted?"

"Maybe."

"Maybe? Are you all right?"

"Yes. Just waking up actually." I tried to get up, but my legs wouldn't move. "Oh, Bast. Let me check and see if he's still here. Hold on a sec."

Like a snake shaking itself out of its skin, my body crawled out of bed. Feet touching the ground, I became human again, but seemed to regress to a toddler wobbling towards the door. I stuck my head out and called "Bast."

Silence. I held onto the wall and tottered towards the attic stairway.

"Bast, are you up there?" I called, first up the stairs inside, and then down.

Silence. A window rattled downstairs. The rest of the house remained still. I staggered back to the bedroom, sat on the edge of the bed and grabbed the cell.

"Only me and the wind blowing here, Fielding."

"D ... D ... Dana, stay put. I'm sending a uniform over right away. Not Marsden, but ..."

"Why not Marsden?"

"Because he's ... shall we say on an extended leave? So Steadman is coming. Don't let anyone else in. Don't let Harker in. Understood?"

"Yes, but why Harker?" Dead air. "Right, Fielding, hang up on me." I dropped the phone on the bed, jumped up and went flying across the floor, landing at the window. Pushing the drapes aside, I peered outside but saw nothing but a sedate backyard. Then a creaking sound—the elevator descended from above. Bast had said something about Trillium coming to fix the elevator, but who let him in?

I wobbled down the stairs like a drunken tortoise. The sound of the elevator stopping and the doors opening reverberated from the hall on the main floor. By the time this tortoise stumbled downstairs, the hall was empty. The hare had descended down an invisible hole. The kitchen also revealed no one, but the back door stood open. After closing it, I took the stairs down to the basement.

The laundry room was cleaner than the night David went missing. But the boarded-up window and my sketches pushed out of the way into a corner gave me no comfort. I returned to the kitchen and checked the dining room and living room.

No one. Quieter and emptier than a graveyard.

The elevator deposited me back on the second floor. In the spare room, Aunt Doris's rosary graced the bedside lamp. When I flung the closet door open, *something soft hit my face*. I jumped back.

One of Aunt Doris's housedresses dangled from the clothes rack.

Next room was David's. Breathing hard, I slid the door open and, with eyes scrunched tight, stepped in. Blinking, I willed my eyes open. A jumble of clothes, toys, furniture and more silence filled the room. A cold wave zapped through me from head to toe, but surprisingly it kick-started me out of this legarthy. I ran out the door, across the hall, up the attic stairwell and stumbled into Bast's room. The covers were piled at the bottom of his single bed. My usually tidy brother had left a pair of shorts and a T-shirt sprawled on the bed.

Silence also filled this room. That didn't seem right. My eyes glanced round the walls, past the shelves of books, the closet door and over to the alarm keypad beside the hall doorway.

Why wasn't the alarm turned on?

I charged towards the office. The door stood open, and I followed the light coming from inside to Bast's computer screen. Two files were open and I began reading the e-mail message and the story by-lined *Sebastian Overture.* This must be the missing unpublished draft.

But it was the e-mail from Oliver that seemed to drain the blood from my head. I now knew exactly who owned Donnelier and who paid Lambton the money in that bar. More pieces started churning into place. Taking a deep breath, I flew from the office and down to my room. Grabbing my sketch pad, I flipped pages back to that oddball shoe I'd drawn in the Mini-Mall the day Jimmie was kidnapped. I tore it off, folded it and shoved it inside my purse, followed by the cell, and pulled on jeans, T-shirt and runners, then headed towards the elevator. When I reached the main floor, the front door buzzer sounded, so I dashed out the side.

It took me less than a minute to get in the car and drive off. Next stop was the Mini-Mall.

Chapter Forty-seven

A few minutes later, Wednesday, August 19, 1998

Dana:

Chalmers Shoe Store appeared empty of customers and staff as I stood in front of the window and stared.

No two-tone runners—just the usual monotone ones. Ray must have goofed that one time last week.

Inside the store there was no sign of Ray or his clerk. No two-tone shoes displayed inside the store or in the backroom. There, I rifled through the extra stock, and after a few boxes of monotone runners, hit two colour combos—navy and grey, red and pink. The big catch was what fell out when my fingers pulled the tissue paper—a plastic bag filled with tiny pills—RU-486. But no signs of Misoprosto, the second anti-abortion pill.

"So that's it," I muttered. I interrupted their sketch search downstairs.

"What are you looking for?"

I swung around. Ray Chalmers faced me. His right hand held a gun but his face resembled white sugar.

"Look, Ray, you better tell me ..."

"None of your business." He waved the gun around causing my heartbeat to accelerate.

"Ray, what if a customer came in, no, what if Lois came in?"

"She won't. She's ... well, she's away."

"Away where?" When I moved closer, the gun zipped across my chest. "Hey, take it easy, Ray." I leaned back and raised my arms. "I don't mean you any harm. I just want my son back."

He stopped waving the gun around and appeared to digest my words. I didn't give him a chance to spew out his conclusion but lunged forward, grabbed his right arm and shook it hard. Ray's hand clamped tighter on the gun. I shoved him and he toppled over backwards. The gun stuck to his hand and he pointed it up at me. His fingers twitched as I reached for a box of shoes and threw it at his right hand. The gun flew out of sight. Squatting down, I grasped Ray's shoulders and shook him.

"I need some answers, Ray Chalmers."

He stared up at me, his eyes locked on mine as if afraid that looking away would bring disaster.

Got you, Ray Chalmers.

"Talk," I said.

When he finished singing, I flew out the door.

"Hey, young lady, watch where you're going," greeted me as I zigzagged through the mall.

"Sorry, my son, my son." I panted, and my heart prepared for the Indianapolis.

"Dana, slow down."

Arms grabbed me and I came to a sudden halt. Aunt Doris glared at me.

"Dana, your manners," she said.

"No time for manners. David ..."

Aunt Doris strengthened her hold and pointed a finger. "Dana, this has to stop. All this rushing around with no consideration for anyone else. After all, you are a mother ..."

"That's why I'm rushing, you old biddy."

"Well, I never ..." She thrust her gargoyle face closer.

"Aunt Doris, you will never forgive yourself if you don't let me go. David is in trouble and if I don't get there he'll be dead."

She let go. I turned and started to run. Footsteps followed behind.

"Dana, gasp, have mercy on an old woman," Aunt Doris said. I stopped and turned around. She chugged up to me, waving a shopping bag at me. "I'm going with you."

"No, you're not. This is dangerous."

"Why isn't your brother here to do all these dangerous things? Because he's queer and yellow."

"Stuff it, Aunt Doris. Bast is ... oh never mind. If you want to come along, fine." I gripped her arm and attempted to steer her forward. She clunked behind, trying to keep up with my gallop. I unlocked the car doors, climbed in, turned the key and started to roll.

"Mercy, Dana, let me get settled," Aunt Doris said.

I glanced to my right. She was seated but the door stood open and her bag was caught on its handle.

"Hurry up."

"I'm 71. I can't move as fast as you young people."

"Well, do your best. David's life hangs on it."

"Wait. My bag. I got Madge some Pepto-Bismol. She's not feeling well." She managed to yank the bag in and tried to close the door.

I was already careening out of the parking lot, but hit the brakes, sending us both forward a little. We sped along Main Street, cutting the corner at Carstairs. Aunt Doris groaned. I pulled up in front of a two-storey house and slammed on the brakes. Aunt Doris screamed.

"Shut up." Leaning in front of her, I opened the glove compartment and hauled out pliers, tweezers, a couple of hairpins, wire clippers, small flashlight and latex gloves.

"Dana, what are you going to do?"

"Aunt Doris, you really don't want to know. Now, if I'm not back in 20 minutes I want you to call Fielding on the cell phone. His number is 905-845-7020. Here use my cell; it's in my bag."

Aunt Doris struggled to open the bag.

"Here." I dumped out its contents. The cell phone hit Aunt Doris on the right knee.

"Ouch." She cringed and picked it up.

I grabbed my purse, threw my tools and other stuff in, and slid out of the car. "Twenty minutes, Aunt Doris; and don't leave the car."

Heading for the backyard, I ran to the back fence, threw my bag into the adjoining backyard, banged my way up and over the fence, then grabbed the bag and charged to the rear patio.

This time at the Robinsons I didn't check any further than the driveway for owner occupancy. No car—green or any colour—in sight. What the house held was of more imminent concern. I pulled on the gloves and picked the door's lock with a hairpin. It opened too easily, for I faced a chain that would restrain even Arnold Schwarzenegger. After a few scary minutes of taking wire clippers to the chain, I tripped into the kitchen, the adrenaline running like sweet honey, fast turning to bitter bile.

The silence stopped me short.

"David." Then "David, David," raising the crescendo with each calling.

Only silence.

I charged into every room but found only emptiness. Downstairs in a dark basement room, a smell of stale food hit my nose. The ceiling light fixture held no bulb. The only light was a night light from the adjoining bathroom. I shone the flashlight around. A dirty dish sat on the floor beside a bed and on top of the bed lay a wad of duct tape. I began rummaging around under the thin bed cover, felt something and yanked it out.

One of David's socks. A sock he wore the night of the Agency's opening.

I crumpled to the cold floor, held the sock up to my lips and wept.

This wouldn't do. Wiping my face with the back of my hand, I stumbled up. Shoving sock and flashlight into the bag, I charged upstairs and flew out the back door. I took the driveway to the street. It was quicker.

There was still one more place to look.

Chapter Forty-eight

Early Morning, Wednesday, August 19, 1998

Bast:

Bast pushed open the main hospital door and rushed inside. A quick glance showed no Fielding in sight. After ascertaining which floor he wanted, he took the elevator up. On the third floor, he called the main desk from his cell. In his best British accent he said he was Detective Sergeant Donald Fielding and he wanted the officer stationed outside Cherry Robinson's room to meet him downstairs pronto. After she returned to the desk and the uniform entered the elevator, Bast popped into Cherry's room. She was talking on her cell and looked up.

"Got to go. Talk later." She closed the phone.

He introduced himself and said he hoped she was getting better. Then he got down to business.

"I want to talk to you about your family," Bast said.

"Family? There's just Ken and me. We have no children."

"It's the other generation I'm interested in."

"What do you mean?" Cherry inched her body to the far side of the bed.

"I think you do." Bast leaned towards her as Cherry pulled the pillow in front of her chest. "I'm talking about your parents—Ray Chalmers who owns Chalmers Shoe Store and Lois Chalmers, owner of The Fashion Shoppe, president of the Mini-Mall Merchants Association and aka L.M. Cole. Her maiden name, I presume."

Cherry pulled the pillow up higher.

"Hiding won't help," Bast said.

"Better listen," a British voice said from behind him.

Bast swung around. Damn. Fielding already. The two glared at each other. Fielding broke the silence.

"You got here first, so you continue the questioning."

Right, Fielding, so you can find out what I know and you don't. But he cleared his throat and pushed on.

"All right, Mrs. Robinson, isn't it true that your mother and your husband both own shares in Donnelier?"

Silence.

"And isn't it also true that Donnelier owns Sprinkle—the Toronto-based pharmacy and the Sonbaker Medical Centre. And ..."

"And you and your husband have a boat *The CK Rob* anchored at Snow Lake harbour?" Fielding butted in.

Bast flinched but swallowed hard. Answers, not anger, might save David.

"What do you want to bet if we search it we find a stash of anti-abortion pills, RU-486 specifically?" Fielding said. "A sort of combination holding point and transport after they got through customs and before they arrived at Sonbaker. Perhaps with some Chalmers's merchandise?" He smiled.

"You need a warrant for that," Cherry said.

"As we speak." Fielding pulled a paper from his jacket pocket and waved it in front of her.

So Fielding had been on the ball. Bast frowned.

"And while we speak," Fielding was saying, "tell me what you know about the kidnapping of David Bowman?"

"Nothing," Cherry said. "Ken and I were away then. We didn't come back until the next morning. I already told that other detective, Harker, I think his name is, all that."

"Mrs. Robinson I don't think so." Fielding leaned forward. "One of you was away all right ... on your boat. And the other one was breaking into the basement of Dana Bowman's home—again, the night of the Attic Agency Opening. What was so important in that basement that you would risk another B and E?"

"Nothing."

"It was some of my sister's sketches, wasn't it?" Bast asked. "Dana caught something about your little operation, didn't she?

What was it? Pills? Shoes? Shoes, that's it." He turned to Fielding. "Dana was always sketching the shoes in Chalmers's store."

"No," Cherry said.

"I don't think so," Fielding said, clearly trying to grab hold of the interview. "I saw some of Dana's shoe sketches. And we've done some checking of Chalmers's recent imports of running shoes, particularly from China. The loading point is close to the factory in China that manufactures shoes carried by Chalmers, but the building next door is a pharmaceutical company specializing in birth control pills and morning after pills like RU-486, which aren't legal in Canada."

"Oh," Cherry said.

But Fielding was already on his cell, giving instructions. Then he turned to Cherry. "Did you or your husband break into Dana Bowman's home last Friday evening and kidnap David Bowman?"

"I told you ... Ken and I were away for a few days."

"On your boat?" Fielding asked. "One of you was on that boat, but the other one was in Dana Bowman's basement." Fielding turned to Bast. "You said you saw someone wearing a baseball cap in that stolen car driving down the street. Women wear baseball caps too."

Bast nodded.

"So what?" Cherry pulled the pillow up tighter.

"Where did you take David?" Fielding asked.

"You're nuts," Cherry said. "First, you accuse Ken and me of hiding drugs on our boat, then kidnapping David."

"Where did you take David?" Bast jumped in.

"You're both nuts."

Bast was incensed at the woman. He moved closer to her so that he was almost in her face "This is my nephew; where did you and Ken take him?" He reached out as if to shake her.

"Overture, that's enough," Fielding said.

Bast moved back but continued glaring at Cherry as Fielding took over.

"Was it you or your husband or your mother or father or perhaps your boyfriend who killed Debbie Sangwell? Think carefully, Mrs. Robinson; if you are the first to tell, it may go easier on you."

Cherry remained quiet but glanced at her cell phone.

"You got some information by phone just as I came in," Bast asked. "Was that your mother or your husband and what did they say?"

"No, it was Dad." Cherry smirked.

Fielding leaned towards her. "And what did he say."

"Just some family business."

"What family business?" Fielding asked. "You better tell me."

"Better listen to him," Bast said.

"Why? Am I under arrest? I haven't done anything."

"Try kidnapping David Bowman, for starters," Fielding said.

"What? I mean we were away."

"Right," Fielding said. "On your boat."

"Better answer him," Bast said. "I think, you or your husband came back to finish off Ray's and your husband's first break-in at our place. You didn't get what you wanted when Dana interrupted your first attempt."

"That's ridiculous." Cherry snorted at him.

"Better talk," Fielding said. "Or I'll have to arrest you for murder and kidnapping."

"No." Cherry sounded scared. "Okay, I broke into your place the night of the reception." She looked at Bast. "But I didn't kill anybody."

"But you kidnapped David," Bast said.

"Oh, all right. But it wasn't planned. He interrupted me and he knew me as the lady from across the street, when he was outside playing with his friends."

"Who called you just now when I came in?" he asked.

"I told you, my dad."

"I don't think so." Bast glared at her.

"Okay, a friend called."

"Would that friend, be your boyfriend, Detective Paul Harker?" Fielding asked.

Bast gulped.

Cherry nodded. When Fielding arrested her and cuffed her to the bed, she started squirming.

"Hey take it easy, cop. It's me who made sure David got fed and took him to the bathroom. And don't forget it's thanks to me David isn't dead ... yet. I don't hold with killing kids."

"You should've thought of that when you kidnapped David," Fielding said.

"You should think of that now instead of arresting me."

"And you should think of telling us what you haven't so far."

"Lawyer." Cherry Robinson clamped her lips shut.

The wandering constable returned and cringed when he saw Fielding. Bast thought the constable would get the third degree like Marsden. But Fielding's cell rang.

"Yes, Steadman ... I see. Stay put in case she returns." He closed his cell and turned towards Bast. "Dana is missing; she wasn't at home when Steadman arrived." Fielding's face appeared ashen. They both leaned towards Cherry.

"Tell us what Detective Harker told you," they both said.

"And none of that lawyer business," Bast added.

She told them.

Fielding looked at the constable.

"Don't let her out of your sight," he said. "She's under arrest."

Bast and Fielding rushed out. In the parking lot a van blocked their exit. Bast swallowed saliva and bit his bottom lip. Two men stepped out of the van, one carrying a camera on his shoulder.

The duo came closer. Bast looked over into the grinning face of Charles Haas.

Chapter Forty-nine

Mid-morning, Wednesday, August 19, 1998

Dana:

Back in the car, Aunt Doris chided me.

"I was just going to call the police," she said. "Whatever is going on?"

"We're trying to get to David before it's too late," I replied as I raced the car through Thurston. When veering onto Snow Lake Road, Aunt Doris lit into me.

"Dana, for the love of God, slow down. We're not going to help David by killing ourselves first."

"Listen, you old biddy, I'm driving. Do you want to drive? Here, you take the wheel." I removed my hands for a few seconds from the steering wheel and Aunt Doris shrieked.

"Christ," I said, under my breath.

"Young lady, don't you swear."

I shrugged. Grabbing the wheel, I sucked in air, swerved the car back into the lane, and turned to Aunt Doris.

"Did you call Fielding on my cell phone?"

"What? No, I forgot the number. Dana, what's the number?"

"It's 905-845-7020. Tell Fielding to meet us at the dock near his sailboat and it's an emergency."

She continued muttering but I tuned her out, my mind on David.

"There, I've just dialled 911," Aunt Doris said. "Now what do I tell them?"

"Oh, for Christ's sake." The car swerved left and Aunt Doris shrieked. I tightened my hold on the steering wheel, righted the car's direction, but kept the fast pace. "Oh, all right, but make sure you tell them to give Detective Sergeant Donald Fielding the message. Tell them it's the Bowman kidnapping case and we have a big lead and we're at the dock on Snow Lake."

Somehow she managed and had about finished when we swung onto the road by the dock. When turning in to park, I saw a figure drag a small boy with blond hair onto a large yacht. *David.* The figure wore baggy pants, a sweatshirt and the head was bent down to the boy, hiding the person's face. But I had a good idea who.

"Change that message. They've got David on a boat leaving the dock."

I slammed the car to a halt, sending both of us flying forward. I banged my head on the edge of the steering wheel, ignored the forehead pain, pushed the door open and staggered out.

"Stay put and wait until Fielding gets here. Aunt Doris. I'm going after David."

"Who? What?"

I pointed to Snow Lake. The boat was now a small box swirling water. I slammed the car door and ran to the dock. As I climbed aboard Fielding's sailboat, thankful that he'd returned it here, I prayed the motor would start. Remembering Fielding's instructions, I pulled on a lifejacket and yanked at the motor handle. It sputtered for a million seconds; then switched into full gear. Grabbing the wheel, I tried to back *The Feverfew* out of the harbour.

The boat carrying David was nowhere in sight

.

Chapter Fifty

A few minutes later in the morning, Wednesday, August 19, 1998

Bast:

"Now Mr. Overture, I just need to know where you and the Detective Sergeant are heading." Haas curled his lower lip.

Bast flinched at his voice. How could he have ever trusted, let alone had feelings for this man?

"Come on Bast. Or do you want me to tell the Detective Sergeant what you were up to last year in Toronto?"

"Me? Don't you mean 'you?' "

"I wasn't drunk when interviewing that rape victim."

"But you got me drunk after that party ... You ..."

"And you cost me my job."

"That's enough." Fielding barged over to Haas. "Kill it. You want a story? You'll have to wait like the rest of the press." He lurched at the cameraman and grabbed the video camera. "Turn it off and if you play one part of this, I'll arrest you and Haas for obstructing police. Now move that van."

Haas shrugged. He and the cameraman climbed inside. Haas started the van and rolled down the window.

"Bast, I'm not done with you yet." He backed up and drove out of the parking lot.

Bast stood stunned.

"I can only guess at what caused the bad blood between you and Haas, but we have to get going."

Bast nodded. They hurried into Fielding's car. Fielding hit the siren as they turned onto Main Street.

Bast hoped they would make it in time for David and Dana.

Chapter Fifty-one

A few minutes later, Wednesday, August 19, 1998

Dana:

I tried to steer the boat faster. The sun beat into my eyes and the beginning of a tension headache crept across my forehead. The wind picked up speed and *The Feverfew* began to rock. Faint voices seemed to come from the right, so I turned.

A large sailboat blocked my way. The six or seven people on it were waving arms and moving their mouths. "Look out ... stupid" carried through the wind. I turned the wheel left and *The Feverfew* swerved left in a spiral of water, spraying a good part of it on me.

"Damn." I shielded my eyes and peered ahead. A swirling speck blinked about 90 degrees ahead. I gassed the boat, causing it to lurch forward into fast gear. Maybe God took care of fools after all.

"Just get me to my son in time, and I'll ... I'll quit swearing," I said to the sky.

I was gaining on the speck, and could now see it was a fair-sized yacht, larger than Fielding's boat. The boat contained two figures, one smaller. The name on the side read "*The CK Rob*."

Cherry and Ken Robinson.

The motor sounds quietened and I thought *The Feverfew* was in trouble. But *The CK Rob* had come to a halt, and the adult in sweats was bent over, back to me and yanking on the gas pull. I slowed Fielding's boat down and tried to cruise forward, gasping for air. Now I could make out a light blue t-shirt on the smaller person. Then blond hair. He turned his head around.

David for sure.

The adult on *The C K Rob* grabbed David and threw him into the water.

I shook into spasms. *The Feverfew* swerved right and left as it picked up speed. Nearing David's entry into the water, I shut off the gas, held my breath and dived in.

The swimming lessons seemed gone as the nightmare took centre stage inside. The lifejacket kept me bobbing but was a dead weight with any movement. Every two seconds I held my breath and poked my head underwater. Just when I thought David was in sight, he vanished. I shook my head above water hoping that would shake some reality into it. Then I dived under.

David's feet and legs appeared at nose level. I grabbed his legs and pushed him up. If I could get us to *The Feverfew*, he might be okay.

I sensed rather than saw the edge of a boat. When two hands reached out I did the natural, grabbed hold of them. The hands pulled us up. Once on the boat I rolled David onto his back and began applying CPR until he opened his eyes and began spitting out lake water. The two hands held a blanket, which I wrapped over David.

"Very touching," a voice said.

I looked up. Lois Chalmers towered above us. Her right hand held a gun and her face displayed a "don't mess with me" sneer.

Chapter Fifty-two

A little later, Wednesday morning, August 19, 1998

Bast:

Fielding was on the blower as they drove, requesting the marine division meet them at Snow Lake Harbour. Bast's mind churned back over the interview with Cherry Robinson. There must be something they had missed ... he had missed.

Harker.

Bast turned to Fielding. "You said something back at the hospital about Harker being Cherry's boyfriend. Do you think he killed Debbie? Maybe to protect Cherry because she kidnapped David. Fielding that doesn't make sense. He wasn't at the Agency opening until after the kidnapping and murder."

Fielding concentrated on his driving.

"Fielding."

"I heard. No, I don't think Harker killed Debbie. It's David I'm concerned with."

"You think he's going to kill David?"

"Maybe."

"But Cherry Robinson said ..."

"Mrs. Robinson said a lot and didn't say a lot and much of it was lies. She might be protecting her boyfriend. Harker has a mixed police record—two reprimands and one suspension for using too much force making arrests."

Bast didn't like the sound of that. Harker hadn't exactly been nice to David at the mall after Jimmie was kidnapped. He shivered and turned to Fielding.

"Can't you drive faster?"

"We are almost there Overture." He drove the car right onto the dock and cut the engine. "And it looks like the marine unit is already here and ready to roll."

The two dashed out of the car. An officer wearing a police marine jacket sat in the boat and a man in jeans, T-shirt, cap and sunglasses stood on the dock. Bast hurried after Fielding towards them. As they neared the boat, the man removed his sunglasses.

Harker. Smirking. And pointing his regulation police gun at them.

Chapter Fifty-three

A few minutes later, Wednesday, August 19, 1998

Dana:

"Ray talked," I said. "So, I'd think twice before using that thing."

"My husband is a weak man." Lois didn't move the gun.

"Not like you, right? You killed Debbie because she saw David's kidnapping and Leila Smythe because she found out about your illegal drug operation." I swallowed saliva and continued. "Worst of all you tried to kill my son now because Cherry or Ken—I'm guessing Cherry because she's your daughter—brought David home after he saw her in our basement. Bet that didn't fit in with your grand money-making scheme, did it? Neither did Ken's little ransom fiasco. You had to wait to do anything with David because you wanted to tie it in with the serial killings of the other little boys. But you waited too long. Cameron Fitzgerald has been arrested and he didn't have David."

"But I do now." Lois sneered.

"Not for long if I can help it."

"And what are you going to do? I always admired your spunk. But you would stick your nose in where it doesn't belong and now you've just sealed it. An accident at sea, in the other boat, which you stole anyway. The boat hit a rock and you and your son were tossed into the lake."

"What rock?"

"Over there." Lois pointed with her empty hand and didn't follow with her eyes. She kept those fastened on David and me.

"If you ditch that boat against those rocks how will you get back? Your boat is out of gas." I tried to sneer back, but my lips quivered in time to the rest of my body.

"I have a spare container of gas."

"But you forgot to fill it up before you left. That's not the efficient Lois."

"No time, thanks to you." She seemed to point the gun a little harder at us and her sneer morphed into a snarl.

I held David tighter and cleared my throat.

"It was the money, wasn't it Lois?" I croaked.

"Of course. Ray is an expensive husband to keep and dangerous. Anyone who would mutilate and kill animals. Did you know he used to strangle kittens when he was a child?"

"No, but I suppose you think it is okay to kill a child."

She pointed the gun closer. I cringed.

"Put your hands behind your back." Lois bent over and pressed the gun against David's head. David, who had been quiet, started crying and shaking. I tried to stand up, but Lois shoved me down. The lifejacket cushioned my back, but my head bounced around and started to pound. The sun glared in my eyes.

"Don't move or he's dead, not fast like I planned, but slow and painful. And don't think I can't do it. I've seen Ray kill animals so I know how."

"David is not an animal, you stupid bitch."

"Don't you call me names, you little bitch. I'm the one in charge here." She removed the gun away from David's head and stood up.

I blinked and squinted past Lois. A boat appeared on the horizon. The police marine unit? Lois stopped, cocked her right ear, and turned her head a smidgeon. I took my chance and jumped up. The lifejacket felt like a dead weight as I aimed for her upper body, but only reached her legs. She pushed me back. Hard. I plopped down and tried to cover David with my body. The gun clicked. Shots were fired, followed by a thud.

My eyes had trouble opening and my head seemed glued to the floor. David was crying nearby and the boat seemed to have hit a storm. I passed out, then was jarred awake and made another try at opening my eyes, succeeding. After three tries, I sat up, rubbed my eyes and looked around.

A Cooks Regional marine boat swayed up against Lois's boat, and an officer appeared to be bent over in it. A groan sounded from behind and I turned around. Fielding crouched a few metres away. He appeared dazed and blood oozed from his forehead. No sign of Lois or David. I hobbled over to Fielding, crouched down and shook him.

"Fielding, wake up. Are you all right? Where's David? Lois? And where's your gun?" My hands trembled as Fielding opened his eyes and said one word.

"Harker."

"Where?" I shook him but he was out again.

"Over here."

I turned around. Harker towered over me. His Chalmers's running shoe touched my hand and he pointed his regulation gun down at me.

"Get up," he said.

I grabbed the side of the boat and tried to stand up. My head vibrated in pain with back and left side joining in aching harmony.

"This way." He motioned with his gun towards the boat's cabin. "You're a slippery little bitch, dodging out of your house."

"It was you I heard in there this morning. I suppose you let the elevator guy in or did you fix it yourself?"

"Shut up and move, bitch." He scrunched up his face.

I perched at the top of the stairs, grabbed the railing, peered down and gasped.

Lois Chalmers stood in the boat's tiny cabin. She still brandished her gun in one hand. With the other she clutched a sobbing David. Bast sat at the boat's table. His face looked mean and constrained.

"I'll give you the same advice I gave your brother," Lois said. "Don't move or David gets it."

"Lois, I thought we were dead anyway." My voice shook in tandem with my body.

"Change of plans. Harker informs me that Fielding arrested Cherry. So we're going to negotiate a trade—Cherry for David." She turned to Harker. "Where is Fielding anyway?"

"Out cold on the deck."

The bile crept up my oesophagus. My head seemed to pound harder and the pain seared into my left lung. The weight of the wet lifejacket further pinched my chest. Then I felt Harker's gun on my neck. I gasped in air. Bast looked up at me and moved his lips.

What the hell was he trying to say?

"Face this way, Bast," Lois said to him.

Bast jerked his head toward her but not before a quick glance at the gun lying on the floor at the bottom of the steps. *Fielding's gun.* So that was Bast's message.

"Lois, it might be easier if I came down the stairs. Harker can stay up to keep an eye on Fielding. He was starting to come to a few minutes ago. That way you can watch us better."

"All right. But no tricks." Lois waved the gun at Harker. "Go keep an eye on Fielding and when he wakes up bring him down here so we can do our little trade."

"But, Cherry," Harker began.

"I can negotiate for my daughter just fine," Lois said. "You've caused enough damage. Marriage-breaker." She muttered the last under her breath.

"Fine. I'll keep an eye on Fielding." Harker released the gun from my neck and his footsteps receded.

"All right, Dana," said Lois. "Come down those stairs slowly."

"Okay. No tricks. See, I'm even putting up my arms." I took two steps, slowly, sucking in air to ease the pain. But my back gave way and I lurched for the railing, almost toppling down the stairs. "Sorry. Head hurts."

I raised my right arm, kept the left hand attached to the railing and continued the slow trek with head down. At the bottom, I clasped the railing harder, sucked in all the pain and swung my right foot forward.

The gun flew in an angle from the floor. For what seemed like long minutes I watched it whack its mark, Lois's right knee. She lost her balance, sending David and her gun in opposite directions. I lunged towards David and from my peripherals saw Bast lunge towards Lois as she attempted the stairs. Halfway up, her right leg gave way. She grabbed the railing and lurched upward.

"Stop right there," an unsteady voice said from the stair-top. Fielding leaned over, his hands clutching Lois. Blood trickled from his forehead onto his shoes. To his left, two feet lying flat protruded. Harker. Fielding read Lois her rights and tried to handcuff her with one hand but Bast had to help. I swung around and struggled towards my son but my feet had difficulty following through.

"D ... D ... Dana, are you all right?"

"Sis, you okay?"

Footsteps galloped down the stairs. Bast tried to steady me, but I could only manage a weak, "David ..." and point. My head felt as if full of bricks being attacked by a blowtorch. I lurched forward into blackness.

Epilogue

Evening, Wednesday, August 19, 1998

Dana:

I sat in David's room, watching him sleep, unable to leave. If my eyes looked elsewhere, he would disappear. My head still hurt. Its dull ache accentuated the emptiness of my stomach.

"Hollow," I whispered.

"Pardon?"

I swung around and winced. Fielding stood in the doorway. Despite the bandage on his forehead, he looked like he had come through better than some of us.

"Just returning these." He dangled my black sling-backed shoes from his left hand. In his right, he held Beechnut. He tiptoed over to the bed and dropped David's stuffed beaver beside his head and the shoes on the floor. He turned around and looked at me.

"And ch ... ch ... checking to see h ... h ... how you two are doing."

"Oh, real great."

"You ... you ... you were pretty brave out there on the boat."

"Yeah, right. I almost got us killed dragging David onto the wrong boat."

"But ... but ... but th ... th ... thanks to you and B ... B ... your brother, we nailed Lois and a bad cop."

"Nailed Lois? Nailed a bad cop? Is that all you cops think of? Catching your man and woman?"

"No. The marine officer who was shot is alive."

"What about David? Look at him. Sure he's back, but he's been damaged."

I stood up and the room rotated, so crashed back into the chair and glared at Fielding. My head burned, but the firewood was hollow. Fielding stepped forward. He crouched down to my level, faced me, and put a hand on my right shoulder. I did not pull back.

"Of course your son is important," he said.

"And catching the murderer?"

Fielding's face turned red.

"Well, come on Fielding, that's true, isn't it?"

"D ... D ... Dana, yes it is."

"Okay, Don, let's be realistic. You got your crooks and I got my son back, so to speak. I'm thankful for that, but shouldn't I feel more? Instead I feel like someone ripped out my heart and left a big empty hollow inside."

"You're numb with shock."

"Yeah, well I don't want to be. I know I should feel happy or at least relieved, but I also know that David is really going to need me now, more than ever, but all I feel is hollow. Ah, shit, why am I telling you this?" I buried my face in my hands and sobbed. I felt arms go around me and leaned my head forward against strong shoulders. All I could murmur between sobs was "Why?"

"Because he's your flesh and blood and you will do anything to keep him intact." Fielding's hand brushed my hair. "When Sandra started to get into drugs at 14, I wanted to beat the shit out of her. It tore me up. So we moved out of Toronto. New school, new friends. Things improved. Then she turned 18, finished high school, went on to university and things have never been the same since. It's all part of being a parent."

"That's it." I sniffed. Fielding let go of me, stood up and handed me a tissue. I stood up also, blew, and wiped my eyes, but the tears continued. "I'm supposed to be a parent but I'm no better than Ron. Did you know that he's left town already? Can't even hang around to see how his son is doing."

"Well, some people are like that, irresponsible. He has to return in October for his trial."

"Maybe I'm that, too. I mean, what business do I have running around chasing criminals? Aunt Doris is right. I'm a lousy parent for it." I wiped my eyes. Fielding placed his right arm around my back.

"No, you d ... d ... did your best under the cir ... circumstances you had to work with."

"Yeah, and just about got my son killed in the process. And look at him now." I glanced at David, amazed that he could even sleep. "I should've figured it out the first night when Ray and Ken broke in. I mean I sat outside those damn stores in the mall and sketched those damn shoes. Why didn't I pick it up sooner? Debbie might still be alive; Madge might still be speaking to me. Did you know she's going up to Barrie with Aunt Doris to stay with her for awhile? But most importantly, and may Madge forgive me ... someday for this ... David would never have been kidnapped and he might still be a happy child."

"D ... Dana don't berate yourself. To answer your question about the sketches—because there was no reason to. It looked like part of the current string of B and Es with the racoon left dead."

"Why didn't I pick it up sooner?" I said, again. "I have no right to be in this business. Bast will have to carry on without me."

"I will do no such thing," Bast said from the doorway. "I just wanted to see how you and David are doing."

"Oh, just great, little brother." I stuck my arms out in front. "Almost got my son killed to catch a killer. Some mother? I think I'll resign as a PI. Maybe take some of those parenting courses. God knows I need something to improve my parenting skills."

"You give your son love," said Bast. "That's the most important thing."

"What do you know about love?" Fielding sneered at Bast.

"Probably a whole lot more than you."

I raised my hands. "Stop, for God's sake stop it. David is trying to sleep. Just leave us alone."

They both left the room. A few minutes later I heard the elevator start up, then stop, followed by Bast shouting "damn, elevator's on the fritz again."

I tuned it out and resumed my vigil, head in hands, contemplating my shortcomings. David stirred in his sleep, kicking my pity party to the back burner. I hurried over to David and touched his forehead.

David would need a lot of love and attention. Since his return, he had not spoken a word. Now he didn't even cry. Worst, he pushed away his beavers.

I only hoped he wouldn't push Bast and me away.

Acknowledgements

Thanks to:

Brent Pilkey for again coming through with information on the correct police procedure, especially in some of my wacky crime scenes. Any mistakes are my doing.

Jake Hogeterp for proofreading *Beyond Blood,* and fixing those pesky ellipses.

My book reviewers for being kind but fair to my first short story collection that led to this novel.

Toronto Public Library, and particularly branch librarians, Janet Nanos, Helen Flint, Susan Zadek (and all the Albert Campbell branch book club members), who let me in to read from my debut short story collection, *Beyond the Tripping Point.* Whether reading on my own or with the Crime Writers of Canada gang, it was fun, and a great opportunity to meet readers.

Aurora Public Library librarians, Reccia Mandelcorn and Bernadette Preyde, for going along with my crazy scheme of a Murder Comes to Aurora reading session, featuring five Crime Writers of Canada authors, including three of us who once lived in Aurora, Ontario.

My friends, especially Tanya, Carol and Marlene for helping me when I cried "help." And to Bob, my good Samaritan, who would land in my driveway to shovel the snow and fix the tree and shrub damage from the coldest and iciest winter in my life.

The gang at Crime Writers of Canada, and Sisters in Crime Toronto (which I finally joined) for being so supportive of my debut short story collection. Special thanks to Nate Hendley, who let me help him organize Crime Writers of Canada readings at libraries and cafés.

All the members of my East End Writers' Group who over the years have critiqued my work, including bits and pieces of *Beyond Blood.* Susan, thanks for being better than a Word's Find feature and finding my repetitious words.

Shane Joseph, my editor at Blue Denim Press and Sarah Jacob my publisher at Blue Denim Press for not giving up on *Beyond Blood* even when the first submission was bloody awful. You saw something there and I followed your instructions to make it better. Special thanks to Shane for his editorial comments about some language and plot that were a little off.

Author Biography

Sharon A. Crawford grew up on Perry Mason and Agatha Christie. She also worked as a clerk at the Toronto Police Services and as a secretary for a legal firm. Those facts may have something to do with her penchant for dreaming up quirky characters and putting them in weird mystery plots. Her 30 plus years as a journalist helped hone her writing skills and introduced her to some real life, eccentric characters whom she profiled in publications such as the *Toronto Star*, *Toronto Life*, cbc.ca, *Check-up Magazine*, *Globe and Mail* and *The Era-Banner*. Today, she works as a freelance book editor, writing instructor, and book reviewer for *Quill & Quire* and *The Prairie Journal*. Her debut short story collection *Beyond the Tripping Point* was published by Blue Denim Press in October 2012. She collaborated with Rene Natan to write a novella, *Fire Underneath the Ice* (Rogue Phoenix Press, 2010).

Sharon founded and runs the East End Writers' Group, belongs to the Professional Writers Association of Canada, Canadian Authors' Association Toronto branch (where she is Writer-in-Residence), Sisters in Crime and Crime Writers of Canada. With the latter, she has helped Nate Hendley set up and host CWC members' reading sessions at libraries and cafés.

In her spare time she walks, gardens, dines out with family and friends, travels by train to visit cousins in southwestern Ontario, and reads mystery and memoir. Her blog sharonacrawfordauthor.com focuses on the craft of fiction writing.

www.ingramcontent.com/pod-product-compliance
Ingram Content Group UK Ltd.
Pitfield, Milton Keynes, MK11 3LW, UK
UKHW020144250726
13967UKWH00002B/851

9 781927 882016